I0626385

Show Me How to Love

Synithia Williams

Copyright © 2016 Synithia Williams

ISBN: 0-9975729-0-6

ISBN-13: 978-0-9975729-0-2

Edited by: Yolanda Barber
Cover Art by: Cover Fresh Designs

Synithia Williams
Columbia, SC

This is a work of fiction. Names, characters, places, and incidents either are the product of the author's imagination or are used fictitiously, and any resemblance to actual persons, living or dead, business establishments, events, or locales is entirely coincidental.

All rights reserved. This book or any portion thereof may not be reproduced or used in any manner whatsoever without the express written permission from Synithia.

ACKNOWLEDGEMENTS

First I'd like to thank my fantastic beta readers who helped me massage this story into what it is today: Danita, Natoya, Kwana, and Liv. I truly appreciate your feedback and the time you took to read over Andre and Mikayla's story. Many thanks to Delaney Diamond, Sharon Cooper, Candace Shaw and K.M. Jackson for your recommendations and advice as I navigated this self-publishing journey. A shout out to my cousin Sharon for sending me little bits of encouragement over the past few years. Thanks so much for looking out with books and contacts who've given me ideas and support. Finally, thank you to my wonderful husband Eric. You've cheered me on during this process better than anyone.

CHAPTER 1

Mikayla Sanders was never one to get drunk at weddings, but this wedding might make her consider getting rip roaring drunk. She quickly made her way to the bar setup in the lobby of the expansive estate. When a family hated each other this much, putting everyone together on a mountain for a weekend of wedding festivities made no sense. The various factions of the Caldwell family were half a step from strangling each other, and the luxury of the surroundings did not make up for the hostility.

She'd finally escaped the bride, who'd gone bat shit crazy about the wrong color ribbons on the two hundred bottles of bubbles. Mikayla's shoulders were tense from listening to the bride-to-be complain about her bow tying ability, and her jaw was in pain from clenching it. But she kept from telling bridezilla where to go and what flaming vehicle to take there. Especially considering Mikayla was the only one who offered to fix the bow fiasco.

As soon as she sat down at the bar, the bartender came over with a highball glass in one hand and a bottle of bourbon in the other. The unofficial Caldwell family drink.

"Care for a drink?" he asked.

Mikayla held up her hand. "Just a ginger ale."

He raised a brow but turned to get the soda. Something stronger would be better. But a stronger drink would lead to an urge for a cigarette. She'd overcome that habit a year ago. Bridezilla and her family were slowly pushing Mikayla off the wagon.

The click-clack of heels against the marble floor came up behind Mikayla.

"Hey, Mikayla, I've been looking for you."

Mikayla turned and smiled, as her best friend, Renee Caldwell was exiting one of the salons. "Well, you found me."

Renee glided over with a natural grace Mikayla couldn't imitate. "I was hoping you'd be with Ryan."

The bartender gave Mikayla the ginger ale that she accepted with a smile. "I haven't seen him since this morning."

Renee sat on the stool next to Mikayla. There wasn't a strand of Renee's perfect pixie cut out of place. She wore a full face of makeup, and Mikayla had never seen Renee without makeup, but she always looked natural and flawless. Renee's genuine heart and smile only enhanced the caramel glow of her friend's beauty. "You two should be sneaking off into a secluded corner or at least still be wrapped up in each other's arms in bed."

Heat spread through Mikayla's cheeks. She clutched the glass of ginger ale and took a sip. Of course, Renee would expect for her and Ryan to be off making love. It would mean Renee's matchmaking skills had once again proven effective.

"How you can talk about your brother's love life without feeling grossed out is beyond my comprehension," Mikayla said while shaking her head.

"Oh please, Ryan's my twin we tell each other everything. Besides, it would be nice if at least one of us could find some romance this weekend."

The bartender came over, and gave Renee the same bedazzled smile most men got in her presence. "Can I get you a drink?"

Renee raised a sleek, arched brow. "What Malbec do you carry?" She turned away from Mikayla to peer at the wine list he had pulled out.

While Renee drilled the guy on the wine selection, Mikayla gave thanks for the interruption. She'd finally agreed to date Ryan and joined him as his plus one at his cousin's wedding. After three years of working and becoming friends with Ryan and Renee, and pushing aside not only his advances but the hope of the rest of his family that she and Ryan would work out.

The moment Ryan invited her she'd known the offer was an excuse to finally get her in bed. She had procrastinated and hadn't gone to bed the night before until after she'd figured he was asleep. Having sex would make them really real. So real, there would be no turning back.

Maybe tonight she'd have her head fully wrapped around the fact that they were in a relationship. Once she overcame the shock of believing that she, former tomboy and fashion police repeat offender, was actually dating the hot rich guy, so many women chased after.

Don't sell yourself to get what you want. Her dad's words rang in her head. She promptly pushed them aside.

When Renee turned back to her, Mikayla spoke up before her friend continued the previous line of questioning. "What did you want with me and Ryan?"

Renee's eyes lit up, and she clapped her hands together. "I was hoping you and Ryan would escape this place with me. My family is driving me crazy."

"Maybe later, I want to lie down for a few minutes. My fingers need a break." Mikayla stretched her aching hands.

Renee froze in the middle of taking a sip of wine set before her by the bartender. She placed the glass back on the bar with a resounding thud. "You didn't help her with those stupid ribbons?"

"I did." Over an hour removing perfectly good grape, a.k.a. dark purple, ribbons from more than a hundred bottles of bubbles and replacing them with passion, a.k.a. light purple, ribbons.

"Why?" Renee asked.

"Because if someone hadn't jumped in to change the ribbons your cousin would have had a major break down. Or destroyed the entire mansion in a fit of bridezilla rage."

Renee rubbed Mikayla's shoulder and spared a better-you-than-me smile. "You should receive a medal, sainthood, and a star named in your honor for doing that."

"Either way, you can't leave," Mikayla said. "Isn't there something else on the wedding itinerary?"

"Don't remind me." Renee dropped her hand from Mikayla's shoulder and reached for the wine. "I didn't come to this wedding expecting to have my entire day planned out down to the minute."

Mikayla sipped the ginger ale and grinned. "You know all brides make demands?"

A burst of laughter came from the opposite end of the lobby. They both glanced that way. Three teenage girls stood huddled near a closet in the corner. They were a set of Caldwell cousins Ryan had introduced to Mikayla the night before

Renee's smoky brown eyes narrowed. "Most brides aren't my crazy cousin."

"As if you and Ryan aren't just as demanding. No wonder you all don't get along."

Renee twisted in her seat and peered at the girls. They continued to giggle and had moved closer to the door of the closet.

"It goes beyond demanding," Renee said. "That side takes family feud to a different level. I still can't believe my dad and uncle came from the same parents."

Mikayla didn't argue. The total cold front that occurred whenever the two men were in the same room validated Renee's statement.

"Plus they're stuck up," Renee continued. "The money they spent on this wedding is obscene."

"Everything is nice," Mikayla said in a voice that tried, but failed, to hide how much she agreed with Renee.

"Nice is a tasteful country club wedding with a few family and friends,"

Renee said not taking her eyes off the giggling girls. "Opulent is renting out a mountain estate for three hundred of your closest friends, importing wine from France, flowers from Brazil, and hiring a celebrity chef to cater."

"It's not as if your side isn't wealthy." Renee's father started Caldwell Development twenty years ago and quickly grew it into one of the top builders in the United States.

"True, but when Ryan or I get married, we won't be giving out iPads as wedding gifts."

Mikayla laughed and raised her ginger ale in a salute. "Point taken."

Renee spared no expense on clothes, accessories and beauty products, but Mikayla would be the first to admit there wasn't an arrogant bone in her friend's size four body.

The girls laughed again. Renee motioned to them. "What are they up, too?"

"Being teens laughing at something silly."

"They're probably laughing at someone instead of something. You never know with Aunt Joleen's kids. Those girls are spoiled rotten."

Renee tilted her head to the side "I wonder what's behind that door."

"A broom closet."

Renee shot her a how-do-you-know-look that she ignored. She gulped her drink, but the liquid did nothing to stop heat from spreading up her face. No way would she admit Ryan had tried to convince her to have a quickie in that same closet. She'd left him pouting, in order to help bridezilla reorganize her seating chart.

"Those kids take pleasure in tormenting people." Renee broke through her thoughts. "They've probably locked someone in the closet. I want to see what's going on." She grabbed Mikayla's arm and pulled her along.

Arguing with Renee when she thought someone was being bullied was useless. Nothing angered her friend more than a person taking pleasure in another's suffering.

"What's so funny?" Renee asked when they reached the girls.

The three teenagers jumped and turned. They looked like cut outs from the latest reality show, makeup that made them look like little adults instead of teenagers, long weave down their backs and clothes that probably cost more than Mikayla's monthly salary. Their giggling hadn't bothered her in the least. She'd missed the opportunity to laugh in corners with girlfriends growing up. Her dad focused on making sure she passed her classes and knew how to change a flat tire.

The oldest of the three twisted her glossed lips. "Somebody's getting it on in the closet."

Renee and Mikayla's jaws dropped. The other two girls burst into laughter.

Mikayla pressed her hand to the side of her face and shook her head.

"You can't be serious."

The oldest grinned. "I know what sex sounds like. And somebody is definitely going at it in there."

Renee grabbed the arms of two of the girls and attempted to pull them away from the hall. "Then you don't need to stand here listening. Go find something else to do."

"Oh, no. I want to know who it is." One of the girls pulled out of Renee's grasp and crossed her arms. "I'm staying here until they come out." The other two followed suit.

Renee sighed and looked at Mikayla. "It's the middle of the day. Who'd do this?"

Mikayla shrugged. "Maybe they're mistaken."

A rhythmic thud against the door along with the unmistakable sounds of a woman's moan undermined her words. The teenagers erupted into another fit of giggles.

Renee rubbed her eyes. "This is a disaster."

"Why are you so upset? It's not your wedding."

"I'm cool with ignoring the itinerary, but watching my cousin have a full blown meltdown because someone is tacky enough to screw in a closet is more drama than I want to deal with."

The thumping increased. Mikayla cringed. "Maybe they're finishing up."

"What's going on over here?" A deep voice said from behind.

Mikayla turned and met the ebony eyes of Renee's cousin Andre. Her heart did a traitorous thump in her chest. Andre was from the other side of the Caldwell family. For him to bother coming over and ask what they were doing was surprising. He'd been brief and cold when Ryan introduced her the night before.

Growing up around a lot of guys didn't give Mikayla many opportunities to feel feminine. But Andre towering over her all dark and imposing made her feel downright dainty. A reaction she surprisingly liked. His dark grey sweater clung to broad shoulders, and dark jeans fit just enough to hint at muscular, strong legs. Add to that a voice that would put the late, great Barry White to shame and it was no wonder her body reacted.

Renee crossed her arms over her chest. "Someone is having sex in the closet." She sneered at Andre. "While it won't ruin your sister's wedding, it will send her into hysterics if she finds out."

Andre's dark eyes narrowed. "Stepsister." He spit out the words like he'd tasted something nasty. The thumping grew louder. Andre ran a hand over his face. "Damn."

"Exactly," Renee said.

Mikayla glanced toward the bar and cringed. "Renee, your dad's at the bar." They swore in unison as the groom and his groomsmen left the billiards room and joined Renee's dad. That meant the rest of the family

9

would soon be returning.

The teens laughed again, and a loud slap against the closet door echoed throughout the lobby. The men turned their way. This tryst wasn't going to be a secret much longer.

A woman's voice came slightly muffled from the other side of the door. "Oh, Daddy, just like that."

"What the heck?" Renee said pressing her hands to her temples.

Andre shifted at Mikayla's side. A scowl twisted his handsome face. His shoulders were rigid. Hands clenched into fists at his side. She glanced at the door then back at him. He took a step forward, and she placed a hand on his arm. His very firm arm. Her stomach did a little twitter that she decided to pretend wasn't happening.

"Don't open the door," she said.

His eyes met hers, coal black and hard with fury. She remembered the way he held onto his girlfriend Angelica the night before. At the time, the prideful manner he'd used when introducing her to Ryan made her assume Angelica was just a pretty armpiece for a rich man.

Another thump from the door came right before the men reached their group. "What the hell is going on?" Renee's dad, Philip Caldwell, asked.

The teen with blonde weave giggled. "Someone's getting it on."

The men's faces lit up with both bemusement and enthusiasm. Mikayla inwardly scoffed. What was it about the idea of sex in a closet that got men so excited?

A slap against the door was followed by, "That's right, whose is it?"

Mikayla's hand fell from Andre's arm. Her jaw dropped. Everything in the background became a dim murmur as a sinking feeling rushed through her midsection.

No.

This couldn't be happening.

He couldn't be the one in that closet. One glance at the astonished look on Renee's face confirmed Mikayla's thoughts.

Everything seemed to move in slow motion, but she had to have moved quickly because she was right in front of the closet door. Vaguely she noticed movement around her, the cackles of the girl's laughter, and maybe even someone calling her name. She snatched open the door.

Andre's girlfriend fell with a loud smack on her back, Ryan bare assed on top of her. They both stared up at the group while the teenager's laughter increased to the crescendo of a pack of hyenas.

Mikayla's gaze swept the spectators. Needles of heat spread over her body. They were laughing at her. The laughter picked at internal cuts she'd thought long since healed.

Mikayla shook her head and stepped back. Disbelief and anguish churned like hot acid in her stomach. Her dad's "I told you so" ran through her brain. Pain tore through her chest while humiliation, an old companion, set her cheeks on fire.

Ryan held up a hand but didn't move from his position between Angelica's thighs. "Mikayla, look, this is not what it seems."

Anger spouted within Mikayla like molten lava. She clenched her teeth and pressed a hand to her rolling stomach. She wanted to scream, curse his ass out. But she refused to act a fool in front of these people.

Ryan's mother Victoria pushed through the group. She took one look at Ryan on the floor and groaned. All hell broke loose as the rest of the family and guests came from the far corners of the estate.

Mikayla couldn't breathe, couldn't think, with the noise and commotion. She spun on her heels and ran upstairs.

When she entered the room she'd shared with Ryan, she wanted to set the place on fire. The king sized four poster bed had been made. Rose petals and chocolates rested on the pillows. Bridezilla had mentioned the resort staff were given instructions to create a romantic setting for all the couples. Her stomach heaved, and her mouth went dry. If she'd come to bed early, he would have had sex with her the night before. If she hadn't caught him today, he might have tonight.

She threw the few items she'd taken out of her bag back inside. Angry tears blurred her vision, but she refused to shed them here. Not where he'd have the chance of ever seeing how much he'd humiliated her.

Ryan burst through the door. She jerked the zipper closed on her bag. Somewhere he'd found his pants. He glanced from her to the bag before stepping forward. "I'm sorry."

Mikayla held up her hand. "Just get out of my way."

"I know it seems bad, but it's not what you think." Ryan's usually perfect posture gave way to stooped shoulders.

She closed her eyes, unable to meet his stare. "Get out of my way, Ryan."

His footsteps on the hardwood floor were slow as he crossed the room. She stiffened when he gently clasped his hands around her shoulders.

"Mikayla, please, let me explain." His voice dripped with regret as if he were actually sorry about what happened.

She opened her eyes. Even with the remorse in his eyes, he still reminded her of the guy she'd considered her friend. Piercing brown eyes that had been full of sincerity when he'd insisted his feelings were real. The same full lips that comforted her when he'd kissed her forehead after she'd come to bed late the night before.

She took a deep breath. The pungent smell of sex coated him. Revulsion twisted her stomach. She pushed his arms off her shoulders. Anger lifted her knee as she sharply kicked him between the legs.

A piercing cry burst from his lips before he curled into a ball and fell to the floor. She stepped around him, gently pulled her coat off the hanger, and walked out the door. She may not be a socialite, but she could hold her head high and walk out like one. The noise in the lobby hadn't died down. Philip Caldwell's voice argued with another that she recognized as his brother's, and they overpowered the other voices.

So much for keeping the peace at this damn wedding.

Renee waited for her at the bottom of the stairs. Her hands wringing and, lips turned down into a frown. Renee opened her mouth to speak, but Mikayla lifted her hand. Right now Mikayla couldn't stomach seeing Renee, she looked too much like her twin.

Maybe her friendship with Renee was just as superficial as her relationship with Ryan. Another person she thought she had a connection with but was only fooling herself. Pain flashed across Renee's features, but thankfully she let Mikayla pass.

She strode out of the estate into the cold February air with her head held high. Quickly, Mikayla put on her coat and stared at the icicle lined trees. What could she do now? She'd ridden up with Ryan, but she'd be damned if she stayed here all weekend. She pulled her cell phone out and searched for a cab company. The list of local cabbies had popped up a second before Andre burst through the front door, a single overnight bag in his hand.

Their gazes locked. Mutual understanding flowed between them. He may be from the wrong side of the Caldwell family, but right now he was the only other person who wanted to get the hell off that mountain as much as she did.

"Can you give me a ride?"

He hesitated. She didn't blame him. They'd barely talked the night before, and she was the girlfriend—former girlfriend—of the man who'd just fucked his woman in a closet. Mikayla considered taking back her request when he held out a hand. The tension in her shoulders eased a bit as she placed her palm in his. The warmth of his grasp traveled up her arm and spread like fingers inside her chest. His brow furled before he looked away and walked her to the black Mercedes S 550 brought out front by the valet.

The snow that fell the night before crunched under their feet. She lowered her head and watched as the fragile crystals shattered by their steps. Shattered, much like her earlier enthusiasm of being invited away for a weekend with Ryan Caldwell. Just moments ago she'd thought her life was perfect. That she'd arrived. Instead, she was once again the outcast who didn't belong with the cool kids.

Andre dropped her hand as soon as they reached the car. The loss of his warmth seemed like another fist to her gut on a crappy afternoon.

Ryan burst through the front door. His concerned gaze darted first to her then Andre. He hobbled toward them. "Mikayla!"

She ignored Ryan and stared at Andre, "Let's go."

Andre cracked his knuckles. She expected him to cross the distance and beat the crap out of Ryan. Instead, he clenched his jaw and entered the car. She followed and slammed the door. Closing her eyes, she blocked Ryan's calls while Andre speed out of the driveway.

CHAPTER 2

Andre whipped his car around a sharp curve. Anger pushed his foot on the pedal every time he remembered Angelica landing on the floor in Ryan's arms. He'd thought he and Ryan were beyond this. Past the childish games and petty rivalry their father's started. What the fuck was he thinking? No matter how much he tried to pull away, this infighting would never end.

He swung around another curve, hit a patch of ice, and jerked the wheel quickly to straighten the vehicle. His companion gasped. One of her hands gripped the door, the other balled into a fist between their seats. Easing off the gas, Andre maneuvered the next curve at a slower speed. The snow and ice from the night before made the roads worse than they were when he drove up yesterday. Killing both of them in the mountains would be an imperfect end to the weekend from hell. His fingers released their death grip on the wheel, and he tried to control his angry foot.

He couldn't believe he'd agreed to let her come with him. In their brief conversation the night before, he could tell she was starry-eyed for Ryan. The desperation on her face when she'd asked him to leave pushed past any preconceived notions from the night before. She may not have had the good sense to stay away from Ryan, but she didn't deserve spending the rest of the weekend on the mountain.

Spotting a bar on the main road, he quickly pulled his car into the parking lot. He needed to calm down. He was too angry to drive rationally. Neon beer signs flashed in the windows of the wood building, old gas station signs hung on the exterior walls. It wasn't his ideal place to stop, but the lack of a Confederate flag was enough to make the establishment suitable.

"Why are we stopping?"

He turned to…damn, he'd forgotten her name already. "You want a drink?"

She scanned the building, her nose crinkled, she drummed the fingers of her right hand against the door. After a few seconds considering, she turned to him and shrugged. "No stars and bars. Why not?"

14

The corner of his mouth lifted in an appreciative smile that she'd looked for the same flag he had. She opened the car door and stepped out. Whatever her name was, she wasn't stuck up, a quality not usually found in Ryan's girlfriends.

They entered the dim interior of the bar. Country music played softly in the background, and a thin haze of cigarette smoke clouded the view of the few people at the bar. The friendly smile of the bartender eased his tension.

"Sit wherever y'all want." The bartender yelled. "I'll be over in a second."

His companion nodded at the bartender before sliding into one of the worn wooden booths near the front window.

"His greeting is comforting," she said.

"I agree."

She looked out the window, and he checked out the inside of the bar. No need for false conversation. There weren't many pleasant things to say after finding your significant others having sex in a closet.

She ran her fingers through her hair. He'd noticed her hair the night before. It was cut chin length and framed her face in a sleek even style. He loved when a woman's hairstyle accented her features. The smoke filtered sunlight didn't diminish the glossy shine of the dark brown, almost black, bone straight tresses. His fingers twitched to touch her hair, and he clenched his fist.

Andre had noticed a lot about her the night before. She wasn't what he'd expect from one of Ryan's girlfriends. Flashy, high maintenance, and beautiful were what Ryan usually went for. Instead, she was stylish but didn't appear fully comfortable with her style. Her steps were hesitant in the heels she wore as if she were still getting used to them. Sexy, in that girl next door kind of way. The biggest shocker, her kindness. While everyone else struggled to get away from his step-sister, she'd jumped right in to help. The mismatch of her and Ryan grabbed his attention the second he'd seen them together.

His eyes strayed to the hint of cleavage revealed by the buttons of her light green blouse. Yeah, he'd noticed her for other reasons, too. He jerked that thought back. No more sleeping with his cousin's girlfriends. His family may be ruthless, but he'd adopted the philosophy of using that tactic only for a specific purpose. Sleeping with her served no goal. Ryan didn't want her, and he didn't want Ryan's leftovers.

He cleared his throat and shifted in the seat. She looked back at him with wide eyes that sparked with her anger.

"Can you believe that just happened?" she asked.

Thoughts of her tempting cleavage were forgotten as the memory of the reason for their departure came back. "No."

She lowered her eyes to her fingers tracing grooves on the table. She had nice long lashes. "How long were you two together?"

He sat back in the stiff seat. "Nine months."

"Was it serious?"

He glanced over his shoulder looking for the bartender. Thought of the engagement ring in his bag. "You could say that."

"You know Ryan begged me to come. After years of listening to my instincts tell me he wasn't ready for a grown-up relationship, I finally broke down and consented. Look what happened."

She opened her mouth then snapped it shut. She gave him a wary glance, before crossing her arms and staring out of the window. Twice she turned to him as if she were going to say something before sighing and turning away with a frown.

He didn't blame her for keeping her thoughts to herself. As much as he wanted to punch the hell out of something or scream, he wouldn't dare do it in front of her. Why tell her he wasn't surprised Ryan had slept with Angelica? This one would probably be back in Ryan's bed after his cousin begged, flashed those dimples, and presented her with an expensive gift.

The bartender finally lumbered over. A tall slender man, with thin blonde hair and a wide smile minus one side tooth. "Sorry, folks. I got to talking to my cousin at the bar. Him and his missus going at it again. Not that y'all came in here to hear about my cousin's problems. What can I get you?"

"Coke, please," Andre said. A bit of rum in it along with a cigarette would go nicely. But not while driving unfamiliar roads. Plus, she didn't seem like the type who would share a smoke with him.

The bartender turned toward...was it Marcella? "And you miss?"

Her brow creased, and she slid him a questioning glance. "I'll just have a Coke."

Andre raised an eyebrow. "Are you sure you don't want something stronger? I know I do."

"But you're drinking soda."

"I'm driving icy mountain roads. Get what you want."

She nodded then smiled at the bartender. "Amaretto sour, please."

The bartender nodded. "Coming right up."

Again, Andre silently watched her as they waited for the drinks. She turned to the window, hair swaying softly against the curve of her cheek. She had a cute heart shaped face, and toffee color skin he'd bet money was silky soft.

A few minutes later, the bartender returned with the drinks. "Here ya go, folks. Do you want me to keep a tab open?"

Andre shook his head. "No, we'll be on our way soon."

A frown creased the bartender's brow. "Where you from?"

"South Carolina," she answered.

The man's frown deepened. "South Carolina...that's I-40. I hate to tell you this, but there was a rock slide on I-40 last night. You'll have to take the detour, and I don't think the roads have been cleared of last night's snow."

His companion's glass hit the table with a thud. "What? No, I need to get home."

The bartender shrugged. "Don't kill the messenger. You might want to find lodgings for tonight. Start over in the morning." He turned and left them to their drinks.

Slender fingers once again raked through her glossy hair. "This is just great."

Andre took a swig from his coke, now would be a good time to add that rum. "Actually, it's pretty damn lousy."

"What are we going to do? I'm not going back to that wedding."

"I agree with you on that."

He hadn't wanted to go to his step-sister's wedding in the first place. But showing loyalty to the family by attending was non-negotiable. Curtis Caldwell demanded loyalty from his kids above all else. Not that Barbara would have cared if he hadn't shown up. They'd disliked each other the day their parents introduced them. Two days after his dad left his mom and informed his sons his best friend's wife would be their new mother.

"We'll find someplace to stay and leave tomorrow." He downed his soda and considered ordering something stronger.

"I didn't see any hotels on the way out."

"We'll figure something out."

"Like what?"

He rubbed the bridge of his nose and tried to ignore the sudden onslaught of a headache. *I shouldn't be in this damn predicament in the first place.* He was supposed to show his face at that wedding, propose to Angelica and secure his lifetime hostess. Then take his butt home to finalize the pieces on a new deal that would undo some of the tarnish clinging to the family business. All Andre cared about was improving the negative image his dad created while building Caldwell Environmental Solutions into a mega house in the waste management world. Angelica effectively ruined part of his plan to show that the next generation of C.E.S. was settling down and preparing for the future. If he were alone, he'd brave the icy roads, but the risk of scaring his companion half to death, was not a viable option.

He pulled out his cell phone to search for nearby hotels. No network signal. He sighed and dropped the phone on the table.

"We can drive downtown, look to see if there are any rooms available." He focused back on...Melissa? But she was gazing out of the window again.

She tapped the foggy glass. "There's a cabin rental place across the street. Maybe they have one we can get for the night."

He turned to the sign visible through the window, Huggie Bear rentals. One cabin sat behind the sign, and a small winding road led up to several cabins along the mountain.

"I'm not sure a cabin makes sense."

She turned to him, her brows creased as she frowned. "Cabin, hotel, does it really make a difference? Since we're stuck together for the night, we might as well make plans soon." She looked at the sky. "We might get more snow."

He mirrored her movements. Heavy grey clouds sat motionless in the sky. As if summoned, a few fat flakes drifted down. With an inward sigh, he resigned himself to the cabin idea.

"Huggie Bear it is. I hope they have something available." He drained his soda.

Megan maybe…took a small sip from her drink. She set the glass on the table and used the tip of her finger to play in the condensation along the cup. Drawing lines until a large drop formed and ran down the side of the glass. She repeated the movement over and over.

"I can't believe this happened…" she said softly. Tears glimmered in her eyes.

Andre shifted in his seat. Please, God, not a crier. Comfort wasn't his strong suit, and this situation called for more than a pat on the back and a gruff there, there. Seduction, shrewd business tactics, and money he knew, not compassion.

"I'm not surprised by anything my cousins do. Especially Ryan," he said.

She blinked away tears. "Funny, Renee said the same thing about you and your side of the family." She took another sip of her drink. "I wonder which side is worse."

Andre cocked a brow. "Both."

She sat up straight. Her confused gaze jumped back to his. "I'm surprised you'd say that. Renee and Ryan never lay the blame on their end."

He caught the bartender's attention and called for a rum and coke. Might as well since they were going to stay across the street. "That doesn't surprise me. The rift within our family is equal on both ends. This stunt your boyfriend pulled today is just another previously used weapon in the Caldwell family arsenal."

"You mean…he's done this before?"

"We both have." He accepted the drink from the bartender.

"But, why. Why would he do that while I'm around? I thought—"

"You thought you were special. That Ryan really cared about you."

Her face hardened at the mocking tone of his voice. "I've known Ryan for six years and in that time we became friends. Or, at least, I thought we did. Despite what happened, I can't believe he would do something so vile just to taunt you."

He thought back to the rivalry. The bogus family reunions organized for the opportunity to claim bragging rights for their kid's achievements in sports and grades. The long lasting rivalry was the only reason they'd invited Uncle Philip and his family to Barbara's wedding. To show off. The competition, suspicion, and disdain drove his dad's ambition to have more, and to some extent drove Andre too. Fighting and backstabbing were all he knew.

"Never underestimate the Caldwell rivalry," he said and then drained half of his drink.

Arms crossed over her breasts, hands briskly rubbing up and down toned arms she diverted her eyes.

"Let's go," she said. "It's snowing harder."

He reached for his wallet, to pay the tab. She pulled two folded bills out of her purse and dropped them on the table.

"I got it," he said.

She shook her head. "You gave me a ride. I don't mind buying you a drink." Sliding out of the booth, she hurried to the door.

He stared at the money on the table. The drinks weren't much, but he'd expected her to wait for him to pay. He turned to where she stood by the door. Arms folded, and head held high, a calm expression on her face. Poised, even though they'd both been hit by a landslide of humiliation. She hadn't crumbled. No hysterics when Ryan and Angelica fell out of the closet. Only a trace of tears. Angelica would have had a world class fit in that lobby if the tables were turned. *She has her shit together. Ryan, what kind of fool are you? Losing a decent woman over a stupid rivalry.*

CHAPTER 3

"You two are in luck. You snagged the last cabin." The rental agent said with a smile. "I hope you don't mind one bedroom."

Mikayla cringed. She turned to Andre, who wore a similar look of uncertainty. "We could look somewhere else."

He shook his head. "No, I'll just sleep on the couch."

The agent glanced between the two then nodded. "Now that that's settled, I just need the rent for tonight and a deposit to cover incidentals."

Mikayla reached for her wallet. "I've got it."

Andre pushed her to the side and passed over his credit card. "Put it all on this."

She didn't know if she should applaud the chivalrous attempt or roll her eyes at his arrogance. "If you're taking the couch, the least I can do is pay."

"We're stranded because of my family. I'll pay."

She couldn't argue. So she stepped back and let him handle the transaction. Once they secured the key and made their way to the cabin, Mikayla tried to push aside any doubts as she followed Andre into the small cabin.

Andre took her bag into the bedroom as she did a quick tour of the place. Besides the one bedroom, there was a living room filled with big wood furniture with stuffed cushions that gave the place a homey feel. A cozy kitchen with a round dining table connected to the living area. Despite the cold, she walked out onto the deck. Snowflakes greeted her along with a burst of air. Mikayla pulled her coat tight. Shades of red, gold and purple splashed along the mountain peaks as the sun set, creating a spectacular view. A covered hot tub sat in a corner overlooking the mountains, a perfect setting for a romantic interlude.

Her chest constricted. What was supposed to be a romantic weekend had turned into a disaster. Maybe even the biggest embarrassment of her life. Childhood taunts about her kinky hair, hand me down clothes, and lack of money were nothing compared to today. The day reality and Ryan slapped her down from the dream that she could really have it all. A successful career, handsome boyfriend, love. She could only imagine the look on her dad's face when he found out. He'd predicted the relationship with Ryan was headed for disaster.

Behind Mikayla, the glass door slid open. She quickly wiped away her tears, and turned and smiled at Andre. His dark eyes examined her. She spun back to the view, remembering the panicked expression he'd had when she became teary eyed at the bar. There was no need to cry. Now was the time to put the pieces of her broken pride together and present a brave front.

"The couch looks comfortable." Andre spoke in a smoother-than-cognac baritone.

A shiver rushed down her spine. Common sense dictated she should be afraid to spend the night in a cabin with a man she'd only met briefly the night before. Instead, Mikayla feared her body's reaction to him. His relative calm in the midst of the disaster earlier was reassuring. The second his warm hand had engulfed hers outside of the estate, she'd felt that things would be okay. But she couldn't trust him. He'd said it himself, not to underestimate the feud between his family.

"You paid for the place, you should have the bed. I don't mind the couch."

Before she finished speaking, he shook his head. "I wouldn't feel right." He walked over. "Take the bed."

She had to lift her head to look into his eyes. The mellow smell of his cologne wafted, crisp in the cool air. She took a step back, to escape the welcoming heat radiating from his body.

"If you insist."

His eyes narrowed, and he nodded. When he headed back inside, she let out a shaky breath.

"Do you want something to eat?"

She nodded. "I'm starving."

"When I came up yesterday, I noticed a small grocery store and a Chinese restaurant not far from the bar. I should be able to make it there and back with no problems. Do you have a problem eating that?"

"No, I'm pretty flexible. I can give you some money."

He held up a hand. "No need. Lock the door and give me your cell number so I can call when I'm on the way back."

"I'm not going anywhere."

"I know, but this way I can reach you while I'm out. Don't want you to think I'm abandoning you."

His sentiment warmed her insides. "You're only going to get food. You don't plan to leave me here stranded, do you?"

Mikayla shivered as an icy wind blew across the balcony. Andre's long fingers wrapped around her arm and pulled her inside. Once again, his body's warmth tempted her as he reached around her to slide the door shut. She should have moved out of the way but found his closeness comforting, his cologne intoxicating. Her eyes closed, and she took a deep breath. When they opened, she stared up into the smoldering depths of his midnight eyes.

"No, I won't leave you here stranded." His deep voice rolled over her like warm chocolate.

Pull it back, Mikayla. Ryan already proved she was crazy to think she could be the perfect match for an overly confident, rich, handsome man. Clearing her throat, she brushed the hair from her face and stepped away. Focusing on pulling her phone out of her purse, instead of the way his presence unnerved her.

"I turned it off after I left." She powered her cell back on and gave him her number. He called her to save it on his phone and then left, with the promise, to be right back.

As soon as he walked out, she plopped onto the couch.

What the hell is wrong with me? Hadn't she just been happy to spend the weekend with Ryan less than twelve hours before? Now she lusted for his cousin. That had desperate social climber written all over it.

One night. She'd stay in her room, watch man-hating movies on Lifetime, and come up with a plan for when she returned. Starting with prospects for a new job. Ugh! She immediately wanted to reject the idea. She was next in line for a promotion to head the acquisitions department at Caldwell Development. Which would put her in charge of locating prospective areas for the company to develop. She wanted that promotion and had worked damn hard to get it.

But was that job worth facing Ryan daily? The idea made her queasy. Potential promotion or not, no way she could continue working with Ryan.

The idea of giving up everything she'd worked for made her head hurt and her body yearn for a cigarette. She'd started smoking while dating her college boyfriend. She'd tried quitting once he died in a car wreck after graduation, but hadn't truly given up the practice until a year ago. The cravings refused to go away.

She rose from the couch and shuffled into the bedroom. The king sized bed, and flat screen television were all she needed to survive the night. She unzipped the overnight bag and pulled out something to sleep in. Thankfully, she'd packed sensible pajamas along with the sexy scraps of material she'd brought to impress Ryan. Not that the lingerie would have helped. Apparently, a closet was all Ryan needed to make him horny.

Ten minutes later, the shrill ringtone of the cell phone greeted her when she exited the shower. Goose pimples sprouted on her arms when she left the warm, humid air in the bathroom and stepped into the cooler air of the cabin. By the time, she grabbed her phone and dashed to the thermostat to raise the temperature a few notches, the ringing had stopped. Renee's number lit her screen. She cringed. She loved Renee but wasn't ready to talk to her friend.

She brought the phone back into the bedroom where she put on pajamas. The cell rang again a few minutes later, and this time Mikayla did not recognize the number.

"Hello."

"Hey....umm…yeah…this is Andre. I'm coming back in and didn't want to scare you."

"Okay."

She frowned at the phone after the call ended. A few minutes later the door opened and she walked out of the bedroom. Arms folded across her chest, she watched as he carried two large brown paper bags into the kitchen. Her stomach growled as the familiar smells of Chinese food wafted over to her.

"What's my name?"

He froze in the middle of pulling out containers and turned to her squinting as if trying hard to remember.

"Uhhh…Marcella?"

Her arms dropped to her sides. "I can't believe you agreed to this, and you don't know my name."

"I was going to figure it out." The corner of his mouth lifted. "Or say hey you all night."

She glared, and his half smile turned into a full blown grin. The first real smile she'd seen. She liked that smile, his relaxed face made his handsome features positively devastating.

"My name is Mikayla."

"Mikayla." Her name spoken in his baritone was way too sexy.

"Andre." She tried to mimic his tone.

Something in his eyes flickered before he blinked and went back to pulling out the food. "Let's eat."

"Good idea."

They settled in at the small table, and she watched as he dished out shrimp lo mein, sweet and sour chicken, beef with broccoli, and chicken wings with pork fried rice.

"Were you planning to feed an army?"

"I wasn't sure what you liked."

"I like it all. And after the day I've had I'm likely to eat it all."

They ate in silence. Numerous times she opened her mouth to start a conversation only to zip her lips and focus on the food. She wanted to vent, but he wasn't the right person. She would normally discuss her issues with Renee, but calling Renee's twin brother a son-of-a-bitch, no matter how deserving, didn't seem like the right thing to do.

Outside of Renee she had a few other female associates, but not one close enough to reveal what happened. Which left her other confidant, her dad. Mikayla stabbed the food with a fork and inwardly cringed. The thought of going through the dreaded I told you so speech made her throat clench up. Her dad had been right. Getting close to the Caldwell family equaled disaster.

They finished the meal. Andre packed up the leftovers while she wiped crumbs from the table. After the limited cleaning, her gaze bounced around the kitchen. Mikayla's skin tingled with nervous energy. She stretched her hand then curled it into a fist. She couldn't talk to anyone. Couldn't smoke. Her nerves were shot. She needed an outlet for the restlessness.

Andre tapped her shoulder, and she jumped. He gave her a wary look. "Do you mind if I take a shower?"

She flexed her fingers again and pushed the craving for nicotine aside. "You don't have to ask."

"Actually I do. The only shower is in your room."

"Oh, I didn't think about that. Yeah, sure, go ahead. I'll watch television until you're done."

He gave a curt nod and pulled some items from his bag on the couch. Once the bedroom door closed, she paced around the room. Humiliation and restlessness hurried her steps.

A vision of Ryan and Angelica falling out of the closet flashed through her mind.

Pulling in a deep breath, then out, she sat on the couch, closed her eyes, and concentrated on breathing. Several minutes later her body relaxed somewhat. She grabbed the remote and turned on the television. Instead of Lifetime she turned to cartoons on a retro station. No need to further weaken her emotional stability with a dramatic movie.

Andre entered the living room after two episodes of Tom and Jerry, along with the fresh smell of soap. He'd changed out of dark jeans and a sweater into a pair of grey sweat pants and a loose fitting t-shirt. Despite the baggy clothes, her eye was drawn to the outline of his broad shoulders and the thick rope of muscles in his arms. He was barefoot, his short hair still damp from the shower. Her eyes strayed to the bulge in the front of his sweats, jerked away, then crept back for another peak. Impressive! As if that mattered at all.

She squirmed in her seat, and her gaze wandered to the television. The intimacy of the moment made her uncomfortable. She hadn't been alone with a man who wasn't family or Ryan in years.

Andre moved his bag and sat beside her on the couch. The scent of his body wash put her body on high alert. Crisp and masculine…it had to be one of those attraction enhancing kind. That was the only way she'd be excited by the smell of soap. Not like he needed the help.

"What are you watching?" He popped open a bottle of lotion, thankfully unscented considering her reaction to his body wash and rubbed some on his arms.

"Umm…Tom and Jerry."

"One of my favorites."

She tried to laugh easily as if his nearness wasn't sending heat traipsing across her skin. Instead, it sounded like a nervous school girl cackle. "Yeah, most guys I know like this cartoon."

"Even pretty boy Ryan?"

Her smile withered away. "I wasn't talking about Ryan."

He lifted one shoulder and quirked a brow. "Your tight expression during dinner made me wonder if you were thinking about him."

"More like wondering if you were capable of talking," Was her clipped reply.

His eyes widened, and she focused on the television. Crap, what happened to not rocking the boat? No need to pick a fight with him tonight. Surviving until morning and going home was more important.

"I'd rather not get in too deep with Ryan's girlfriend." He continued rubbing lotion into his arms.

Her head snapped around. For a second, she watched the fluid movement of his hands as they smoothed lotion into the firm muscles of his arm before her eyes narrowed in on him. "Ex-girlfriend. Though I hate to call myself that."

He placed the bottle of lotion on the coffee table, then turned to study her. His gaze slowly raking across her features. It was clear from the questioning look in his eye he didn't believe her. His doubt rattled her nerves and woke up the frustration she'd learned to ignore whenever people tried to get a rise out of her.

"Are you sure you two are through?"

Her anger revved up. The humiliation, hurt and disappointment from earlier seeking an outlet. What she had with Ryan, a relationship and friendship had ended today.

"I'm positive it ended today," she said in a slow deep voice.

Andre leaned back on the couch. He shook his head as if her words were meaningless. "That's what all you women say. No matter how badly a man treats you, you get mad and curse his name, and then after he apologizes you're right back in bed with him."

She jumped up from the couch and faced him her hands perched on her hips. Andre thinking she would go back to Ryan easily, pissed her off as much as finding Ryan in that closet. She wanted the glamorous life but not enough to sacrifice her pride.

"I don't know who you think you're talking about, but I'm not some simple-minded female. Do you think it was easy for me to believe he was ready for a monogamous relationship after watching his string of one-night stands? Ryan didn't just lose some woman he was toying with tonight. He lost a friend. He can come crawling on a bed of glass, promise me the moon, and I'd throw it in his face. It took too long for me to realize I'm worth more. I deserve more. Ryan Caldwell damn sure isn't going to steal that from me."

Andre's prolonged stared added speed to her already racing heart. He held up his hand. "I'm sorry. I shouldn't have said that. I won't bring it up again."

Doubt still lingered in his eyes. She clenched her teeth at his almost mechanical apology. If she were in his place, she wouldn't believe her either. She'd witnessed plenty of Ryan's exes come back after he flashed a smile and said sorry. Disgust churned her stomach. Despite all of her good intentions and beliefs that Ryan would treat their relationship with more respect than his others, he'd behaved no better. And worse, he had humiliated her beyond redemption.

"You know, the next time you decide to become such a chatterbox go for polite conversation over dinner. Don't sucker punch me with this type of foolishness out of the blue." Her voice wavered with pain.

She rushed into the bedroom and slammed the door. Her tears refused to be suppressed any longer and streamed down her cheeks before she fell onto the bed.

CHAPTER 4

Andre stood at Mikayla's bedroom door and listened to the quiet sobs. Each hiccup a kick to his conscience. He shouldn't have taken his anger and frustration out on her. They were both victims of Ryan's stupid game. The look of disgust on her face when she'd listed the reasons why she wouldn't go back to Ryan nearly convinced him she meant what she said. But he'd seen women forgive men for a lot worse. His mom still slept with his father after all of the hell Curtis had put her through.

Apologizing to Mikayla was a given, but not while she cried. Tears in a woman's eyes always rendered him useless.

Stepping away from the bedroom door, he headed outside. Thick snowflakes and icy wind met him as he hurried to the car. Andre grabbed a pack of clove cigarettes from the glove compartment and sprinted back into the cabin. Bypassing the closed bedroom door, he opted for the balcony. One day he'd give up smoking, but today qualified as bad enough to fall back on the habit. Digging the lighter out of his pocket, he lit a cigarette. The sweet smell of tobacco immediately melted the tension from his shoulders. The smoke drifted to the closed balcony door connected to Mikayla's room. He huddled in a corner away from the door.

A rush of other emotions replaced his tension. A knot formed in his stomach. How could he have been fooled by Angelica? His mom's warnings that she was a gold digger echoed in his brain. But since her divorce, his mom believed most young and beautiful women were gold diggers.

Angelica waltzed into his life with her five nine height, supermodel looks, and amazing sexual prowess. Her slight Parisian accent was the cherry on top. She played his body and ego, like a violin in the hands of a professional violinist. That's all it took to keep him happy. Love wasn't real. He'd seen that long before his parents split up. But a wife, and eventually children, would go a long way to securing the future of C.E.S.

Marriage was just another business arrangement. Angelica wouldn't have brought any real connections to the family, but the moment she batted those cat-like eyes, the blood in his brain rushed to his dick and decided on the trophy wife. Andre had strutted like a peacock with her on his arm and accepted the praise and envious looks from other guys with pride.

He took another drag on the cigarette. Their relationship was built on bullshit, and he deserved to lose her. He wasn't hurt by their split. Pissed off, yes, but not hurt. Luckily she'd revealed her true colors before he'd given her the ring in his bag. A cynical laugh escaped him and echoed in the night. That could have been his wife in the closet instead of his girlfriend.

His nose tingled from the cold. He took one last drag of the cigarette when the curtains along the door leading to the bedroom twitched. Mikayla slid the dark blue fabric back. Her glare was fierce but not as fierce as the halo of her body in the lamplight from the room. His breaths hitched. She may not have Angelica's exotic looks, but she more than made up for what she lacked in glamor with down home southern girl attraction. The curves he'd wondered about were on full display in her pajamas: thick thighs, round ass, small waist, and full breasts. He blew out a lungful of smoke and tugged on the front of his sweatpants.

The easiest way to forget a woman is between the legs of another. The thought whispered in his brain, but he dismissed it. Or tried to anyway. She seemed like a nice woman, so for once, he'd play the nice guy.

"I smelled smoke." She said after sliding back the glass door.

"If the smoke bothers you I'll put the cigarette out." He leaned down to snuff the tip when she rushed over.

"Don't."

He straightened and watched her. Mikayla's arms crossed full breasts to protect against the cold, and her hands ran frantically up and down her arms. The sleeveless pajama top was useless against the breeze, even with the purple flannel pants and matching slippers she wore. He'd never been around a woman in real lounging pajamas. Surprisingly, he liked the comfortable look more than the silks and satins he was accustomed to seeing. An overwhelming urge to reach out and pull her curvy body into his arms and protect her from the chill made him shift his stance. Instead, he took another drag.

Her eyes followed his movements. He recognized the look of someone who hadn't quite kicked the habit.

"I have another in my car."

She shook her head. "I quit."

"So did I," he said with a lift of one shoulder.

He held out the cigarette. She hesitated, chewing on her bottom lip before finally taking it from him. His gaze was glued to her as she inhaled. Mikayla's eyes closed, and her lips curved into a sinful smile. She slowly exhaled and licked her lips. A steady drumbeat of desire started in his chest and ran down his body.

When her eyes opened, he couldn't look away. Her lips parted before she quickly pressed them together and lowered her lids.

She shoved the cigarette his way. "Thanks."

"You can finish."

She shook her head. "No, I really did quit."

He wanted to put his lips on the filter and see if he could taste her. Badly. Which wasn't what a good guy would do.

He shook his head, "I'm finished."

She stared at the smoldering tip, before crushing the cigarette in the ashtray and tossing it in the trash.

"It's freezing out here." Her voice trembled a little and, she rubbed her arms.

"I know."

She glanced at him. "Well, goodnight."

"I'm sorry for what I said earlier. I didn't mean to make you cry."

In the cold, Mikayla's heavy exhale was just as visible as the cloud of cigarette smoke she blew earlier. "You didn't make me cry."

"Then I'm sorry for reminding you who did."

She tightened the grip on her arms. "It's not as if I can forget. It's the reason we're stranded here. Besides, I can't blame you for what you thought. Most of the women Ryan dated forgave him easily. Believe me, I saw the tears of his previous girlfriends."

She shivered. He stepped closer and ran his hands over her shoulders. Her soft skin was cold beneath his fingertips.

"You're different. You're stronger than I expected. In the middle of all the drama, you kept your head up and didn't cause a scene. Since then, you've handled being forced to stay in a cabin with me with class. I shouldn't have misjudged you."

"I'm not that strong."

Pleased that she didn't pull away, he took a step closer. "You are. To walk away like you did…"

"Is what any other woman with a bit of sense would have done. Before that, I wanted to scratch his eyes out." She shook her head and lowered her eyes. "I kneed him in the balls."

He chuckled. Back at the estate she didn't seem to possess a lot of fight. But Mikayla had proved him wrong yet again. He liked a woman with a bit of fire. Time to rein in those types of thoughts. Liking her would be a mistake. Still, he didn't take his hands off her shoulders. "Better you do that than me realign his esophagus."

She raised her head and laughed. The soft sound was like a warm breeze in the cold night. "Maybe we should've acted the fool. I think they both could have used a good beat down."

Moonlight shone on her hair, turning the brown tresses silver. Without thinking, he lifted his hand and took a few strands between his fingers.

"We'll tag team them next time," he said.

Her body barely shifted forward, surrounding him with her sweet floral scent. "I like that idea."

He continued to toy with her hair. The fine locks were soft like silk against his skin. He wanted to bury his fingers in it, pull her close and see if her lips were just as soft. He pushed the strands behind her ear. Then trailed his fingers slowly down the side of her face. One taste, that's all he wanted. The urge had nothing to do with revenge, and everything to do with a cold night, a beautiful woman, and one bed.

Her eyes widened, and she shook her head. The cold air rushed around him when she stepped back, dousing his desire and bringing common sense back into play.

Her chest rose and fell with short quick breaths. She cleared her throat, "I'm gonna call it a night."

He sucked in a lungful of the frigid night air, wishing it would cool the hot thoughts in his head.

"I think that's a good idea." He hoped the roads would be clear tomorrow. He couldn't do this another night.

"Good night, Andre." She slipped back into the bedroom.

Andre watched the doors close. Fought the ridiculous need to knock on the glass. Sure he could explore the spark between them, but what good would it do to follow her? He would not sleep with his cousin's ex-girlfriend. Would not make this a pissing match between him and Ryan. *You weren't thinking about Ryan when you touched her.* True. But getting involved with Mikayla was a bad idea. He wasn't convinced she wouldn't forgive Ryan. No, he needed to ignore this attraction and drive her home first thing in the morning.

*

Andre jerked up to a sitting position. Bright morning sunlight dragged away the remnants of sleep and reflected off the snow covered trees through the balcony's glass doors. Squinting he held up a hand and blocked his eyes. Pushing back the blanket Mikayla had tossed to him the night before, he surveyed the room. The door to the bedroom was closed. The kitchen appeared undisturbed, and the only sound was the faint humming of the refrigerator. But something had woke him.

The front door cracked open as Mikayla slipped inside. She was still in pajamas, her hair hidden behind a bright orange scarf, and dark red slippers on her feet. One of her hands was pressed tightly against her chest as if protecting something as she quietly shut the door. When she turned and caught his eye, she froze.

She shuffled, and bit her lower lip. "I didn't mean to wake you."

"What were you doing outside? Looks like more snow fell. It has to be freezing."

She avoided his eyes but dragged her feet along the floor and crossed the room moving slowly toward him. When she stood at the back of the couch, she uncurled her hand and held it out.

He shook his head and chuckled. "I thought you had quit."

"I did!" She came around the couch, and he moved his legs so she could sit on the edge. "This is crazy. I haven't smoked in over a year and after one terrible afternoon I'm craving a cigarette as bad as I did in college."

"Because of what happened?"

She threw the cigarette on the table and rubbed her eyes with the balls of her hands. "I shouldn't let this get to me. I shouldn't be so surprised that Ryan did what he did." Her head fell back on the sofa, and she frowned up at the ceiling. "I'm mad at myself, more than I am at him." She said softly.

He peered at the cigarette on the coffee table, then back at Mikayla. He could either let her get her thoughts out or remain distant and watch her fall back into the habit she was trying to fight. The urge for a cigarette gnawed at his insides. Even now, he wanted one.

His mouth dried up at the thought of confiding in her. He glanced at Mikayla's stooped shoulders and pensive frown and something tugged in his chest. A new, almost uncomfortable sensation. Having a "let's talk" conversation wasn't high on his priority lists. Dealing with the problem head on without examining his feelings was more his style. Her unease made him want to soothe the discomfort. What the hell. He could continue to pretend to be a good guy. Indulging her for a few minutes would, hopefully, bring a smile to her face, and then they'd go their separate ways.

"I understand how you feel," he said. "I knew things with Angelica weren't…ideal, but I let myself believe marrying her would be okay."

Slowly, Mikayla's head turned to face him. He saw the same conflict in her eyes that he'd battled. He had to choose, open up with the person who was connected to his enemy or keep the churning emotions bottled up inside.

"You were going to marry her. I'm so sorry."

He shook his head. "Don't be. I'm lucky to have seen her true colors before proposing."

"But, you must hurt more than me. I wasn't in love with Ryan. If you were thinking of marrying Angelica, then you were betrayed, by the person you loved."

He shifted to avoid the empathy in her eyes. His stomach churned. He couldn't tell her that he was only marrying Angelica to improve the company image. He didn't want to witness the disgust in her eyes when she realized he'd let lust, and Caldwell pride chose his bride.

"I'm better off." He turned back toward her. "And so are you."

Her soft tempting lips curved up into a small smile. She didn't have the tension around her eyes and shoulders like she'd had the day before. No tightness to flatten her full lips, and no stiffness in her speech. All of which made her infinitely more desirable.

"My dad would agree with you. He never liked Ryan."

"Smart man."

She shook her head and leaned back staring at the ceiling. "About a lot of things." Her chest rose and fell with a deep inhale and release of air. Andre zeroed in on her nipples, hardened by the cold that also added inches to his morning erection.

"Being with Ryan was…something I thought I wanted." Her voice jerked him out of his thoughts. "Maybe too much. I wasn't so ordinary with him."

"I wouldn't call you ordinary."

Surprise and pleasure danced in her soft brown eyes. "Believe me, I am." She brought her knees up on the couch and wrapped her arms around them. "I used to think I was less than ordinary. I felt plain and forgettable. I don't want to be that anymore."

Ordinary was the last thing he would have used to describe Mikayla. Even now, with her hair wrapped in an orange scarf, and wearing pajamas, she was sexy. Though she had been hurt, she'd proven herself emotionally strong, practical, but not afraid to admit to her flaws. A good woman. How had Ryan snagged her?

"I think Ryan had someone extraordinary and didn't realize it."

Her tongue darted across her bottom lip, and they parted with a silent sigh. The air thickened around them, and he held her gaze.

"Thank you." She sat up, broke eye contact, and cleared her throat. "More snow fell last night. I wonder if the roads are clear."

The part of him thrumming with attraction hoped they weren't. The sensible part of him prayed they were.

"Let's see if there's anything on the news."

He flipped on the television and clicked through the channels until they came across the weather report. Two more inches of snow and an additional half inch of ice. Travel was not recommended until all roads were cleared, and highway travel was unlikely with the rock slide.

"Well, at least they think the detour roads will be open tomorrow," Mikayla said.

"It means another night together."

"If they let us keep the cabin."

They both cast a long glance at the cigarette on the coffee table. The thought of the relief that would come from taking a drag clouded his brain. Maybe she felt the same. An uncomfortable silence filled the space. He wanted to fill the void, keep her talking, and learn more about what made Mikayla fall for Ryan of all people. He wasn't much better than Ryan. But her smile, and the tiny bit of trust she had to feel in order to open up with him was nice. He liked the feeling.

He stood, lifted his hands over his head and stretched. "We can walk down to the main office together."

She didn't immediately answer. Her widened gaze focused on the front of his sweatpants and his erection. Masculine pride and slight embarrassment heated his insides. He pulled on the waistband of his pants to try and diminish the effect. Not easy knowing she'd sized him up.

She covered her face and turned her head. "I'm sorry, what did you say. I'm still a bit…groggy."

He couldn't help but smile. "Walk with me to the main office to see if we can keep the cabin for another night."

"Good idea."

She jumped up and at the same time he took a step forward. They bumped into each other. Her warm body sent a rush of excitement over his skin. He reached out to steady her, to get another feel of her, but she backed away quickly. Her eyes avoided his.

"You can shower first," she said.

"Do I smell?" he teased.

Her gaze flew to his. He smiled, and she chuckled.

"No, just being nice," she said.

"That's good to know. Once we get the cabin situated, we'll figure out what to do for the rest of the day."

He could think of several things he'd like to do. A few of them involved keeping warm with her. As if she had read his thoughts, desire sparked in her eyes. The need to reach out and kiss her was overwhelming. He jerked his gaze away.

With a gasp, she uncrossed her arms and turned away. "Go shower, and we'll figure out how to get through the day. We'll need something to eat and a distraction from…the urge to smoke."

Nicotine wasn't what his body craved. He grabbed his bag off the floor, put it on the couch, and pulled out some clothes. "I'll only be a few minutes."

He quickly got the rest of his things and went into the bathroom, before he gave into his craving for a taste of Mikayla.

CHAPTER 5

They secured the cabin for another night. Once they took care of the second night, again Andre insisted on paying. They searched for food. With the roads blocked, they were limited to the breakfast options in the rental office and the Chinese Restaurant he'd found half a mile from the resort that wouldn't open until later. They grabbed doughnuts, granola bars, and coffee from the office before walking back up the hill toward the cabin.

"Want to walk the trail, instead of going back inside?" Andre asked.

Mikayla eyed the paved trail circling the perimeter of the Huggie Bear property. The rental agent had mentioned that many of their visitors came to the resort for the passive recreation. Hiking wasn't on her short list of favorite activities. Too many memories of trekking through the woods with her dad, followed by teasing from the popular girls for her scratched arms and knees when she returned to school.

She took one last sip of coffee then pulled up the collar of her grey wool coat. "It's freezing. Besides, I'm not really a hiker."

"Once you start walking you'll warm up." When she gave him a skeptical look, his lips spread into a smile that would melt the ice in Antarctica. "I'm going to walk. Maybe it'll help clear my head."

"I'll wait for you inside."

The corners of his smile dipped, and some of the light left his eyes. She could go inside and watch television alone, or hike a trail that appeared wonderfully absent of briars with a handsome man who seemed to want her company.

"Come on," he said. "Better than sitting in there alone." He held out this hand.

She stared at his hand. Taking his hand wouldn't be that big a deal in a normal situation. Except this wasn't a normal situation. The warmth spreading beneath her skin from the small gesture wasn't a normal reaction to a guy she shouldn't be attracted to.

"I was just thinking the same thing."

She tossed the coffee cup in the trash and slid her hand into Andre's. He led her to the section of trail near their cabin. The resort staff had spent the morning shoveling snow from the paved trail. She and Andre were the only two taking advantage. Wooden signs marked various detours that lead from the regular paved trail onto more rugged hiking areas.

Even bundled in jeans, boots, coat, and gloves, the coldness seeped into her bones. Not surprising, she'd picked this outfit with Renee because it was cute not hardy. A strong gust of wind made her shiver, and she moved closer to Andre. He noticed and shifted to walk in front of her, and blocked the wind with his body. She lowered her head and smiled at his kindness. Slowly, she warmed as they tracked up the hill. He didn't talk much as they walked. Occasionally he'd stop and study their surroundings while she ducked the wind.

She kept her head down avoiding the cold and looked for patches of ice that would have her falling on her rump. He stopped suddenly, and she bumped into his back. A strong hand kept her from falling over.

"Oh, sorry," she glanced around. "Why did we stop?"

He pointed to the mountains. "Check out the way the mist rises." His voice held a sense of wonder and appreciation that she didn't expect from a guy previously described as devious.

She shifted her gaze to where he indicated. The mist clung to the peaks like a translucent white veil. "It's beautiful," she whispered.

"It's better in the summer after it rains," he said, staring at the view.

"Do you often visit?"

He frowned, and shook his head. "Unfortunately, no. I don't get out as much as I used to." A wistful note in his voice.

She pulled her coat closer to block the wind, and then turned to him. "I've always been indifferent to the mountains. Not too excited about getting attacked by bears."

"Bears?" His rich laughter floated in the wind and sent a shiver down her spine that had nothing to do with the cold. "You're joking."

She pulled her coat tighter. "No, I'm serious." His deep laugh continued, and she couldn't help but smile. "Look, I'm only walking with you now because its winter and they're hibernating."

He shook his head. "Let's go back down. Don't want a bear to get us."

She giggled, then pressed her hand to her lips. What the hell? Giggling wasn't something she did…ever.

On the way down the mountain, a sign on the trail indicated a detour to a cabin that was restored from the late 1800s. Andre read the sign then spun to her with an eager grin.

She rolled her eyes but followed the gesture with a smile. "Fine, we'll check it out."

Their breathing, along with their footsteps in the snow was the only sounds as they hiked to the cabin. Views of the mountains were visible through the trees. The size of the peaks brought home how small her problems were in the grand scheme of things. It was a philosophical thought that wouldn't be remembered on Monday when she returned to work.

Pushing aside the idea of going back to face Ryan and his family, she hurried along the trail to the cabin. Dark gray clouds hung in the sky, and the air had the quiet calm that usually preceded snow.

Inside was tiny. She paused and observed the one room cabin. "Could you imagine raising a family here?" She eyed the small living area.

"People didn't need so much back then." Andre ran his fingers along the walls wooden beams.

"Everyone needs privacy," she said. "I spent the night at my cousin Sheri's house once when we were little and overheard her parents having sex." She shuddered at the memory. "I was mortified. I still can't look them in the eye. Can you imagine if you were in the same room with your parents on one of those nights?"

He turned to face her. His dark eyes studied her face. "That's the first thing you think about?" He said in a teasing drawl. "Sex?"

Andre's silky baritone wrapped around her. Heat crept up her face. The man said the word sex with enough smoothness to tighten her nipples and send her thoughts places they had no business going.

She spun away feigning interest in the fireplace. "It wasn't the first thing on my mind."

Heavy footsteps crossed the room and stopped behind her. "You can have sex without making a lot of noises." His voice dipped enough to make her wonder if he cared to demonstrate.

"Apparently so," she said. He stood close and the heat from his body beckoned her. She shifted away to peer out the window. "It's snowing." She brought a hand to her head. "My hair is going to be messed up."

He chuckled, and she lifted her chin. The tangled mess her hair was whenever her dad tried to arrange it was the reason she now spent too much money at salons. She'd refused to be ashamed of not wanting her hair to get wet.

Andre's warm hand engulfed Mikayla's, sending a shockwave of awareness up her arm and straight to her core. "It's barely coming down. But let's go before the snow and bears get us."

She couldn't suppress her chuckle. They hurried back to their cabin as the snow fell harder. Andre turned up the thermostat the second they were inside. She paused blowing into her hands when he came over and peered at her head.

Mikayla raised a hand and checked for flyaways. "Is everything okay?"

Andre reached over and brushed snowflakes from her hair. She didn't move. When the crystals were either gone or melted and he ran his hand through her hair. She remained still. Usually, Mikayla hated anyone touching her hair, but his fingers soothed rather than irritated.

His eyes darkened, with an emotion she wasn't foolish enough to identify. She stepped away and made a show of brushing away non-existent snow.

"I'm sure it looks terrible."

"It's fine," He cleared his throat and removed his coat and gloves.

She glanced at Andre as he walked over and sat on the couch. Andre possessed the Caldwell good looks. Maybe not so much of the charm, but he was nice. Ryan's side had described their uncle's children as cutthroat.

"What are you watching?" She sat beside him.

"Just flipping through channels." He held out the remote. "You want to pick something?"

She shook her head. With a shrug, he turned back to the television. She pulled the quilt he'd folded and placed on the edge of the couch around her and snuggled into the other end of the couch. Sleep came quickly. Her eyes opened to slits when Andre lifted her into his arms.

"You'll be more comfortable in the bed." His deep voice lulled her eyes closed.

Andre carried Mikayla into the bedroom and gently placed her on the bed. A soft sensation brushed across her forehead. A kiss? It couldn't be. Still, she smiled and fell back asleep.

CHAPTER 6

Andre came into the cabin and set the DVDs he'd gotten from the rental office on the table. The lights were off. The only sound in the room was the hum of the HVAC unit heating the space. Mikayla must have still been asleep. He'd fallen asleep watching television earlier. After waking up and realizing she still slept, he figured it would be better to go out and find something they could entertain themselves with for the rest of the night.

Much to his surprise, he'd enjoyed her company earlier. She liked to talk but did not fill the space with useless words. Several times that afternoon, he found himself just enjoying the sound of her voice. She didn't require many conversations, unlike most women he knew. Most women tried to drag information out of him. Mikayla's lack of prying made opening up to her easy.

He knocked softly on the door. When there was no answer, he peaked in. She lay curled on her side, hugging a pillow to her chest. Without the orange head wrap from earlier her hair fanned across the pillow and his fingers itched to run through the soft strands.

Clearing his throat, he called her name. She didn't move. He edged closer into the room and gingerly approached her.

"Mikayla," he said. He poked her shoulder a few times.

She groaned and swatted his hand away before rolling onto her back. His throat constricted. The tops of her breasts swelled above the neckline of her shirt. Her nipples, pebble hard beneath the soft material, stoked his admiration better than the mist rising from the mountains. He clenched his hands when he really wanted to reach out and take the swells into his hands.

He shook his head. Be the good guy, not the jerk. He would not sleep with or fondle his cousin's ex-girlfriend, no matter how delectable her breasts appeared.

"Mikayla," he called loudly.

She jerked awake and sat up. He took a step back, and she looked frantically around the room. When her eyes focused on him, her face scrunched into a scowl.

"Did you yell at me?"

"You didn't move when I called you from the door or when I poked your shoulder." He shrugged. "I had to yell to wake you up."

"I haven't slept that long in the middle of the day in…" her brow crinkled. "I don't know how long." She swung her legs to the side of the bed and stretched, her breast straining against the fabric of the shirt she wore.

Andre diverted his gaze to the crown molding along the ceiling.

"You were pretty tired, huh." He felt foolish for stating the obvious.

"I'm not usually this tired." She said behind a yawn. "But somebody had me out hiking." She stood and strolled into the bathroom.

His lips quirked. Their tour around the property was hardly a hike, but he'd enjoyed getting out and stretching his muscles. He hadn't had the chance to enjoy nature in years. He'd allowed too many Caldwell family responsibilities to take over his life.

"I got some snacks from the rental office and a few DVDs."

She poked her head out of the bathroom and ran a comb through her hair.

"What kind of snacks?"

"More doughnuts and a few cookies."

She stopped combing her hair and smiled. "Thanks for getting something. I forgive you for making me hike."

He smiled, and Mikayla ducked back into the bathroom. He sauntered over and leaned against the door jamb. Watching as she squeezed toothpaste onto her toothbrush. An innocent act, but for some reason watching her do the mundane task seemed sexy.

"You might want to hold your forgiveness until after you hear what movies I brought. I hope you don't mind horror or action."

She met his eyes in the mirror. "As if I'm really in the mood for some sappy romance."

He grinned. Then it hit him. He liked her. It was one thing to want to have sex with a woman, but to like her and want to have sex with her meant he was heading down the wrong path. She bent over to rinse, and his eyes dropped to the delectable swell of her ass. His dick twitched in agreement. They were both wronged. Could they really be faulted for seeking comfort with each other?

He jerked away from the door and took a step back. He wouldn't take comfort now only to see Mikayla on Ryan's arm at another family wedding in the future.

Andre cleared his throat. "I'll put in the movie and put the food in front of the television."

She turned. Their eyes met, and her hand paused as it wiped the excess water from her mouth. She pulled in a stuttering breath. Then quickly glanced away. His body heated. *She felt it too.*

"I'll be out in a minute," she said softly.

He nodded before spinning on his heels and walking out. When she joined him a few minutes later, he sat on the couch with the first movie, Zombie Invasion, already in the DVD player.

She rubbed her arms and eyed the food. "You know what would be great with this."

He smiled. "A cigarette."

With a sigh, she flopped on the couch. "Isn't this sad? I haven't smoked in a year, but after one incident, I'm ready to pick up the habit again."

He handed her a plate. "Tell me about it. I quit two years ago, but we had a few rough months when we thought we'd lose a major client. Before I knew it, I had a pack in my car, home, and office again."

"Do you smoke every day?" Her full lips pursed as she slowly sucked lo mein noodles into her mouth, followed by a long circular sweep of her tongue.

His balls tightened before he swallowed hard and averted his gaze. "When I'm stressed. Which isn't every day, but more than I like."

Bullshit. He was tense daily after doing the dirty work required to make the company successful.

She nodded. "It makes me mad all over again, knowing this thing with Ryan is causing me to backslide."

"How about we agree not to let this take us down that road again."

"Yeah, you say that now then you'll be back home smoking a pack a day." She said a teasing glint in her eye.

"You don't trust me?" He smirked and took a bite of food.

Mikayla's light laughter filled the room. "I didn't say that."

"Check in with me whenever you want. I'll let you know if I had a cigarette."

She slowly chewed and watched him. He wanted her to agree. Wanted to prove she was just as intrigued by the attraction between them. Wanted her to accept his obvious attempt to keep in contact.

Her shoulders relaxed and then she nodded. "It's a deal."

He released a breath, and only displayed his satisfaction by smiling and starting the movie.

*

Later that night, a shriek jerked Andre from his sleep. He pushed the covers off and shook his head to clear the fog of sleep. He sat still, listening, but heard nothing. He pulled the covers up and laid down when he heard the shriek again, it had come from the bedroom.

That had him rushing to Mikayla's door as if one of the zombies they'd watched earlier chased him. He burst into the bedroom, and Mikayla thrashed around on the king size bed. She mumbled and swung her arms as if fighting off an attacker. He hurried over and grabbed her flailing arms. She struggled more. Eyes closed, her head jerked from side to side.

"Mikayla," he said giving her a soft shake. "Come on, baby, you're dreaming. Wake up."

One of her arms broke from his grasp, and she fought harder. He didn't want to pin her against the bed. He wasn't a dream expert, but holding someone down who was fighting while having a nightmare couldn't possibly help the situation.

He pulled Mikayla against his chest. Her body jerked.

"No…please…leave us alone," she murmured.

He wrapped his arms around her. "Shh, baby, it's okay. You're having a dream. It's okay." He ran his hand up and down her back and gently rocked from side to side.

She stiffened. He sucked in several deep breaths, to calm his racing heart as she lay rigid against him when suddenly her body relaxed and collapsed into him.

The tension left his shoulder, and he pulled back enough to see her face. Her eyes were closed, and her breaths came smooth and even. She slept like the dead. A nightmare and a strange guy holding her and still she hadn't awakened.

She appeared calm now. He could leave. Lay her back down, tuck the sheets around her, and go back to the couch. He smoothed the hair away from her face. He watched and slowly the fear from seeing her thrashing around on the bed evaporated.

He pulled her close again. Burying his nose in the crook between her shoulder and neck, took a deep breath, and pretended she was his while he inhaled the sweet floral fragrance she wore.

Andre's heartbeat slowed, and his body temperature steadily rose. A reminder that his good deed for the day was done. He gently laid her back on the bed. He ran the back of his hand along her cheek, then moved to get up.

Her hand shot out and grabbed his. His body froze. Her eyes opened, and she observed him through sleepy eyes.

"It was a nightmare," she said in a low husky whisper.

He smiled. "I kinda figured that out. Do you want to talk about it?"

"You'll think I'm crazy."

He rested his arms on his knees. "I doubt that."

She brought his hand back to the side of her face and placed a warm cheek against his palm. Her light breaths brushed against his wrist, sending a tremor through him.

"I was being chased by zombies."

A relieved laugh burst from him, and his shoulders relaxed. He'd expected some deep-seated trauma to be the cause of her nightmare.

Synithia Williams

"Then it's my fault for bringing those movies."

She shook her head. "No, my fault for not telling you. I sometimes have nightmares after watching horror films."

"Then why did you watch?"

She opened her eyes and met his. "I needed the distraction...you know."

His thumb trailed down the side of her face, stopping at the corner of her mouth. Her full lips parted. Moonlight streamed in through the windows, reflecting off her cocoa skin and that damn orange head wrap. He wanted to snatch the thing off, dig his hands in her hair and chase away the remainder of her nightmare with a kiss.

"I should go back to the couch," he said, though the couch no longer held its previous appeal. He moved to get up, but her hand tightened.

"Don't go," she whispered.

He cleared his throat and shifted on the bed. Her quiet declaration tightened his groin.

"That's not a good idea."

She shook her head. "Maybe not. I know there's this...attraction between us, but we're both smart enough to realize that it would be stupid to follow up. I would feel better if you stayed with me a little while longer."

She sucked in shallow breaths and her hand clung to his. Asking him to stay after acknowledging the attraction meant she was either really afraid or really stupid.

He was really stupid.

He pulled his hand out of hers and shifted. "Slide over. I'll sleep on top of the covers."

She scooted out of the way. Then lifted the duvet. "No need for you to be cold. We can keep the sheet between us."

Suppressing thoughts of how only a sheet separated him from her beautiful warm curves, he slid under the covers next to her.

CHAPTER 7

Somebody lay beside her. Mikayla hadn't opened her eyes, but she recalled asking Andre to stay. Her face heated. If she'd been fully awake, and not wrestling with leftover fear, she wouldn't have made such a crazy suggestion. He must think her all kinds of dopey for dreaming about zombies then asking him to sleep beside her like a toddler.

Slowly rolling onto her back, she peered at Andre out of the corner of her eye. He lay on his back, with one arm draped across his eyes. His mouth slightly open, a soft snore escaped with each exhale. A slight nudge would probably push him to the floor he lay so close to the edge of the bed.

She frowned; he didn't look comfortable. Well, what should she expect, for him to be curled up against her back? Handsome, wealthy, and used to dating women as beautiful and polished at Angelica; there was no way he'd be flattered that Mikayla asked him to protect her from imaginary demons. Still, thoughts of the day before made her smile. Even though Andre didn't talk much, he seemed to enjoy himself. He wasn't like Ryan, who always needed to talk and be the center of attention.

She stared at the ceiling. The vision of Ryan and Angelica falling out of that closet was so vivid it could've been projected on the flat surface. Tears burned her eyes, and she let them fall. She'd have to face him, and the humiliation of what he'd done, on Monday. A sinking feeling assaulted her midsection.

Mikayla sniffed, and Andre rolled onto his side. Panic flashed across his handsome face. Oh yeah, he didn't do crying. Grabbing the edge of the sheet, she tried to dry her cheeks.

"Are you okay?" Andre's sleep filled voice was a deep sexy rumble.

She sat up and tried for nonchalant. "I'm good."

"Are you sure? I mean…I can get you some…whatever it is you may need."

His helpless expression made her smile. "Do you have a new job you can pull out of your hat?"

He groaned and sat up beside her. "Sorry, can't help you there."

"I figured."

They both sat silent for several seconds. When Andre's smoky eyes met hers, desire burned away the sinking feeling in her stomach. Barely a few inches separated them. His body would still be warm with sleep and perfect for snuggling.

She pushed back the covers and scurried off the bed. Crossing the room to the bathroom, Mikayla stopped at the door and faced him. He watched her with a slight frown.

"Umm…sorry about last night. I didn't mean to make you uncomfortable by asking you to sleep beside me. You could have left. I would have been alright."

One of his shoulders lifted, and his mouth curved into a too sexy for this early in the morning grin. "I didn't mind lying beside you, Mikayla."

She nodded, met his gaze, and her heart thudded. So, so wrong to be attracted to him. Spinning around, she went into the bathroom and closed the door. She furiously brushed her teeth. Each stroke came with a mental chide to stop thinking about how Andre in a t-shirt and sweat pants lounging on the bed created a pretty damn good visual of the word sexy. After giving her teeth and gums an undeserved trashing, she stepped into the shower. Once she finished and stood cold, wet and dripping in the bathroom, she cursed herself for running in there without any clothes.

She wrapped one of the thick burgundy towels around her torso and peeked into the empty bedroom. A relieved sigh escaped her. Padding across the room, she unzipped her bag and pulled out an outfit to wear. Andre knocked on the bedroom door.

Mikayla tightened the towel before crossing the room and cracking the door. Andre held his body wash, toothbrush, and a t-shirt in his hands. And a pair of red plaid boxers. A mental image of him in his boxers filled her brain, and her cheeks flamed.

"Do you want me to wait to take a shower?"

"No, I just finished." She stepped back and opened the door wider.

"Thanks. I checked the news and apparently the detour roads are clear. We can leave as soon as we're dressed."

He stopped just inside the door. Gave her a quick once over in the towel. Her skin tingled. Andre's hot stare made her body come alive. The soft towel rubbed against her puckering nipples creating a delicious friction that scattered across her skin everywhere the material touched. She twisted one foot into the carpet and ignored the sensation that made her want to drop the towel.

"Good. I need to get home," she said.

He blinked then stepped around her. "Yeah, me too."

She didn't watch him go into the bathroom, just waited tensely for the door to close. Once the door was shut, she let out a shaky breath. *Thank goodness for the men and women of the Department of Transportation for clearing the roads.* Another day in the mountains and she'd make a monumental mistake.

Mikayla dressed quickly putting on a pair of jeans and a red sweater. By the time Andre emerged from the bathroom—bringing a burst of steam and the sexy fragrance of that damn body wash—her packed bag sat near the door. He'd put his sweat pants back on but wore a clean t-shirt. And probably those boxers. In his hand, was the old t-shirt, toothbrush and body wash. No underwear present; maybe he hadn't slept in any. A slick stream of excitement rode down her spine as the thought of the various possibilities that could have happened if he had curled up next to her beneath the covers.

"I've already packed my bag. We can leave whenever you're ready," he said.

She jerked her thoughts away from Andre's underwear preferences. "Same here. Whenever you're ready. I know our situation is weird," she smiled. "But thanks for making a terrible weekend a little easier."

"It wasn't a chore to be with you."

She sat on the bed, grabbed a pair of socks and put them on. "You did act like it was a chore when we first arrived."

He crossed the room and sat on the bed. They didn't touch, but she still slid over a few inches. "I didn't know what to expect spending the night with Ryan's girlfriend."

She glared, and he held up a hand. "Ex-girlfriend."

"I guess I can understand that." Mikayla relaxed, then cocked her head to study him. Andre seemed to be handling the split tremendously well. "How are you doing?"

"What do you mean?"

Mikayla turned on the bed, to face him. "Yesterday you mentioned things were getting serious between you and Angelica. Are you doing a good job of distracting yourself, or are you crying when I'm not looking?"

The deep rumble of his chuckle sent a quiver through her stomach.

"I can promise you I'm not crying."

"Why not, if you two were getting serious. You paraded her around the night before so everyone could see how much you loved her."

A frown replaced the smile on his face. "I paraded her around, but that wasn't love." He sighed heavily and met her eyes. "You don't understand my family...Well, maybe you do. When you're raised to idolize certain things, it's hard to let go." A hint of disgust clouded his voice. He rubbed his hand over his face and shook his head as if he could clear it of the bad memories. "Long story short, Angelica fits the bill of what I need in a wife."

"What bill?"

"Angelica's beautiful, she knew how to entertain, and is a perfect companion for social events."

An armpiece, Mikayla thought. "Then how could it possibly be serious?"

He shrugged. "I thought she was a nice person. I did like her, we were compatible, and she wouldn't make a fuss about the demands of my family or the business. I planned to marry her."

"You would marry her, but you didn't love her. Why?"

He smirked and shook his head. "My family doesn't marry for love. You only briefly met my dad and step-mom, but a few minutes in a room with them will quickly reveal there's no love between them. They started as an affair that resulted in both of them dumping their old spouses for a newer model."

"Don't you want to love someone," she asked.

"No."

Simple, abrupt, with no explanation.

"I've been in love." Some of the wistfulness of what she'd once felt floated with her voice. "It's not so bad."

He leaned back and crossed thick arms over his wide chest. "Ryan?"

She shook her head. "No. My college boyfriend. We met during our junior year and dated all of our senior year. He asked me to marry him."

"What happened?"

"He died in a car wreck." She said simply.

Andre's dark eyes lowered briefly. "I'm sorry."

She shifted and toyed with the edge of her shirt. "I've come to terms with my loss. Cried enough tears to fill Lake Michigan. And yes, I still miss him. But his mom insisted that I live after it was over. He wouldn't want me to cry every day."

"What was his name?"

Brown eyes that crinkled when he grinned in his thin, tanned face flashed across her mind. "Brenden." She smiled. "He made me laugh, all the time at the silliest stuff. He was such a great guy."

Andre slid closer, wrinkling the quilted bed cover and her will to slide away. "The look on your face. You didn't have that look with Ryan."

She lifted then lowered her shoulders. "No, I didn't."

Andre lifted a hand and brushed the hair from the side of her face. His fingers trailed down the side of her cheek, sending shivers across her skin. A warning flared somewhere deep within her. They were getting too comfortable again. Mikayla ignored the warning and turned to rest her cheek against his palm.

She met his gaze. His dark eyes were alive with desire. Heat sparked between them. She took a stuttering breath and blood pounded in her veins like a rushing stream. Too many emotions swirled inside of her. She hadn't talked about Brenden in years, mainly because she didn't want those old feelings brought up. Andre was the last person she should trust with those feelings, but after he'd spent the night keeping her nightmares away it seemed silly not to trust him.

"You don't talk much, but when you do you get right to places I don't like going," she said in a wobbly whisper.

"If you're going to talk, it might as well be about something." He slid a hand to the back of her head. Long fingers gently twisted in her hair, which was probably now a mess. He pulled her closer.

Anticipation ignited and flared along her skin. As much as she'd wondered about Ryan's kiss, she'd never longed for his kiss, not the way she did for Andre's. She called on reason, to stop her now. "We shouldn't do this."

"No, we shouldn't." If she loved his voice before, she was completely enamored with the thick layer of desire flavoring the deep rumble. "That's why it's just going to be a kiss."

His lips touched hers. A spark, then bone-numbing need blasted through her body, tightening her nipples and sending trickles of desire to her core. She jerked back. Her breaths were short ragged bursts, struggling to supply oxygen to her brain. The same confusion, she was sure, shone in her eyes swam through his. With Andre, heat and intensity that powerful was something she didn't need. She made a move to pull away and at the same time he came in to kiss her again. This time the shock was expected, but no less explosive. Her skin tingled from the crown of her head to the soles of her feet. His tongue gently pushed past her lips.

Strong hands eased Mikayla back on the bed, and he settled muscular hips between her thighs. His large body covered hers and infused her memory with the smell of his body wash mixed with an underlying spice that was uniquely him. A hypnotic fragrance too consuming for her to forget, ever. Her arms wrapped around his neck, and she arched her back and pressed her breasts into his solid chest. Andre responded by sliding his body along hers; sending delicious currents of awareness to every nerve in her body.

His skilled tongue played with hers in an intimate dance that ripped all coherent thought from her brain. Tasting, teasing, and tormenting with deliberate exploration.

Her arms tightened around his neck and were a silent request for more. She moaned when his strong hand went up her shirt and caressed her midsection. Squirming under him her legs spread and he settled more firmly against the damp heat of her center. The hard ridge of his thick erection strained against the material of his sweat pants, taunting her and increasing the wetness between her thighs.

Andre's large hand engulfed her breast, then squeezed gently. The smooth skin of his palm made slow sensual circles around her swollen nipple. With each rotation, her body tightened and twisted beneath him, and the pleasure thrummed to the depths of her stomach. Low wanton moans interrupted Mikayla's short breaths. Breaking the kiss and gliding his mouth across her cheek, Andre snaked a skillful tongue to her ear. His probing mouth played with the sensitive lobe, and he nibbled and sucked while his hand massaged her breast.

"Andre," His name erupted with an unsteady breath.

His lips lightly pulled her ear. "Mikayla."

Oh, man, why did he have to say her name like that? All deep, rumbly, and full of a promise to take her places she'd never been before. He pushed his hips forward then rotated them against her aching flesh. Her eyes rolled in her head; her thighs quivered. How long had it been since she'd had sex? Too long. Not since that banker nine months ago. Long enough to convince her it was okay to go from friends to lovers with Ryan, even though, common sense said it wasn't. Long enough to make her seriously consider sleeping with Andre after only meeting a few days before.

"We really need to stop," she said firmly.

The soft kisses he pressed against her neck stilled. He lifted his head. "I'm stopping." He slowly withdrew his hand from her shirt. Mikayla bit her lip to keep from begging him to continue the proficient exploration. Swiftly, he rolled off of her and stared at the ceiling.

"I'm going to need a cigarette," he said between heavy breaths.

She nodded. "I think one more won't hurt either of us. Then we'll quit tomorrow. Again."

The sporadic rhythm of heavy breaths echoed through the room, almost drowned out by rapid beats of her heart.

"We can't do this," he said.

"No, we can't."

They didn't move for several minutes. Eventually, Mikayla's heart rate returned to normal, but her body buzzed.

Andre sat up first. "I think it's time to go."

She nodded, even though he couldn't see the gesture with his back to her. He stood, took a deep breath, and then marched out of the bedroom. Mikayla sat up, covered her heart with a trembling hand and tried to ignore the unsatisfied desire crawling beneath her skin.

"I need to go home." She said to the empty room. Gazing at the door, she yearned to call him back. "I need to go now."

CHAPTER 8

Mikayla glanced at Andre out of the corner of her eye. Uncertainty danced a jig in her brain. She wanted to spend more time with him, but couldn't keep seeing Andre. Yes, the kiss they shared had been exactly what a first kiss should be. Surely after a few weeks this weekend would fade in her memory just like her zombie dream. Once the rush of emotions faded, maybe she'd realize the kiss wasn't so fantastic.

Yeah, keep trying to convince yourself of that.

"I appreciate you taking me home," she said.

He darted his eyes away from the road and glanced at her. "It was a given that I'd take you home on Friday."

She shrugged. "I know, but I still appreciate it. You didn't even know my name yet you took me. Especially knowing how you feel about Ryan."

"From what I can tell, Ryan doesn't deserve you."

And now, her insides radiated all warm and tingling. "Angelica doesn't deserve you."

His dark eyes slid to her again. She gave him a small smile then turned to look out of the window. "So, I guess when you drop me off its goodbye." She stared out the window at the trees whizzing by.

Several beats passed with no response. Of course, this was goodbye. They had no reason to stay in touch.

"Not necessarily. You did agree to check and see if I pick up a cigarette again."

The tension in her shoulders eased and she faced him. "I did. But I probably shouldn't. Not after this morning."

He nodded slowly, but his thick brows furrowed as if he didn't like the comment. She turned back to the window while he changed the satellite radio from a talk show to a classical station. She recognized the song from television, but not being a classical fan wasn't sure of the composer.

"Won't that put you to sleep?"

"Classical helps me think."

She shifted away from the window to watch him. "What are you thinking about?"

He ran his hands along the steering wheel. "Work. We're launching a new project soon. I really should have worked on that this weekend instead of going to the wedding." His voice lacked its usual warmth. Now cool and aloof it was the same tone he'd used before they were stranded. He'd already begun to distance himself from the weekend and her. Something she should do as well.

Resting her head on the back of the seat, she closed her eyes and pushed back the sense of loss until the music lulled her to sleep.

Several hours later, Andre pulled into her apartment complex, and she woke up. With the back of her hand, she smothered a yawn. Mikayla checked the clock on the dash. He'd made excellent time.

"We're here already?"

Andre chuckled, then looked at her with remnants of the softness she'd witnessed at the cabin. "Do you fall asleep every time you ride in the car?"

"Actually I do," she agreed with a grin.

After giving Andre directions to her building, they rounded the corner to her place. Renee's Cadillac sat in front of the building. Mikayla groaned. Her friend must have left at the butt crack of dawn, to arrive before them. Not surprising since Mikayla hadn't answered any of her calls. Knowing Renee, she was worrying herself sick wondering where Mikayla was.

"I'm not in the mood for this," Mikayla said, unbuckling her seat belt.

Andre parked and raised his brows. "In the mood for what?"

"That's Renee's car next to us."

"Oh."

"Look, thanks for the ride, Andre." She opened the door and jumped out. Half a second after, Andre hopped out and followed her to the back of the car. "I can take it from here."

"I'll get your bag."

Mikayla gazed up at the window of her second-floor apartment. The blinds shifted. Renee had a key and was probably watching them now.

She accepted her bag from him, pivoted on the balls of her feet taking two steps before changing her mind, and turned back. She opened her mouth to say...what? Call me. Hey, let's hook up one weekend. Please kiss me again? He admitted he didn't want love, picked women who fit his lifestyle and had expressed no desire to change. Their two nights in the cabin were an anomaly.

"Take care of yourself," he said. At least the warmth had returned to his voice.

"You too." She gave him one last parting smile before turning and heading toward her apartment.

On the way upstairs, she tried to prepare herself mentally to talk with

Renee. No matter how touching Renee's show of concern, Mikayla didn't want to re-hash the weekend. Or blurt out that Renee's brother should be crowned king of the bastards.

Her door swung open before Mikayla could reach the knob.

"I've been worried sick about you. I've called and called, and every call went straight to voicemail. I even called your dad."

Mikayla groaned and pushed pass Renee into her one-bedroom apartment. The tan carpet muffled her stomps. "Why did you call my dad? Now he's going to be worried sick." She dropped the bag in the living room next to the off-white leather sofa. Back in her space, the scent of the apple cinnamon candle she frequently burned lingered in the air and eased the coiled tension tightening her body.

"When you didn't answer your phone I checked with him just to make sure you made it home and wasn't crushed beneath the rockslide on I-40."

She could forgive Renee for checking because of that. "Did you tell him what happened?"

"I just told him you left early. I know he already hates my brother, I didn't want to give him a reason to go ballistic."

Mikayla flopped down on the couch and considered covering her head with one of the orange throw pillows to block out the brewing headache. There would be no easy way to tell her overprotective parent about what happened between her and Ryan.

"I'll figure out something to tell him." She dropped her hands and met her friend's eyes.

Renee frowned and walked over taking the seat beside her. "Where were you?"

"The detour roads weren't clear. We rented a cabin."

"You spent two nights in a cabin with Andre." Renee's voice rose to a high pitch.

"No, I spent two nights with Bigfoot."

Renee sucked her teeth. "This isn't funny, Mikayla. Why would you spend the weekend with Andre? I know what Ryan did was beyond messed up, but to jump in bed with Andre—"

Mikayla bolted up in the seat. "Whoa, whoa, I didn't jump into bed with Andre, okay. You know me better than that." Or did she assume Mikayla would be that desperate? If Renee could believe that, then their friendship was just as superficial as her relationship with Ryan. "When have I jumped into bed with anyone?"

"I'm sorry. I just know Andre and the history between him and Ryan."

"Yeah, your family is quick to jump to assumptions." Mikayla grabbed her bag and marched across the room and into the bedroom.

Renee's footsteps followed. "Please don't be mad at me, Mikayla. I already feel horrible about what Ryan did."

Mikayla dropped her bag and turned back to her friend. Renee stood in the door twisting her hands together, uncertainty in her eyes. This was the first time Mikayla had seen her very confident friend appear uncomfortable.

"I'm not mad at you, Renee."

"The way you looked at me when you left the estate. It was like you couldn't stand the sight of me. I know I've teased about us being pretend sisters, but I really feel that way. I encouraged you to date Ryan. I understand if you blame me a little, but I don't want to lose my best friend over this."

The rest of the tightness in Mikayla's chest lifted. Mikayla walked over to her friend and took Renee's slim hand into hers. "I don't blame you. This is Ryan's fault. I only blame myself for believing he could be different with me."

"Then what was that look for?"

"I was angry. You two are twins. Facing you was just too much at the time." She squeezed her friend's hand. "We're good." Mikayla turned away and ran a hand through her hair.

Renee moved and sat on the edge of the bed. "So…what did happen with Andre?"

"Why are you so worried about that?"

"Because. Ryan and Andre have stolen each other's girlfriends since we were in high school. What Ryan did is bad, but to have my cousin take advantage of you would be horrible."

"Nothing happened, Renee, I promise." Except the best kiss of my life.

"What did you do all weekend?"

Instead of meeting Renee's eyes, she checked the leaves on a plant in the window. "Watched television and checked the news for information about when the roads would be cleared. Yes, we both wanted to find ways to keep our mind off what happened. But, sex wasn't a part of it."

Renee sighed. "Good, besides it's not like you're seeing him again."

Mikayla's stomach clenched. "I'm not." She stopped fiddling with the plant and faced Renee. "And pretty soon I won't have to see Ryan either."

"I was afraid of that. Look, you don't have to quit—"

"Yes, I do. I can't keep working for your family after this." She didn't want to quit. She wanted that promotion. Deserved it. But to face Ryan every day would be too much.

"It'll only be awkward for a few weeks. You two were only officially dating for a short time. Everyone in the office will take your side."

"I'm not worried about people taking my side."

Renee stood and crossed her arms. "What about the acquisitions position, and the land you worked so hard for Caldwell Development to purchase? Are you going to forget all of the work you did to secure that deal and move on?"

Mikayla cringed. Hell, I'm no quitter. She prided her ability to start and finish projects. She'd always pushed herself to do more in order to get away from the pitiful girl she once was. To be like the glamorous, ambitious, and confident women who had it all in the television shows and movies, she had watched as a kid. Mikayla's ambition is why she urged Caldwell Development to purchase the land Renee referred to after learning of a yet to be disclosed influx of new jobs. Jobs meant workers who needed housing. Not seeing the deal to fruition stung worse than the hurt of Ryan's betrayal.

"I don't know, Renee…"

Renee clasped her hand. "I know things are bad right now. Believe me, Mom, Dad, and I gave Ryan hell after you left. None of us want to lose you. You're practically family."

I'm not family. "What happened after I left?"

Renee scrunched her nose. "They…stayed together."

Mikayla's jaw dropped. "What?"

"Apparently, Angelica is the mystery woman Ryan fell in love with in France. Even though everyone hated what happened, Ryan is viewing this as a second chance." Mikayla sank onto the bed. She had some familiarity with Ryan's broken heart after falling in love with a mystery woman in Paris. He didn't say much other than he'd met, and lost, the woman of his dreams. Knowing he had been in love before once tugged at Mikayla's compassion. Now that same fact sickened her.

"I'm quitting."

Renee held up a hand. "Don't be rash. Just talk to my dad tomorrow. We'll make sure you never work on a project with Ryan. Give you a raise, whatever it'll take to keep you."

"My pride isn't for sale," she said.

Renee's flawless features froze with that steely Caldwell family determination. "Here's the deal. You don't have a new job, so there's no need to quit until you find one. And, you know it would kill you to walk out before at least settling the low country deal. To hell with Ryan. Don't let him ruin your career."

Renee made a valid point; quitting without a plan would mean she'd have her pride, but no money to pay the bills.

"Fine."

Renee gave a curt nod, but her shoulders sagged. "Good."

Mikayla dropped her head into her hands. What the hell am I doing?

CHAPTER 9

Tension vibrated throughout Andre's body as he walked into the corporate headquarters of Caldwell Environmental Solutions on Monday morning. Known as C.E.S, the company headquarters rested in a high rise in Greenville's Central Business District. He gave tight nods to those he recognized as he made his way to the elevator. The freedom and relaxation of the weekend with Mikayla faded with each beep of the elevator; replaced with the anticipation of what lay ahead. What deals would need negotiations, and if they failed, who would be paid off to get what C.E.S. wanted. That's how his father ran the business. The way Andre and his brother Isaac had learned to run the business.

Andre couldn't deny his dad's influence had made C.E.S. successful. What started out as just his dad with a truck was now a multi-million dollar enterprise with fleets in ten states and over 100,000 employees. He took pride in what his father had built. Not so much in the lengths his family took to get there, but cut-throat practices were the way of the business world.

He walked off the elevator on the top floor of the building. Thick beige carpet cushioned his footsteps. Kimberly Griffin, the administrative assistant, sat at her desk in front of large pane windows overlooking downtown Greenville.

"Good morning, Mr. Caldwell," Kimberly said crisply. Her thick brown hair was pulled into a tight French braid. She wore her standard conservative pantsuit in an equally bland color, navy. The unadventurous clothing didn't hide her full curves. Kimberly was his brother's hire. Isaac loved eye candy. Luckily, Kimberly ignored Isaac's flirtations. Unlike the four previous administrative assistants.

"Everyone is waiting in the conference room. Your dad has already called twice to see if you had arrived." Her phone rang, and she pressed full lips together after checking the caller ID.

Andre waved a hand to stop her from answering. "I'll announce myself."

A rare expression of relief reflected in her hazel eyes before they deadpanned. Behind the square rimmed glasses, the usual no no-nonsense expression returned. "Have a good morning, sir."

He strode down the hall and entered the door on the right. The top C.E.S. executives sat around a long cherry wood conference table. A 60-inch flat screen television showed the various faces of executives from the other states.

Curtis Caldwell's dark eyes pierced Andre. Curtis despised delays and interruptions. Isaac checked his watch. Andre ignored both men and sat in the empty leather chair to the right of the senior Caldwell.

"I apologize for the delay, everyone," Andre said with a tight smile. "We can get started."

Kimberly slipped in quietly behind Andre and sat in the corner where she took minutes.

His dad sat back in the high back Italian leather chair. A dark grey three piece suit stretched over his brawny arms, and he braced his hands on the table, still calloused from the early days of hard labor despite the latter years of manicures. "We start at eight every Monday. Nothing's changed."

Andre tilted his head to the side and leveled a cool stare at his dad. "Then there's no need for further delay."

Curtis's coal black eyes hardened, and for a second Andre expected a challenge. But his dad swiveled to the rest of the people at the table. "Let's begin."

Andre leaned back in the chair and reached for a pen and pad. Kimberly stepped forward and slid his iPad in front of him. He nodded his thanks.

"What's going on with the landfill in the low country?" Curtis's authoritative tone commanded the room.

"We're having trouble with the closing," Scott Morrison, VP of Operations spoke up. He sat beside Isaac and leaned forward resting his hands on the table.

"What type of trouble?" Curtis asked in a low voice.

Scott shifted and pulled on his tie. "There are rumblings, small ones, of possible contamination from the landfill to the well water system of the residences nearby. The state health department is quietly reviewing the claims. I've held up closing until I learn more."

"Fuck," Curtis said.

Isaac tossed his iPad on the table. "I warned you there would be risks with this deal. The health department shut down that landfill in the seventies and, since then the owners haven't complied with the regulations."

Andre leaned forward. "This deal is still good. We've got to wait until the department completes the testing before we make our next move."

Isaac tented his fingers beneath his chin. "Good deal or not, we need to figure out our next step."

"I'll tell you what the next step is," Curtis made eye contact with Andre. "We're abandoning the landfill project."

"What?" Andre slapped a hand on the table. He'd decided to purchase the landfill so C.E.S. could expand into methane gas recovery. They could sell to nearby manufacturers. Not only was the landfill in Hartsville County an inexpensive investment, but the word was Dalmtrix, Inc., a manufacturer of car engine parts, had considered moving nearby. Dalmtrix ensured each of their facilities implemented sustainable energy methods.

"Are you questioning my decision?" Curtis glared.

Andre slowly inhaled and then exhaled tamping down his frustration. "No. But I don't want to abandon this opportunity at the first sign of trouble."

"If there are rumors of contamination, no one will welcome us taking over the landfill no matter how useful the project," Curtis said.

Scott raised his hand like a school kid. "We can bury these rumors."

"Easier to abandon the project," Curtis countered.

Andre clenched his fist. Typical. His dad would quickly abandon a project that wasn't his idea.

Scott's hand popped up again. "We've already begun a soft leak of our plans to get into the landfill gas market. Dalmtrix is issuing a press release next week with their intentions to locate in that county."

Isaac cursed. "Why did we do even a soft leak of our intentions?"

"I ordered it," Andre cut in, rubbing the bridge of his nose.

"I'm pulling the plug on this project," Curtis said.

Andre pulled on his tie. "You can't."

Curtis made a swift cutting motion with his hand. "It's too risky."

Andre refused to let the deal die. Not when there was an opportunity to take C.E.S. into new territory. "They can move their facility to another part of the state. You know enough people to pull strings. Get Dalmtrix to move near another landfill that we can use."

Curtis's eyes lit up with the possibility. "What are you thinking?"

Thoughts of ways to save the deal swirled in Andre's head, and he drummed his hands on the table. "We're going to Columbia for the legislative session next week."

Curtis shrugged. "And?"

"Senator Leventis supported Dalmtrix locating in his county. We can make sure he changes his mind."

Narrowing his eyes and rubbing his hands, Curtis eyed Andre. "You're willing to do whatever it takes to make this project happen?"

"I am. Dalmtrix is a multi-million dollar corporation. Wherever it goes will generate nationwide buzz. By tying C.E.S. to their press and providing energy through methane recovery, we'll be a household name. If they're coming to South Carolina, we're getting the business."

Isaac slid forward. "If we're going to push Dalmtrix to another location we need to leak the story about the contamination to the local press."

Andre's last bit of good guy contentment drifted away. "Then circulate rumors that the addition of Dalmtrix will exacerbate the situation," he said. "That'll help convince Senator Leventis to push against the deal and provide a reason for the change of plans."

Curtis nodded and smiled. "Great idea. Kimberly, strike that conversation from the minutes. Now, on to more important things."

They dragged through the updates from each area of the business. As the meeting progressed, Andre thought of Mikayla. The way her face lit up like he was a hero after he'd agreed to take her off the mountain. The memory brought an uneasy churn in his stomach. He wasn't that guy. He was this guy; the guy who did what it took to get a job done including starting rumors for professional gain.

Andre had to get his head out of the mountains and back in the game. The weekend with her was nice, but hiking in the snow and lounging on the sofa watching movies wasn't reality.

After the updates from each executive and the new account progress reports, the meeting ended.

"Andre, Isaac, give me an hour then meet me in my office," Curtis said while the other meeting attendees filed out of the conference room.

Andre met his brother's eyes, and Isaac raised an eyebrow. He didn't need ten guesses to figure out what his dad wanted to talk about. Curtis wanted to know what happened between him and Mikayla. Andre had no way to explain something he couldn't figure out himself.

*

"Tell me why the hell you ran from your sister's wedding?" Curtis asked. He sat behind a large polished mahogany desk in his corner office decorated with classical paintings. Paintings he cared more about revealing how much he paid for than their artistic value.

"Stepsister," Andre said sitting in the leather seat across from his dad.

Isaac plopped down in the seat next to him. "Family is family."

Andre snorted. "For normal people, not Caldwell's."

"I'm not in the mood for that crap," Curtis cut in. "You should have stayed and snatched Angelica back from your cousin? Instead, you run off like a scared rabbit. Your behavior was embarrassing, and your absence devastated your sister."

Andre crossed one leg over the other. "My *step-sister* was only devastated because something outshined her grand event. And I didn't run. Angelica wasn't worth the fight. If she had sex with Ryan in a closet after just meeting him, she damn sure wasn't worth trying to get back."

Isaac turned to him. "They knew each other."

Andre waited for anger or indignation to show up. Nothing happened. Not surprising since he hadn't loved her. *Don't you want someone to love?* A vision of Mikayla, soft and delicious in his arms after they had kissed flashed in his head.

He shifted in the chair. He sucked at love. "I guess that means she won't fall in bed with a stranger."

Curtis grunted and leaned back in his chair. "It's a good thing we found out before you married her."

Isaac dropped his hand and glared at Andre. "Hold up? You were going to marry her?"

Andre nodded. "She's beautiful and understood the demands of my career. Why not?"

"Sometimes you're too much like him." Isaac motioned to Curtis with his head.

Curtis slapped a hand on his desk. "You're both just like me. No need pretending any different. The fact is, marriage is a business arrangement. People trust a man that has a wife and kids behind him. If either of you are to take this seat," he rubbed his chair, "you'll need to remember that."

Andre cut his eyes at Curtis. "We'll run the company together."

Curtis gave a curt laugh. "That's the same bull my brother spat, but you see where that landed us."

Taking a deep breath, Andre slid a glance at his brother, who shook his head. Curtis couldn't fathom, despite all his warnings about how the people closest to you would stab you in the back, Andre and Isaac had formed a bond. In a mixed up world of rivalry and dysfunctional parents, their only sanity came from their brotherly connection.

Curtis pointed a finger at Andre. "It was cowardly to leave instead of making some sort of stand. I don't blame you for not wanting Angelica anymore, but you could have at least done something to prove you were still the winner. Get caught sleeping with her one last time during the reception. Let Ryan see you can still make that girl go on her knees for you. It wouldn't have taken but a few dollars."

"That's about all the fatherly advice I can stomach," Andre stood.

"Where were you all weekend?" Isaac asked. "I called your house and stopped by yesterday."

Curtis glared through narrowed eyes. "Don't tell me you were hiding out?"

Andre crossed his arms and glared at Curtis. "I didn't hide out. The roadblock meant I had to spend the weekend with Mikayla."

"Who in the hell is Mikayla?"

Isaac turned in his seat and gaped at him. "Ryan's girlfriend?"

Curtis's sharp gaze bounced between the two. Comprehension flashed in his eyes and he let out a hearty laugh. "That's a good one, boy. Not as good as what I recommended, but good. I hope you wrapped it up. I want legitimate grandchildren."

"I didn't—"

"Too bad you didn't do it at the wedding." Curtis wiped a tear from his eye and leaned back in the chair. "But that's neither here nor there. Philip was upset that Ryan had hurt that girl. She's worked her way into their good graces. My brother always was a pansy ass. It'll be worth the look on his face when he learns she's just as no good as Angelica. Hell, he was singing her praises to anyone who would listen after you two left. I can't wait to burst his bubble and let him know she ran straight into your bed."

"No," Andre said taking a step toward Curtis's desk. "You are not going to put her in the same category as Angelica."

Curtis's laughter faded. "You don't like this girl. Do you?"

Andre's hand sliced the air. "She doesn't have anything to do with our family's bull."

"Bull?" Curtis stood, pressed his fists into the desk and leaned forward. "This family's bull paid your way to college. Allowed you to grow up in a house full of servants. Gave you the ability to run a large corporation. Are you trying to turn your back on me? On what I did for you and your brother? Do you want to go back to being on the outside of this family?"

"You've made it perfectly clear that you don't tolerate disloyalty." Andre ground clipped words through clenched teeth.

"Don't forget it. My brother said I was only good enough to take out his trash. I proved him wrong and built this empire. I'll keep on building C.E.S. until Philip can't help but acknowledge my success. And while I'm doing that I'm going to humiliate him and his family until he wished he'd picked up trash with me." Curtis said in a voice laced with spite.

Spine ramrod straight Curtis glared at his sons as if he were their lord and master. Andre believed Curtis truly thought he owned them. "You had your fun with that girl, and now it's done. Don't see her anymore. She'll probably run back to Ryan and then you can let him know you spent two nights between her thighs. But until then, we're going to get them back for what he did. Either you're with me or you're against me."

Curtis leveled both his sons with a stare. A cold knot tightened in Andre's stomach. The one time he defied his dad had ended in pain and humiliation for him and his mother. And ultimately proved Andre was all Caldwell. Andre had tired of the ruthless lifestyle. Tired of the constant need to prove he wasn't the enemy. But, no matter how dysfunctional the family dynamics were he agreed with his dad. Family and the business meant everything. A pleasant reprieve, that's how he'd view the calm during those two days with Mikayla. A part of him yearned for more of that. But doubted he'd ever experience peace again. He was too much like his father.

Caldwell men didn't know peace.

CHAPTER 10

"So, how was the wedding?"

Mikayla froze in the middle of putting her purse in the desk drawer. With a stiff smile and a sick feeling rumbling in her stomach, she turned to Charity York. Charity officially worked as an administrative assistant to the current head of the acquisitions department. Her unofficial title, office snoop.

"Fine. I didn't stay long." Mikayla said, straightening the already organized items on her desk.

"Why not? Did you and Ryan decide to come back early?"

"No, I did."

Charity's eyes gleamed. She sashayed into Mikayla's office and propped a curvy hip on the desk. "Don't tell me you and Ryan broke up already."

Mikayla's heart beat increased and heat crept beneath her skin.

A woman's laughter floated from the hall. She and Charity looked to the door. Ryan paused in front of her door; Angelica clung to his side. They made a handsome couple, Angelica's tall, shapely figure, long highlighted hair and caramel skin a perfect match to his towering height and muscular build. Seeing them together shouldn't hurt so much.

Angelica lifted her chin. Pouty lips curved in a satisfied smile, and she tugged on Ryan's arm. "Come, show me your office."

Ryan rubbed the back of his neck and gave a sorry lift of the shoulders before walking away with Angelica. Charity's eyebrows rose to her hairline. She placed a hand over her heart as she looked from the door to Mikayla.

"Who is that?"

Mikayla swallowed hard and brushed the hair from her face. "His new girlfriend."

Charity's eyes popped, and her jaw dropped. "What? That is just wrong, Mikayla. I thought he really liked you. To think, you were just another notch on his belt. After the way the family took you in and everything. Just wrong."

Charity chatted on full of righteous indignation. Charity's words of comfort were as fake as she was loud, and only served to make Mikayla's stomach twist like a psychotic pencil sharpener. Everyone would know Ryan dumped Mikayla over the weekend and picked up a new girlfriend as easy as shopping at Nordstrom Rack on a one day sale.

"Charity." Mikayla cut off the diatribe. "It was a mutual breakup. Ryan can date whomever he chooses. I'm cool."

"Well, I'm not," Charity strutted to the door. "And I'll make sure the women in the office realize how he treated you. We won't have them sighing over his smiles anymore. No ma'am, not when he played with one of our own." The last words trailed over her shoulder as she breezed out the door.

Mikayla rubbed her temples. There was no way she could stay here. She would not be the butt of jokes. Not again. Her hands trembled and Mikayla jerked open the desk drawer. She rummaged inside her purse until she found the pack of cigarettes and the box of nicotine patches she purchased. Trembling fingers closed around the box of cigarettes.

No. She'd quit, and wouldn't let embarrassment make her go back to that addiction. Maybe ignoring the craving would be easier if Andre were near. A picture of Andre's full lips closing around the tip of a cigarette popped into her head. Andre would be a good distraction.

A knock on the door broke into her thoughts. She dropped the box and slammed the drawer shut. When she spun around, Philip Caldwell stood at the door.

"Mikayla, my office please," he said stiffly and marched down the hall.

She straightened her shoulders and followed. They passed Charity in the break room huddled around the coffee pot with a few other women. Mikayla sucked in a shaky breath. *Please, please, please, don't let them find out what really happened.*

Philip, Ryan, and Renee occupied the three largest offices in the rear of the building with Philip's in the middle. Mikayla noted Renee's closed door. It was unusual for Renee to arrive at the office late. When Mikayla entered the plush interior of Philip's office, she didn't feel the usual comfort from the homey feel of large wood furniture, thick carpet and family portraits on the wall. This was where Philip gave her advice, mentored her on her career, and even encouraged her to accept after Ryan asked her out.

Philip crossed to the bar in the corner and poured bourbon into two crystal glasses. He held one out to her. She shook her head, and with a shrug, he poured the drink intended for her into his glass.

"Renee told me you want to quit," he said.

Thus, Renee's reason for coming to work late. "I do."

"Dammit, Mikayla," he took a sip of the drink. "Don't throw away a promising career because my son is a jackass."

Mikayla raised a hand. "With all due respect, Mr. Caldwell—"

"Oh, it's Mr. Caldwell now. Last week it was Philip." He downed another swallow.

"Mr. Caldwell, Philip, no matter what I call you. You're my boss, and I overstepped my boundaries by dating your son."

"Don't spout a bunch of professional bull crap at me, Mikayla. Talk to me like you would before Ryan screwed his ex-girlfriend in a closet and embarrassed the hell out of you."

Mikayla flinched. Typical Philip Caldwell. Bulldoze through the crap and get to the point. "Fine. I can't sit in my office and pretend as if what Ryan did wasn't completely disrespectful. I won't go to board meetings and act as if everyone in there isn't thinking poor Mikayla, another notch on Ryan Caldwell's bedpost. Or worst that I plotted to sleep my way to a better position and the plan backfired."

He scoffed. "To hell with what the people in this office think. This is my company. The only opinion, that matters, is mine." He stalked over and pointed at her, the highball glass half full still in his hand. "You're a damn good employee and a damn fine woman. I thought Ryan had finally gotten some sense in his head when he asked you out. I like to keep business in the family, and you and Ryan being together was perfect."

"But, Philip, I can't..."

"Yes, you can. As soon as we close the deal in the low country, that acquisitions job is still yours."

"I don't want the position out of pity."

"Damn, woman, you know it's not out of pity." He marched to his desk. "That job was yours as soon as Kelly announced her retirement. Still is. Now I can't change what Ryan did, and I'm damn sorry he screwed up a chance with a woman who has common sense. But I'll be damned if I let you throw away this promotion over Ryan's romp in a broom closet. Turn in a resignation and I'll tear the damn thing up."

"But—"

"No buts," he downed the rest of his drink. "We've got a board meeting in thirty minutes. You give Ryan the virtual finger by doing your job. Now get out of here and get to work."

Mikayla watched him with a mixture of annoyance and pleasure. She deserved the job, but, man, sometimes she hated the arrogance that came with working for the Caldwell family. She spun on her heel to leave.

"One other thing."

"Yes?" Mikayla glanced over her shoulder.

"My nephew Andre. Renee told me about the two of you, too. Don't trust a word that boy says. He's just as sneaky and dirty as his dad. I believe nothing happened. Keep it that way." His voice was straight forward, each word a bullet strong to the chest. With a stiff nod, she walked out.

*

Mikayla escaped the words of comfort, delivered with varying degrees of false pity from the women in the break room. She'd gone there hoping for a fortifying cup of strong coffee. She should have known better than to enter Charity's gossip stronghold. After breaking free, she exited to find Ryan leaning against the wall waiting in the hall. He straightened and headed in her direction.

"No!" She shook her head, shooing him with her hand Mikayla stalked pass.

"Mikayla," he followed.

"Not now, not ever, Ryan," she hurried down the hall to her office and shut the door.

Tears welled in her eyes. Her lungs burned from the paltry amount of air delivered by her short, shallow breaths. Stupid Caldwell men. She paced back and forth from her desk to the door. What if Philip was right? Andre wanted to sleep with her. Maybe just for revenge.

After a knock on the door, Renee peaked inside. "Can I come in?"

Mikayla stalked over to her desk and sank into the chair. "You own the building."

Renee stepped inside. Despite the uncertainty in her friend's eyes, she looked fabulous in a dark maroon dress and sleek cream trench coat cinched at the waist. "I know you're upset that I spoke with my dad, but I had to let him know you're considering leaving. I hope he talked some sense into you."

Mikayla leaned back in the chair. Her toe tapped against the floor beneath the desk, and the craving for a cigarette kicked up a notch. "I won't abandon the deal in Hartsville. But I can't stay forever or take that position. You should have seen the gleam in Charity's eye when Ryan walked in here with Angelica."

Renee placed a hand on her hip, and then she held up the other hand. "Wait. He brought her here?"

"Yes. But since your dad is refusing my notice, and I have no other means of income, I'll deal."

Renee sighed. "It'll get better."

"Yeah...time heals all wounds and other such philosophical crap."

Renee came around the desk and tugged Mikayla up from her seat. Drawing her in for a hug. "It does, I promise." She pulled back and scrutinized Mikayla from head to toe then smiled. "At least you look fabulous today."

Mikayla couldn't help but smile. The top of her white V-neck dress separated from the black skirt by a thick gold belt accented her figure in all the right places. Renee insisted Mikayla buy the dress despite Mikayla's protests about feeling ridiculous during their first shopping trip together.

The garment was now one of Mikayla's go to outfits. No wonder Renee loved it.

"Thank you, Renee. Only you would consider a fashion choice the bright side to public ridicule."

Renee grinned, reached over and smoothed a stray hair on Mikayla's head. "Looking good on the outside makes every obstacle easier to face."

Mikayla smiled in return, which quickly died when Ryan stuck his head in the doorway. Her stomach knotted.

"You work with him. Might as well get it over with." Renee glared at Ryan on her way out the door.

Ryan tapped the side of his leg with his fist. He opened his mouth, closed it, and then blew out a breath. She wanted to scratch his eyes out. Instead, she curled her hands into fists.

"Mikayla," he finally said taking slow, measured steps toward her. "I don't know what to say."

Her spine stiffened. "Then leave."

He blew out a heavy breath and ran a hand over the waves of his perfectly faded haircut. "I'm sorry."

"Sorry? Sorry? You're damn right you're sorry. I'm not even mad about the cheating really. I almost expected it from you."

"That's not fair."

"Apparently it is fair. Because did you not fuck somebody else in a closet this weekend!" She sucked in a calming breath. Placing a hand over her rapidly beating heart, she stepped back, even though the desk separated them.

"Mikayla, I didn't plan to cheat on you. I never intended to cheat on you. Everything I said about wanting to be with you, trying to get my life together, and finally settling down, was true. But...Angelica...she's the one. The one I told you about. The one I fell in love with. I do care about you, Mikayla. I swear I never meant to hurt or embarrass you."

She broke eye contact, not wanting to see the pain and sincerity in his dark gaze. He gave her the same sad look he'd used when he described the way Angelica left him years ago. The look that used to make her feel sorry for him.

"You could have said something. Explained who she was. I would have understood."

"I know. That was my plan, but things happened. The situation spiraled out of control, and I hurt you. You know you're more than an employee to us...to me." He leaned on the desk, lowered his head and tried to make eye contact. "Can we still be friends?"

She met his gaze. Saw the guy who teased her and Renee about their obsession with hair. The guy who came to her for advice on a new development or brought in her favorite bagels for breakfast. She saw her friend and was surprised a part of her wanted to say yes.

She shook her head. They weren't friends. He'd run this same game on every other woman, and she'd watched from the sidelines as they easily fell. No wonder Andre thought she'd be back with Ryan in no time.

"We can't be friends, Ryan. We never were friends."

He jerked back.

Mikayla straightened her shoulders and grabbed her a portfolio off the desk. "Don't talk to me unless it has something to do with work. Otherwise, you don't exist." She stalked around the desk and out of the office. Wishing she had a cigarette, and that she could smoke it with Andre.

CHAPTER 11

By Wednesday afternoon, Andre craved a cigarette and Mikayla. Getting over the mid-week hump didn't usually mean much to him. His work days tended to blend into the weekends. Last week with Mikayla was the first weekend he could remember actually relaxing. A few days with a woman had him reevaluating his belief that only unmotivated people counted down to a weekend of doing nothing.

He left work, and the hustle of downtown Greenville traffic, and drove toward Simpsonville. He kept a condo downtown and usually stayed there during the week. But the small house he owned out in the country was home. The place provided an escape from the headaches at work, whenever he made the time to visit. In the year since he'd purchased the place, he'd only made it out there to stay twice. He didn't really have the time to stay in the country tonight but needed the break.

He bypassed the driveway to his place and turned down the long paved driveway to his friend Jonathan's house. The ranch style brick house sat at the bottom of a hill in the middle of acres of pasture fields. Large pecan trees surrounded the house and the driveway. Light from the motion sensor illuminated when he pulled next to the house. It was almost seven and already dark, but he knew Jonathan's property almost as good as his own. Andre couldn't see the cows in the pasture as he stepped from the warmth of his car to the frosty night air, but their soft moos wafted on the breeze. He pulled his overcoat close and hurried through the open garage into the kitchen.

"Yo, John, you in here?" Andre called.

The latest sports updates echoed from a small television into the empty kitchen. He walked through the kitchen into the attached living area.

"John," he called again. When there was still no answer, he figured Jonathan was still out tending to the cows and went back into the kitchen and pulled a bottle of beer from the fridge.

He settled in at the bar with his beer just as Jonathan entered the kitchen through the garage.

"Are you comfortable?" Jonathan pulled off his thick coat and work boots and set them beside the door.

"Don't leave your door wide open if you don't want company."

Jonathan shook his head. He hung his baseball cap on the wall rack and ran a hand through his curly hair. When Andre first met Jonathan in college, he'd taken one look at Jonathan's light skin, curly hair, blue grey eyes, and assumed he was soft. After hearing Jonathan's country boy drawl, he'd figured his assumption was right. He smiled now when he thought about the fist fight they had that not only revealed Jonathan was no softie but landed him a best friend.

Jonathan lumbered over to the sink and washed his hands. "I don't usually get company in the middle of the week. Your dad and brother must really be driving you crazy to send you to the country on a weeknight."

Andre took a swig of his beer. "Long story."

"I was wondering when I'd get to hear it. I figured something was up when Isaac came looking for you on Sunday. Was the wedding that bad?"

Jonathan went to the fridge and took out a bowl with what appeared to be a marinade inside. He set the bowl on the counter and pulled a stovetop grill from beneath the cabinet.

"I only got one steak, but I'll split it with you."

Andre shook his head. "I can find something at the house."

Jonathan scoffed. "You haven't been in your house for at least two months. There's leftover chicken in the fridge. Have at it, then tell me why you're here."

Andre cringed and ran a hand over his face. Had it been that long since he'd taken a break from the family? He forgot about the food and recounted the Angelica and Ryan fiasco. His friend didn't look surprised in the least. Jonathan had never liked Angelica. And, the feeling had been mutual.

"I hate to say I told you so," Jonathan leaned back against the counter next to his steak cooking on the grill.

"You might as well. I'm just glad I found out before asking her to marry me."

Jonathan grimaced and crossed bulging arms over his brawny chest. "I can't believe you even considered marrying that woman. You deserve what you got with that one. Whenever you do something because it's expected, you end up getting burned. Angelica was the type of pretty side piece you thought you needed. And like most pretty girls, she wasn't about a damn thing."

Jonathan had a deep aversion to beautiful women. It wasn't that he dated women who could be considered unattractive, but any woman, who spent a fortune on clothes, jewelry, and beauty treatments instantly turned him off. One of the reasons he hated Angelica.

"Lesson learned," Andre gulped down his beer. "It doesn't change the fact that eventually I need to find someone. As much as I hate to agree with Curtis, if we want the business to stay in the family then eventually I need kids to pass the legacy on. I'll be damned if I let my step-sister and her husband get their claws in the business. They'd suck all of the money out in no-time."

Jonathan pulled the steak off the grill. "I can understand, but damn, man, you're only thirty. No need to rush. Next time, pick someone worth having kids with and not just a pretty face with a big ass." Jonathan paused then pointed his finger at Andre. "On second thought, don't give up completely on the big ass."

Andre laughed and thought about Mikayla's pajamas hugging her backside. She wasn't just a pretty face. There was more to Mikayla, and he might as well face the fact that he wanted to learn more. He hadn't heard from her since they returned. Not that he was surprised. They'd both agreed they didn't need to act on the attraction between them. He was dying to know how things went when she returned. Had she held her head up and handled the reunion with grace, or had she forgiven Ryan.

Jonathan dropped the bowl with the cold chicken from the fridge on the counter. "Why are you frowning?"

Andre relaxed his face. "Just thinking about this woman I met over the weekend."

"You didn't like her or something?"

"No, that's the problem. I want to see her again. I just don't know if I should."

Andre recounted the rest of the weekend in the mountains, including his dads order to stay away from Mikayla.

Jonathan grabbed his steak and sat across from Andre. "As difficult as it is to say this, I agree with your dad."

"And, usually I'd agree. Look, nothing's wrong with talking to her. She's cool. We can be friends."

"Since when did you ever want to be just friends with a woman? Come on, man, I know you better than anyone. You want to sleep with her."

"That doesn't mean I will."

"Are you dumb as well as ugly?" Jonathan grinned then took a bite of his steak.

Andre flipped Jonathan the bird but chuckled. "To hell with you. I can see her without something happening."

"Yeah, tell yourself that. You didn't listen about Angelica and look where that landed you. Stay the hell away from this woman. The rift in your family runs deep, and both sides play dirty. Don't fraternize with the enemy."

"She's not with Ryan anymore."

Jonathan shrugged. "You don't know that. She still has to work with him every day. Do you really want to find her in the closest with Ryan next? Leave that woman alone."

Andre stood and put the cold chicken in the microwave. If Jonathan said leave her alone, then he should consider the advice. His friend could read women easily, and he couldn't deny his friend had been right about Angelica.

Andre's phone rang. His mother's number appeared on the screen. "Hello, Mom."

"Hi, Andre," his mother's over-exuberant voice replied. Dawn Caldwell always tried too hard to sound happy. "I heard what happened at the wedding. Are you okay?"

"I'm fine. Who told you?" Though he already knew the answer.

"Your father. I spoke to him yesterday." She hesitated. He could picture his mother twisting her shirt in her hands. "You know I'm visiting next week."

He gripped the phone blood draining from his hands. "Yes. I know. Where are you staying?" He held his breath and hoped in earnest, she'd say a hotel in the area.

"You know where I'm staying. Let's not get into that. I just wanted to make sure you were okay."

Andre's didn't lash out, but his muscles quivered with tension. She always stayed at his father's apartment in the city. The only reason Dawn gave for becoming Curtis's mistress after he cheated on her with his best friend's wife, left her, and then married his mistress was because she still loved him. If what his parents had was love, he could do without.

"Thanks for checking, but I'm fine. I'm at Jonathan's. I'll call you later."

"Oh, okay. I just...I just wanted to make sure you were okay. I love you, Andre. You can do better."

"Yeah...you too, mom." He ended the call.

"You cool?" Jonathan asked.

"I'm good." He punched a minute warm up time on the microwave. "I'm going outside to smoke."

Jonathan didn't say anything as Andre walked out. That's what Andre liked about Jonathan; he knew when to talk and when to shut the hell up. Andre went to his car and pulled the pack of cigarettes from the glove compartment. His family's bullshit had tired him out. The headaches weren't worth the lies, deceit, and stress. He wanted an outlet. Hell, he needed an outlet.

His cell phone chimed. He yanked the phone out of his pocket. The cold outside seeped into his fingers as he punched in the code, to read the text. His heart raced. Mikayla finally reached out to him.

"Hey you."

He stared at the screen. Contemplated what to do. Already, his tension had eased.

He texted back. "Hey you."

To hell with staying away from Mikayla.

CHAPTER 12

"I think there's a problem with the deal in the Hartsville." Ryan poked his head through her office door.

Mikayla turned away from her computer and cut her eyes at him. "What do you want, Ryan?"

Hurt flashed briefly across his face. Yet, he still walked into her office and made himself comfortable in the chair across from the desk. She clamped her jaw shut fighting the urge to yell for him to leave. All week long he'd tried to rekindle their friendship. Popping into her office, to say 'how are you doing' and sending jokes via email the way he'd done before. Every time she ignored him and deleted any correspondence not related to work. Angelica popping into the office every day to ooh and aah over him didn't help his cause. Their constant display combined with sympathetic stares from coworkers made Mikayla's stomach twist and roll like she'd gorged on a toxic honey bun.

"I've heard rumblings that the deal in Hartsville may fall through. The land we bought is useless if Dalmtrix doesn't locate there," Ryan said.

Mikayla scowled and crossed her arms over her chest. "I got that information from a good source. Dalmtrix has Senator Leventis's approval. Dalmtrix plans to announce the location of their manufacturing plant in the coming days."

Ryan shook his head. "They should have announced it already. There's word of possible contamination from the nearby landfill into the wells of the neighboring residents. Concerns are spreading that having Dalmtrix move in will further degrade the environment. If this deal falls through, we're stuck with 100 useless acres."

Mikayla's stomach dropped. She turned away from Ryan and struggled to take in steady breaths. Her cousin's tip that Dalmtrix was moving into the area was the reason she researched available land nearby for a potential new subdivision. With the location of a worldwide manufacturing facility also came the need for housing. She'd gone to Ryan with the information and convinced him to persuade Philip to purchase the land. Once they discovered the deal was almost closed, they'd bought the area and planned to have the engineer design the layout in the upcoming months. This deal made her a shoe-in for the acquisitions position. If things fell through, her brilliant plan would be nothing more than a million dollar mistake.

"How could Dalmtrix possibly have anything to do with the pollution from the landfill? They aren't even there yet. This is no reason to kill the deal." She turned back to Ryan.

His elbows remained on the armrest, but he lifted his hands. "I agree, but somebody must have something on Senator Leventis. I gave him a call earlier to ask about the announcement, and he acted as if he didn't know what I was talking about."

Mikayla's hand slapped her desk. "That's ridiculous. We talked to him last week."

"I know. Which means either he's going senile, or someone's convinced him to hold out on the deal."

She fell back into her seat. "This deal can't die. What are we going to do with all of that land?"

"We'll figure that out. We bought it cheap; maybe we can sell cheap."

She raised a brow and Ryan tried to smile. They both knew that was unlikely. They'd gotten the land so cheap because there was nothing going on in that county. The previous owner held onto it even though he could barely pay the taxes. At the time, they were able to easily convince him to sell because the Dalmtrix plans were secret. If the deal had been public, the land would have cost a lot more. But with no deal, the land was useless.

She sat up. "I'll find out what's going on. You work on Senator Leventis and find out why he shifted his position. Just because the landfill is crappy doesn't mean Dalmtrix can't locate there."

"This wouldn't be the first time a deal fell through. It'll be okay."

"No, it won't." she said sharply.

Ryan froze and she lowered her eyes. Of course, he wouldn't understand she needed this deal to go through. Her first big deal. The deal was supposed to be proof she could make the decisions required to head the acquisitions section. That she belonged.

"Why don't we get a drink and think about our next step," Ryan said.

Her eyes snapped to him. He appeared...hopeful. In his world, ex-girlfriends didn't harbor hard feelings for long.

"I'm not having a drink with you. In fact, now that you've delivered the bad news, you can leave." She turned back to her computer.

"Mikayla, come on, baby, don't be like that."

Her head whipped around. "Like what, Ryan? Like the girl you cheated on, with some woman in a closet."

He sighed. "I explained that."

"And everything is supposed to be okay now? Well, it's not. We are not friends. Will not be friends, and I doubt we ever really were."

He slid forward in his chair and reached across the desk. "You know that's not true. I don't want there to be hard feelings between us."

"There are no hard feelings, Ryan. You are exactly who I originally thought you were. Selfish, conceited, and not worth my time."

His face hardened, and he pulled away slowly. Her words were intentional, meant to inflict the blow, and she wouldn't feel guilty. He'd confided about hating the way people viewed him as a rich boy with no depth.

Angelica glided to Mikayla's door. As if sensing her man's feelings had been hurt. Her pretty face twisted into a fierce frown when her gaze landed on Mikayla. A second later, she smiled and called to Ryan.

"My dear, isn't it time for you to leave? We have plans."

Ryan stared at Mikayla. She raised her chin then turned away. Without another word, he trudged across the room. Ryan's voice, low and urgent, trailed behind as he hurried Angelica away from Mikayla's door.

Mikayla released a shaky breath and rested her head on her hands. Damn this deal falling through. She couldn't keep playing this back and forth game with Ryan. She could barely stand to look at him, much less watch him and Angelica fawn over each other. If the deal in Hartsville were actually falling through the repercussions would be devastating. Everything she'd strived for in her perfect life completely ruined. She wouldn't let that happen.

She lifted her head and pushed a lock of stray hair away from her face. Now wasn't the time for a pity party. Now was the time to find a solution. Reaching for the phone, she called her cousin, Dennis. He managed the Dalmtrix facility in Chicago and oversaw the plans for the move to South Carolina. Although Ryan had no reason to lie, she needed to find out for herself if her brilliant career move would turn into a career-killing mistake.

*

Mikayla slammed her apartment door and threw her black Kate Spade purse onto the floor. Lipstick, a calculator, mints, a pack of cigarettes and coins scattered. She stared at the pack of cigarettes in the middle. Her head ached, she had cramps, and her skin itched with the need for a nicotine fix. She snatched up the pack and step over the mess.

The phone call to Dennis confirmed some of what Ryan told her. Someone warned Dalmtrix about the landfill contamination, and though the company hadn't originally planned to cancel the move, rumors circulated they were no longer welcome. He planned to continue to push for the move, and Mikayla hoped that her cousin's efforts proved useful.

A small glimmer of hope at best. Ryan's idea, that Senator Leventis no longer backed the move is what really pissed her off. The man represented the area, knew the need for a boost to the local economy, and avidly supported Dalmtrix. To learn, he would flip on a decision that directly impacted his district, for no apparent reason, didn't seem right. She wanted to believe that all politicians weren't corrupt, but there was something wrong about the Senator's change in plans.

Mikayla stomped into the kitchen and turned on the faucet. With one hand, she clutched the pack of cigarettes, the other filled a glass with ice from the freezer. When she made her way back to the sink the water slowly backed up instead of going down the drain.

"What…not again," she said. Scowling, she flipped the switch for the garbage disposal. The machine gave a sorry hum. She threw down the cigarettes. "Damn."

She turned off the water and went back into the hall and snatched up her cell phone. She made a quick call to the after-hours maintenance line and left a message.

A few seconds later her phone rang. That was quick. She glanced at the number and froze. Her heart seemed to stop and then jump back to life.

Her terrible afternoon faded with the sight of Andre's number. "Hey you."

"Hey you." Andre's deep sexy voice sent her heart rate into a frenzy. "I decided to call instead of text to see how your week went."

She sighed heavily and slumped against the counter. "Terrible."

"Was it that hard working with Ryan?"

"Ryan was only part of the overall crappiness that was my week. A deal I was key in getting may be falling through. I found out right before I left work. Then I came home to a broken garbage disposal."

"What was the deal? Maybe I can help."

She smiled. His offer to help sent a comforting warmth through her body. "I don't want to talk about that right now. I'm just glad today's Friday."

"Big plans. A hot date."

"I wish. No, just me and whatever movies I recorded on my DVR."

"What about the disposal?"

She scowled at the water in the sink. At this rate, the water would drain by the next millennium. "Hopefully maintenance will call back tonight."

"I've got one better. How about I help you out?"

She gripped the phone. Giddiness did a fairy dance across her skin. Right now she didn't care what Ryan, Renee, or Philip Caldwell thought. She wanted to see Andre.

"You can help me from Greenville?"

Again he laughed. Again heat took over her insides. "I'm actually on my way to Columbia."

"Why is that?"

"I've got some things to do at the state house next week. I'll be in town all week. Maybe we can get together for lunch…or something."

Her body nearly seized from the invitation and his smooth baritone. She could enjoy his company without getting wrapped up in the situation.

Yeah right.

"Lunch sounds good."

"Only lunch?"

"Maybe some smoking cessation classes." She laughed. Funny she hadn't thought about smoking since getting on the phone with him.

He joined in. "I'll stop by tonight and take a look at the garbage disposal for you."

"I'm supposed to believe you know something about plumbing? You don't have to pretend to work on my sink, to visit."

"For the record, I don't need an excuse to see you. I planned to come by tonight anyway."

His declaration froze her flirty comeback. "Why?"

There was a short pause before he answered. "I miss you." Surprise wrapped around his voice. She missed him too.

"I'll see you soon," she answered, then rushed to end the call before changing her mind.

CHAPTER 13

Since Andre called, Mikayla checked her reflection in the mirror for the third time in the hour. She changed out of her work suit into her usual Friday night attire, pajama pants, and a t-shirt. Then changed again into a pair of jeans and a long sleeve yellow V-neck shirt. Renee's advice to always look cute had her considering changing into a flirty cream top. Her plan was to appear casual. Difficult to do when nothing about Andre coming to her apartment induced casual feelings. Instead, anticipation coursed through her body like electricity through a power line.

She checked her reflection in the mirror for the umpteenth time, and someone banged on her door. She jumped and dropped the cream top. Who in the hell would hit the door like that? Andre didn't come across as the door pounding type.

The banging came again. Frowning, Mikayla crept from her bedroom. She grabbed the baseball bat that she kept next to the door before looking through the peephole. With a sigh of relief, she unlocked and opened the door.

"What are you doing?" She asked with a laugh.

Andre grinned back. He must have come straight from the office. Beneath his dark overcoat, he wore a light blue button up shirt with white cuffs and dark blue slacks. Gold cufflinks gleamed at the base of his sleeve and his tie was perfectly knotted around his neck. He balanced a pizza box with DVDs on top in one hand, and several grocery bags and a small toolbox in the other.

"Sorry for banging on the door. My foot is the only thing free." He lifted the pizza box. "I stopped for food. You said you'd come home to a broken disposal, so I assumed you didn't have time to eat."

She forgot how delicious his voice sounded in person, or how quickly the sound heated her blood.

Friends, just friends.

"I haven't eaten yet." Mikayla stepped back and let him in. "But I'm more curious, you plan to fix my disposal wearing that."

"Kitchen?" he asked. She led the way down the hall where he dropped the pizza and bags on the island in the middle. "You don't like my outfit."

"It's a little fancy for a plumber."

"I left my overnight bag in the car."

Her hand froze in the act of lifting the top of the pizza box. She turned wide eyes on him as her insides quivered. "Really?"

The corner of his mouth lifted. He pulled off his coat and hung it on the back of a chair at the dining table. "I'm spending the next few days in Columbia. If I mess up this shirt, I have more." He turned to the sink. "So what's the issue?"

Her shoulders slumped. "Um…it's clogged. The disposal is jammed."

He nodded before flipping the switch. They both frowned at the humming noise. Without hesitating, he removed cufflinks and rolled up his sleeves. She watched the play of muscles as he moved his arms. The man had fantastic arms, strong, lean, and with just enough dark hair to be sexy.

"You don't have to do this. I've already called the maintenance guy. He'll be here if not tonight then tomorrow."

Andre turned dark eyes toward her. "You don't think I can."

"No…I mean…I'm sure you can. But you're in a suit."

"I don't mind getting dirty. They're only clothes. Besides, unclogging a disposal is relatively easy."

He kneeled to look under the sink. Her mouth fell open. She'd assumed his offer to come had been just an excuse to see her again. His actions were definitely not what she'd expect from the callous jerk Renee described. She dropped to her knees beside him and peered over his shoulder.

"Do you really know how to fix this?"

He unplugged the disposal. "I hear doubt in your voice."

"I've never seen a corporate executive play plumber."

Warm dark eyes turned to her, and a sexy smile spread across his full lips. "I'm not playing plumber."

She giggled and almost rolled her eyes at her silliness. "If you permanently break my disposal I won't balk at asking you for the money to replace it."

"When I finish, you'll be calling me every weekend to fix broken things around your apartment." He stood and stuck his hand into the drain.

And that's not all she'd be calling for. *Don't go there, Mikayla.*

He pulled pieces of the apple cores she'd shoved down the disposal that morning. Her previous thought flew out of her brain. The man couldn't possibly be thinking about sex as he pulled her junk from the sink. He lowered back to the floor and pulled the toolbox onto his lap.

"How did you learn to work on plumbing? Ryan never…" she let the sentence drop.

When his eyes met hers, she dropped her gaze. Not here ten minutes and already she'd compared Andre to Ryan.

"I've always been interested in how things work. When repairmen came to our house, I usually tagged along." He removed an L-shaped piece of metal, she recognized it as an Allen wrench and slid under the sink. "Some of them consider you an annoyance, but most are willing to show you what they're doing. I picked up what I could. In college, my friend Jonathan taught me other stuff."

He used the Allen wrench to screw something on the bottom of the disposal.

"What are you doing?"

"The blades are jammed."

He talked about what was going on, but she didn't hear a word he said. Instead, focusing on the way he spread one leg out, bent and swung the other back and forth while he worked. Her gaze locked on that simple movement; the muscles of Andre's thigh bunched and flexed beneath the material of his pants. Desire slowly spread through her limbs like hot chocolate on a cold night. Seeing Andre in her kitchen, working, had her long neglected libido revving up.

She startled out of the trance when he popped up and once again stuck his hand into the sink. He pulled a few more pieces of apple from the sink before plugging up the disposal. This time when he tried the switch, the familiar whirling of the blades filled the kitchen.

Mikayla grinned from ear to ear. "You fixed it."

He laughed. "It was simple."

"That's fantastic." She flipped the switch off, then on again. "Thank you."

She spun around and nearly collided with him. He stood close enough for the subtle scent of his cologne to reach her. Dark eyes took her breath away. The pride in his gaze from her words was evident, but something more…something hotter also flared in the obsidian depths. The air thickened with the awareness between them. Her body ached with the memory of the one kiss they had shared.

"I've got to do this." His baritone hit her and knocked away all of that *just friends* nonsense.

"Do what?"

His dry hand lifted and cupped the side of her face. "Kiss you." Slowly, too slowly, he brought her face to his.

Her body shuddered, and his firm lips connected with hers. He didn't hesitate to slide his tongue across her lower lip, and she swiftly let him deepen the kiss. The spark and eruption happened again. The feeling of plunging off a cliff that was both scary and exhilarating. Their tongues danced against each other, increasing her need. Mikayla clutched the front of his shirt and pressed her hips forward. He pulled her closer but not close enough. The softness of her breasts flattened against the hard surface of his chest. Her nipples, stiff and aching for attention, tingled. One of Andre's hands plunged into her hair, and the other gripped her waist.

He pulled away too quickly. His lips pressed firmly together, his nostrils flared. Andre's short heavy breaths echoed in the room. Her fingers slowly loosened their grip on his shirt but didn't let go. Not when she wanted to jerk him back down. She held her breath. Each pound of her heart vibrated through her body, and her sex, slick with need, pulsed in tandem.

"We should watch the movie." He said between rough breaths.

"Yes…we should."

"But what we should do, and what I want to do, are two different things."

She licked her lips, took a steadying breath. "I can relate."

Heat flared in his eyes. Her fingers tightened on his shirt. He closed his eyes, took a breath and then met her gaze again. The passion was still there, but not as intense. "But we're friends. And friends don't make love when the other friend just had his hand stuck down a sink."

Her shaky laugh was half-hearted at best. "I guess you're right."

The perfect white teeth of his grin sent her heart into overdrive again. "I'll freshen up. Then we'll watch the movies. Catch up on what happened over the week."

She nodded. "I'd like that."

Untangling his fingers from her hair, Andre dropped his other hand from her waist. Reluctantly she released her grip on his shirt. The cool air in the room replaced the warmth of him. Slowly, as if she were backing away from a coiled snake, she stepped away. Her eyes sunk to the prominent lump in his pants, definitely like backing off a snake. An anaconda.

She turned to the cabinet and pulled out two burgundy ceramic plates— her idea of fine china. "Are you ready for pizza?" Desire thickened her voice.

"Do you mind if I bring my bag up and change into something less confining."

She imagined him changing clothes, naked, in her room. One plate slipped out of her hand onto the counter and spun in fast circles. She slapped a hand down to stop the spinning and cleared her throat. "Not at all."

He eyed the plate then her before the corner of his lips twitched. "I'll be right back."

After twenty minutes he'd gone to the car, washed up in her guest bathroom and was back in the kitchen. Dressed casually, he wore dark jeans and a white t-shirt that clung to his back and shoulders better than paint to a wall.

She opened the pizza boxes and frowned. "There's no meat on the pizza?"

He walked over and stood close to her. The smell of his body wash cloaked her and sent her senses careening out of control. "I like cheese. It's hard to go wrong when you don't know what your companion likes."

"Cheese is fine. I just never met a man who didn't want pepperoni or sausage on his pizza." She pulled out two large slices and placed them on the plates. "I've got beer if you want one."

He twisted his head and gave her a surprised look. "Beer, no wine?"

Crap! Sophisticated women would offer a guy wine. "Is that a problem?"

He grinned, and her heart did a quick thump. "I never met a woman who liked beer. I've been hanging around the wrong type of women."

A butterfly flutter vibrated through her belly. "I agree." She opened the fridge and pulled out two bottles. "Although Renee would say I'm hanging around the wrong man."

Arms crossed, Andre leaned on the island. "I think my friend Jonathan would like you. He's a good judge of character, but the fact that you like beer, pizza, and horror movies would put you on his approval list."

She popped the top on the bottles and handed one to him.

He raised an eyebrow when he looked at the label. "Abita, strawberry lager?"

"Lager is beer," she said.

"Strawberry lager is not beer."

"Well, it's all I've got so drink up."

"I may have to take back what I said about Jonathan liking you." He took a sip then licked his lips. A sensual reminder that he'd just licked her bottom lip. Mikayla mirrored the gesture, and automatically licked hers. He tipped the bottle toward her. "It's alright."

What were they discussing? Oh right, his friend's approval. "You mentioned Jonathan in the mountains. Does his opinion matter that much?" She picked up her plate and motioned with her head for him to follow.

"Outside of my brother, Jonathan is the only person I know who tells me the truth. Especially when I don't want to hear it. He warned me about Angelica. I should have listened."

"You two met in college." She took a bite of pizza then licked some extra sauce from her lower lip.

"Yeah, freshman year. I took one look at him and thought he was a pretty boy. He took one look at me and saw me for the stuck up know it all I was. Instant dislike."

She took a swallow of the sweet lager. "So how did you two become friends?"

"We fought over a petri dish."

"Excuse me?"

"We were in biology lab and reached for the same petri dish to plate some bacteria. Before you knew it, we were wrestling around on the floor. We broke thousands of dollars' worth of equipment. Nearly got expelled from school."

"What happened?"

"My dad bailed me out," bitterness crept into his tone. "I insisted he do the same for Jonathan."

"Did Jonathan appreciate that?"

"No. He was mad as hell that we were the ones to save his ass, even though his father was working to do the same thing. Long story short, our ensuing argument ended with us both agreeing on what a hassle it is to have overbearing parents. From then on we were cool."

"Parents," she sipped her lager and thought of her dad. "I haven't told my dad about what happened with Ryan."

"Why not?"

"Because he never liked my relationship with the Caldwell family. I mean, he likes Renee alright, but even so he's not happy about the changes I've made since meeting them."

"What type of changes?"

"Nothing drastic, but my dad sees my interest in being successful and fashionable as losing his little buddy. Before I met Renee, I didn't know what to do with my hair, couldn't match clothes, and the thought of accessorizing made me hyperventilate."

He considered her words and nodded. "I can see that."

Her hand collapsed onto her lap, plate and all. "Is it that obvious I'm out of my league?"

"I don't mean it like that. You're stylish, but I think you'd be more comfortable as you are now, and the way we were in the mountains. Jeans, t-shirts, chilling on the couch watching television."

"Well, I'm working to change that."

"Why? It's what I like about you."

Her head slowly tilted to the side. She watched him for signs of teasing or an indication that he was just being nice. Most men she came across liked a girlie girl. Women like her...correction women like she used to be, were delegated to the friend zone or called when a man didn't know how to change his own tire. Something one of the men Renee set Mikayla up with actually had her do.

"In my experience, guys like the polish and glamour. Even you said that a woman like Angelica fitted perfectly into your world. That alone made her good enough to marry."

"I was never comfortable around Angelica. Our relationship was always about the show, how we looked together. Last weekend, with you I was able to relax." She cocked a brow, and he grinned. "After I realized you weren't what I expected. But even before that, I'd noticed you. Why would you want to change what makes you stand out?"

She picked off a section of cheese from the pizza. "I wasn't considered cute when I was younger. My dad did the best he could, but he raised me like a son. My hair was a knotty mess, he hated pink and frills so my clothes were usually the least girly thing he could find, and we spent the weekends working on his cars or camping. To say I was a tomboy is an understatement. The guys ignored me and the girls teased me. It's one of the reasons I hate to be humiliated. I suffered enough of that growing up."

"What changed?"

Her gaze met his eyes and she smiled. "In college, away from dad, I picked more feminine clothing. Though I lacked style, anything was better than overalls and Power Rangers t-shirts. After college, I started working for the Caldwells. Renee took one look at me and made me her personal makeover project. Now I can at least pretend to know what I'm doing fashion-wise."

"I bet your dad didn't like that."

She laughed. "Not at all. He thought I was changing too much to fit in with their lifestyle. Basically, selling my soul just to jump into a higher class."

"And Ryan?"

She turned away, took a gulp of the beer. "I got too comfortable and started to believe me and Ryan being together made sense."

"You still care about him?"

She shook her head but didn't meet his gaze. She had cared for Ryan. How could she not care for him just like she had for Renee and Phillip? But those feelings for him had withered up in the span of a few seconds.

"I hate seeing Ryan daily. But I can't quit yet. Now that Dalmtrix isn't moving to Hartsville. My credibility as an acquisitions person is shot to hell. I have to fix that, before moving on."

"What?" The word cracked like a whip.

She turned back to him. His lips pressed into a thin line, and his brows nearly met above his eyes. "I pushed Philip and Ryan to purchase a hundred acres in Hartsville County. Dalmtrix was putting a manufacturing facility there which meant new jobs and people needing a place to stay. Today I found out the deal may be dead.

Shifting forward, Andre dropped his plate on the coffee table. "Things may still…work out," he took a long pull from his bottle of lager.

"It's probably for the best. I can't stay at Caldwell Development. Once I help salvage what's left of that land purchase, I'm looking for another job."

The tension left his shoulders as he blew out a breath. "I will admit, it will be nice to know you're not working for my uncle and cousin anymore."

"And why is that?"

He turned on the sofa, to face her. "Mikayla, I've thought of you every day since leaving the mountains. My dad, brother and best friend have all said I should forget about you. But here I am."

Her skin tingled, and the blood pounded in her veins. "Why?"

"Because, I want to be here. With you."

CHAPTER 14

"So, how many cigarettes did you smoke this week?" Mikayla asked.

Andre grinned at Mikayla sitting opposite him on the couch. By talking throughout, she'd avoided paying attention to the horror movie. Too bad. He'd hoped she'd ask him to stay and keep away the nightmares. He should've left the second she mentioned her connection with Dalmtrix, but he enjoyed playing her hero and wasn't ready to stop.

He stretched his arms out on the back of her off-white leather couch until his fingers brushed the back of her shoulder. "I had three," he answered her question.

He liked her apartment. Nicely decorated with warm earth tones and abstract paintings on the wall. Her furniture was modern, but she included a lot of traditional features, a grandfather clock, a bright blue and white quilt and a rocking chair. The two styles blended into a welcoming feel, reminding him of her personality.

"Cheat."

He chuckled and took a sip of the second, surprisingly good, strawberry lager. "If you worked with my dad, you would too."

"I work with his brother. I know what you're going through, if they're anything alike. And I didn't smoke."

"I might let you backslide tonight."

Temptation flashed in her eyes. An image of the two of them, lying in her bed, sweaty and spent after sex, sharing a cigarette swept through his brain. He shut the thought down. This visit was about getting to know her better, discovering if what happened in the mountains was real or a fluke, not getting her in bed.

"I've done well this week," she said pointing at him. "Let's keep it that way. You've heard about me and my dad. Now tell me about your dad."

"If you know my uncle, then you know my dad. That's what's so crazy about this entire family feud. They're too alike to get along. Sometimes I think Phillip is growing tired of it all."

She pulled her feet up onto the couch and wrapped her arms around her legs. A dark burgundy polish adorned her toenails. Simple, not flashy, just like her.

"What actually happened?"

He shifted closer. "My grandfather owned land in Columbia and passed it on to my dad and Philip. Philip wanted to sell it in pieces to developers then reinvest the money in more land. My dad didn't intend to give up what the family had. He'd started collecting trash for businesses. Dad wanted

Philip to go into business with him. Philip said our family deserved more than picking up other people's trash. He sold his half, bought more land and started developing neighborhoods. My dad moved to Greenville, and through…any means necessary…grew Caldwell Environmental Solutions."

She tilted her head to the side, and the soft waves of her hair floated around her face. "It sounds like your dad is smart."

"He's ruthless."

"But you're proud of him. Of the company. I can hear it in your voice."

"Of course I'm proud. He started with one truck, and now we have contracts with businesses and governments all over the Eastern United States. Before long we'll expand west, and we're looking into utilizing the methane gas from our landfills to power nearby businesses."

Her head popped up. "There's a landfill near the spot Dalmtrix is considering. Maybe you can buy that landfill and supply gas to them." Her lips twisted in a self-depreciating smile, "Maybe then the deal will go through."

He turned away and drained the remainder of the lager from his bottle. He couldn't tell her the real reason he was in Columbia. As soon as he ended this deal with Senator Leventis her land acquisition would be a waste of millions of dollars. Guilt rode his back like a crazy monkey, but not enough to make him confess his family's plans. From the moment, she'd opened the door and smiled, the stress that tightened his neck and shoulders after a week at work dissolved. He liked her, and it was much too soon to destroy what had barely started. He wouldn't think about how much he wasn't the good guy she thought he was. Or how the soft smile on her face would turn to a look of disgust if she found out.

"Maybe." He sat his empty bottle on the coffee table. "So, tell me about your family."

"Nothing remarkable to tell. My mom died when I was four. I don't really remember her."

"What happened?"

"A heart attack." She downed the rest of her ale. "She was older than I am now, almost forty, but still her death was a shock to my dad…my family."

He reached over and placed a hand on her shoulder. "I'm sorry for your loss."

She shrugged and shifted until his hand fell away. "It's alright. I was young, and despite his lack of female style, my dad did a great job raising me."

He brought his hand back, watched as she pushed her hair behind her ears and gave a brave smile. Just like she'd done in the mountains. When things were tough, she plowed through, said things would work out. He wondered how many times it actually had worked out for her. Losing her mother, then later the man she loved in college, only to have Ryan humiliate her. Then there's the deal falling through. He couldn't control that...not really. But a part of him wanted to make sure she never suffered a loss again.

"I take it he lives nearby," he asked.

"Not too far away. I grew up near Rock Hill. He's an inspector for the County's Public Works department. You know roads, pipes, stuff like that."

"Sounds interesting."

She laughed. "It was. The man drilled in my head just how dirty men could be. How they'd lie, tell you they love you and do everything up to murder just to get you in bed."

"Rough on the boyfriends, huh?"

"You can't imagine." Her shoulders relaxed, and the smile on her face softened. "He liked Brenden, said he could tell Brenden cared."

His body stiffened. He forced himself to relax. He wouldn't be jealous of a dead man. "But he didn't like Ryan."

"He liked Ryan alright, he just didn't like Ryan and me together."

Three guesses weren't needed to figure out what her dad would say about him. Difficult to imagine the man would encourage her to date another Caldwell man.

"Are your feelings usually in line with your dads?"

"Most of the time. Guys in high school pretty much ignored me. Brenden was the first guy to pay me any attention. We met in class and just clicked from the start. Brenden was easy to love."

"And Ryan?"

She sighed, and then ran a hand through her hair. "Ryan and I got along great at work. I knew he was a playboy, but through my friendship with Renee, I saw past that. He flirted, but I didn't believe he could seriously be interested in me. But he kept on. I trusted him with not so good results."

"And with me," he asked softly.

Her lips parted with a staggered breath. Eyes warmed to the consistency of hot chocolate. She wanted him. That was no secret. And he wanted her. He wanted to talk to her, see that smile on her face, and impress her with his plumbing skills instead of his family name. He was interested in more than a quick bedroom romp. Something near panic hit and made his heart pound against his ribcage. He didn't know how to do the long term, loving type relationships.

"It feels natural...like it did with Brenden," she said. "But it's also different. Something says I shouldn't do this, something bigger says I should."

Her words dissolved his panic. Desire thrummed through his body and slowly hardened his dick. Now was the time to pull her close, kiss her, then carry her to the bedroom and do what the not so good guy in him wanted.

What he'd tried not to think about since leaving Greenville and driving down I-26 to Columbia. One thing stopped him, her budding faith in him. If he slept with her, and she found out about C.E.S.'s involvement in Caldwell Development's loss when Dalmtrix fell through, she'd view his actions as part of the whole family feud.

Letting the deal go through wasn't an option. His family's business tactics were ruthless, but every step they took, made C.E.S. more successful. Getting Dalmtrix to move somewhere else, and expanding the landfill gas program was the best business decision. He'd just have to make sure Mikayla never found out the extent of C.E.S.'s involvement in the company's change in plans. No matter how much he wanted her, he had to move slowly, earn her trust. Show her that there was more to the attraction between the two of them than revenge against Ryan or even Caldwell Development. Then she'd have some reassurance if she ever learned about his involvement.

The rationalization caused a guilty burn in his stomach. But her admission that their attraction felt right doused the flames.

He cleared his throat and broke eye contact. "You want to watch the other movie. Or are you tired of my company already. Do you want me to leave?"

"No, this one is fine." She turned back to the television.

He swung one of his legs onto the couch then slid it behind her.

"Come here," he reached over and tugged on her arm.

She hesitated, then settled her back against his chest. A two by four was less stiff than her body. He ran a hand up and down her arm. Gradually she relaxed. Having her this close, with her sweet floral scent encasing him, and the soft strands of her hair brushing his chin, the arousal between his legs slowly grew.

Andre tried to focus on the human killing thing on the screen. The distraction proved useless. He could only focus on Mikayla and her reactions to the movie. Her body tensed during a suspenseful part, pressing her back and her curved rear into him. A ridiculous chase followed the suspense. She chuckled, her breasts bounced, and his fingers flexed on the couch. Bloodshed came next, and Mikayla squirmed, sliding her legs back and forth along the couch. His breathing hitched, and pictures of Mikayla sliding her legs along his, naked and warm in bed flickered through his mind. The longer they watched, the more his arousal drugged his system.

She snuggled closer, rested her head against his chest. The move brought her backside right against the hard ridge of his erection. He wasn't going to sleep with her. Yet. But if this kept up, he damn sure was going to need a cigarette. Or another taste of her. Andre buried his nose in her hair, breathed deeply, inhaling her scent. Her body tensed, and he was sure this time not because of the movie. He settled one arm under the weight of her breasts and propped the other hand on the back of the couch. She shifted, her back increasing the friction between her body and his hyperaware dick.

She sucked in a quick unsteady breath, and her beautiful breasts rose and fell again. Andre licked his lips. The outline of her nipples beneath the close fitting t-shirt captured his attention. He shouldn't touch her. If he did, he wouldn't remember he was trying to move slowly. Trying hard not to lift her shirt and see those hardened tips between his fingers. His hand twitched against her stomach. She gasped.

Enough with the good-guy stunt. He slowly brought his hand up until the full weight of her breast rested in his grasp. His head lowered to nip and lick the softness of her ear.

Her lips parted. Heavy lids lowered over soft brown eyes. Carefully he pulled on the tail of her shirt. Taking his time to reveal the smoothness of her flat stomach, and then tugged higher until the satin cups of her beige bra showed. Her stomach caved in, and he ran eager fingers lightly across her skin. With the other hand, he tugged the thin barrier of the satin bra down and revealed two of the most delectable breast he'd ever seen. Pecan brown, with a plump chocolate drop nipple. His mouth watered. A sharp breath hissed between clenched teeth and his fingers wrapped around her luscious flesh.

Mikayla's head twisted to the side, a silent gasp escaped her full lips. He lowered his head to the smooth skin along her neck. He kissed her and tasted the sweetness of her flesh. Each flick of his tongue increased the pounding of his heart. He wanted to flip her around and take her hard nipples between his lips. Draw them deep into his mouth while his hands squeezed and caressed the pliant mounds. Instead, he casually rolled the rigid tips between his thumbs and index fingers. Her body tensed. Then suddenly relaxed. Only to tense again. Her legs rose up and down as she ran her feet along the couch.

Mikayla's chest rose, a silent plea for more, and he gave her what she craved. Gently plucking and teasing her nipples until they protruded stiffly. She whimpered, and sweet feminine noises filled the room.

Her eager response sent a surge of I'm the man pride through his body. Each twist, sharp inhale, and light moan of her body revealed she was also caught up in the pleasure of the moment. And urged him to go with the impulse blasting in his veins. He slid one hand down her stomach and stretched his fingers, longing to slip in the treasure between her thighs. His fingertips breached the edge of her pants, and he let out a ragged exhale.

Mikayla stiffened, then scrambled up. He sat frozen for a second and stared at the now empty space between his legs then at her. Slowly, he sat up and watched her shaky hands struggle to pull the wrinkled bra over her gorgeous breasts and yank her shirt down.

"We have to stop."

He ran a hand down his face. It trembled. Hell, his entire body trembled.

"If…that's what you want." His voice was tighter than the underwear struggling to contain his erection.

"It's not…I mean it should be. But it's not." She shuffled from side to side. Her hands twisted underneath her shirt behind her back. To fasten her bra, he supposed.

"Can you be more specific?"

Mikayla pulled in a deep breath, her shoulders rose and fell. After a few seconds, she turned and met his gaze. Then looked away. Then met his gaze again.

"I can't have sex right now." She cleared her throat, ran a hand through her hair. "It's just not a good time." She drew out the last word.

He stared in confusion.

"Of the month."

It dawned on him. His face burned. What the hell! Was he actually blushing? "Oh… well…I understand."

"Besides, it's for the best, anyway. We're just friends."

They were beyond that. Biology kept them apart tonight, but something far deeper pulled them together.

"What just happened says we're more than friends."

"But, are we going there?"

"Apparently not tonight." He took a deep breath. "Let's watch the movie."

She hesitated, and then sat on the other end of the couch. To hell with that. Andre slid his hand around her arm and pulled her beside him. He wrapped his arm around her shoulders, ignored his throbbing penis, and tried to watch the movie.

CHAPTER 15

Mikayla stretched and rolled over on the bed, and her knee bumped into something warm and hard. Her eyes popped open. Andre slept soundly next to her. Fully clothed from the night before. They'd watched movies until late, so she'd offered him her couch. They ended the night with another horror movie, which lead to another nightmare and Andre getting off the couch, and sliding in bed with her. Regardless of their "just friends" efforts, the night before ranked as one of the best dates of her life.

He lay closer to her this morning than he had in the mountains. Still no spooning, but he faced her, and his feet touched hers. Mikayla's long neglected body parts heated with the memories of the previous night. She would have forgotten all about not letting things get intimate if Mother Nature hadn't intervened.

Slowly she eased out of bed and grabbed a t-shirt and flannel pajama bottoms. She tiptoed into the connecting bathroom. After washing her face and brushing her teeth, she hoped into the shower. When she left the bathroom, all thoughts abandoned her mind as she drank in the sight of Andre's large body sprawled out on his back across her queen size bed like he belonged there. His long arms and legs took up the limited space she'd left behind. The temptation to crawl back in and curl herself around him hit hard. She liked seeing him in her bed. Despite the odds, they clicked, but so many things made trusting that easy connection scary.

She could fall for him. Hard. She wouldn't let herself do that until she was clear about what was actually happening between them.

A knock on her apartment door jolted her out of her thoughts. She checked the clock beside the bed. Damn! My hair appointment with Renee.

The knock came again. Andre shifted and stretched. Mikayla ran to the side of the bed.

"Good morning," Andre's voice, deeper and sexier with the gruffness of sleep, filled the room.

She pressed a finger to her lips. "Shh. Renee is at the door. She can't know you're here."

Frowning, he sat up on the bed. "Are we a secret?"

"No, but there's no need for her to find out like this. She's already upset about what happened between Angelica and Ryan. She'll think you're here for revenge and release that famous Caldwell temper."

Andre's frown deepened. "You can't believe that's my motivation after last night."

She couldn't answer when she'd just wondered if this thing they shared, were real. "Regardless, do you really want to announce our...relationship to the family like this?" He opened his mouth as if he wanted to argue. Mikayla held up a hand. "Just stay in here and don't say a word. I'll tell her I overslept and will meet her at the salon. It'll only take a minute."

She turned and hurried out the bedroom before he could respond. After, closing the bedroom door behind her, and hiding his overnight bag in the entryway closet, she took a breath then snatched the front door open.

"I'm so sorry, I overslept." The words rushed from her mouth.

Renee pushed past her and marched down the hall to the living room. "Where the hell is he, Mikayla?"

Mikayla's heart leaped in her chest. She shut the door and followed her friend. "What are you talking about?"

Renee spun around, her high heeled boots knocking hard on the floor when she marched through the kitchen and then to the living room. She looked like the angry host of one of those modeling reality shows. "I recognize Andre's car. I can't believe this. Didn't you listen when I explained what it's like between him and Ryan? I know you're hurt—"

"I'm not hurt," Mikayla retaliated. She hurried down the hall to stop Renee from barging into the bedroom.

"Then why? Are you doing this to get back at Ryan?"

"Ryan doesn't give a damn what I do."

"That's a lie and you know it, Mikayla. If Angelica hadn't come back into his life, you and Ryan would be happy right now. We both know his heart never really healed after Paris. I don't condone what he did to you, but I know why he took the chance with her. And you do, too. You may not have loved Ryan, but you were friends. Sleeping with Andre will hurt him...you and my cousin know this."

Renee's words struck, and she'd ignited Mikayla's guilty button. She didn't want to think about how Ryan would feel about her friendship with Andre. Ryan's feelings stopped counting the moment he stepped in the closet with Angelica.

Mikayla crossed her arms over her chest. "This isn't about Ryan."

Sympathy filled Renee's eyes. "Maybe not for you, but I know my family."

Mikayla dropped Renee's gaze and glanced at the bedroom door. Her confidence waivered. What was his goal? Cloud her judgment; make her want him so that he could get even with Ryan? Why would he even think Ryan cared if that was his plan?

"Ryan chased after you in the mountains," Renee said as if Mikayla had spoken her questions. Renee stepped toward Mikayla. "One thing, that's drilled into us, is to not lose our cool in front of our cousins. Ryan did that, first with Angelica and then with you. Andre knows Ryan still cares."

Pain sliced through Mikayla's chest. Tears blurred her vision. She blinked them away.

Another knock on the door interrupted them. Renee touched her shoulder, but Mikayla pulled away. "It's probably the maintenance guy. My garbage disposal was clogged."

She wiped the wetness from her eyes and crossed to the door. A glance through the peephole and her stomach sank. Swearing beneath her breath, she sucked in several deep breaths and turned to Renee.

"No one is here, and we're on our way to the salon, okay," Mikayla said with steely determination.

Renee's arched brows scrunched together, but she slowly lifted and lowered her head.

Pasting on a broad tight smile, Mikayla opened the door. "Hi, Dad. What are you doing here?"

Evan Sander's dark eyes studied his daughter carefully. He stood a few inches taller than Mikayla but made up for his lack of height with burliness. A brawny man with wide shoulders and strong arms and legs, the fruits of lifelong manual labor. He wore a dusty ball cap with Titans, the name of the Pop Warner football team he coached, stitched across the front over his bald head, and a thick leather jacket over worn jeans.

"Do I need a reason to visit? I wanted to make sure everything is okay. When you called after your trip, you didn't sound good."

"Everything is fine. I've been busy with work and traveling."

"You know I need to make sure my baby girl is okay."

She pushed back her frustration and sighed. No matter how hard she tried to prove she could take care of herself, he believed that was his responsibility.

"I'm perfect. In fact, Renee is here. We're on our way out to the salon."

He examined her from head to toe. "You're not dressed, so you've got a few minutes."

With a silent sigh, she stepped back and let him in. He scrutinized everything on his way down the hall. Panic squeezed her chest. Andre's coat was still in the kitchen.

She pushed him past the kitchen to the living room. "Just a few more minutes, Renee. My dad just stopped by for a second."

Evan's square jaw hardened, and his bushy brows formed a line over his eyes before he pulled away. "No need to push."

"Sorry," she mumbled.

"Hi, Mr. Sanders." Renee rose from the couch and shook Evan's hand.

A quick sweep of the room and Mikayla realized Renee had hidden the empty lager bottles from the night before. She mouthed "Thank you." Renee may not have agreed with Andre being there, but hiding the evidence meant she had Mikayla's back.

"Good to see you, Renee. So how was the wedding?" Evan pulled back and took stock of everything in the living room.

"The wedding was nice. Beautiful with the snow and everything."

Evan nodded. "I was worried when you called to see if Mikayla stopped to visit me. I thought maybe it didn't go so well. I know how much you and Ryan were looking forward to it."

Mikayla cringed. "Want some coffee, Dad? Sit down while I make some."

She spun and went into the kitchen before he could answer. She grabbed Andre's coat off the chair and opened the pantry door.

"Whose tool box?"

Mikayla threw the coat on the pantry floor and slammed the door. She turned while her dad examined the box and the tools.

"The maintenance guy. I'm out of coffee."

He opened the box and shuffled through the tools. "The garbage disposal again? They charge you too much rent to have things breaking down every day." He opened the cabinet under the sink and kneeled to take a look.

"Dad, please, it's fixed now. And I really need to get dressed."

Thankfully, Renee hurried into the kitchen "We're going to be late. You know Cathy hates when we're late."

Mikayla crossed the room to Renee, hoping her dad would follow. Instead, he pushed past her and opened the pantry door.

"Whose coat is this?" Evan picked up Andre's coat from the floor.

Renee raised an eyebrow and speared Mikayla a what the hell look.

Heat rose in Mikayla's cheeks. Deal with the most pressing issue first. With a straight face, she turned to her dad.

"Ryan's. He left it here before the wedding."

Evan's eyebrows met over questioning eyes. "Why is it on the pantry floor?"

"I may have thrown it in there without thinking. So the maintenance guy wouldn't get it dirty."

He looked at the label. "This is an expensive coat."

She walked over and pulled the coat out of his grasp. "I know it's expensive. I've got to get dressed. How long are you in Columbia?"

"Just drove down to see you. Let's talk, Mikayla." He looked to Renee.

"If you'll excuse us." He placed a firm hand on Mikayla's shoulder and gently guided her forward.

Renee stepped out of the way. When Mikayla stopped outside of the kitchen, he plodded pass and went straight into the bedroom. Mikayla's heart jumped in her chest. She sprinted across the hall and into the bedroom. Evan stood at the foot of the bed. His arms crossed, a scowl marring his face.

Rumpled sheets, but an empty bed. The bathroom door closed. Swallowing hard, she willed Andre to stay out of sight.

"Close the door." Her dad said. Once she did, Evan continued. "Now tell me the truth. You and Ryan are through, aren't you?"

She nearly sagged with relief that she could answer truthfully. "Yes."

Her dad's nostrils flared. "Did he hurt you?"

"I don't want to talk about it."

"Did that rich boy hurt you?"

The vision of Ryan and Angelica on the floor flashed in her mind. She shoved the embarrassment away. "No, dad. It was mutual. You were right. Ryan and I are better as friends."

He studied her then slowly his face relaxed, and he uncrossed his arms. "One day, you'll learn the advice I give, is solid. I know you want to be independent, and that you like the fancy clothes and parties."

"It's not the clothes and parties, Dad. My job requires me to attend events with a dress code that doesn't include camouflage and overalls."

Evan flinched. The jab was petty, but he had to accept that she wasn't his little sidekick anymore.

"The point is, they're not your family. You can always depend on me. You may not be able to depend on them."

Mikayla walked around him and tossed the pillows on the bed to the floor before jerking the sheets up. "I know."

"Is that why you haven't called because you were embarrassed to admit that you were wrong about Ryan?"

She bit back a smart reply and continued to make up the bed. Wrong when it came to Ryan, she had no one to blame but herself for her dad believing she deserved an 'I told you so'.

"I've been busy with work."

He sighed and placed a hand on her shoulder. She turned away from the bed to face him. Evan gave her an awkward pat on the shoulder, just like he'd done when she was a little girl. "Don't work yourself so hard. Life is too short." Concern filled his eyes.

Guilt swept over her. After her mom's heart attack, her dad became extra diligent about their health. He feared she'd work herself into an early grave.

"I will. That's why I'm going to the salon with Renee. To relax."

He nodded, initiated another that-a-boy pat. "Alright, you don't have to say it again. I did bring my fishing gear. Thought I'd fish over on the lake. I was hoping you would join me."

"Not today, Dad. Hair appointment and all. But, look, I'll come up next weekend okay?"

"We'll go out to dinner tonight, alright. My treat. You can even wear one of your fancy dresses." He turned toward the door. "Get dressed, I'll say my goodbyes to Renee and you can go."

"Dad wait," she hurried over and gave him a hug. "I look forward to dinner."

An easy smile relaxed the hard lines of his face, and he nodded. "Me too."

The bedroom door shut quietly behind him, and the bathroom door opened. Andre stood in the doorway. His dark eyes boring into hers. Renee's warning came back, but it didn't prevent the memories of the night before from resurfacing.

"Why did you cover for Ryan?" he asked quietly.

She raised her chin. "I didn't cover for him. I kept my dad out of my business." She whispered back, in case her dad hadn't left yet. "I think you should go."

He crossed his arms over his broad chest. "Why?"

"We should end this."

A dark scowl covered his handsome face. He stalked across the room and towered over her. "After last night, you want to end this?"

"What was last night really about, Andre?"

He pointed at the door. "You're listening to Renee? You're going to believe that bullshit instead of what we both feel."

She pushed past him and snatched the pillows off the floor. "It's not bullshit." She slapped one pillow down at the head of the bed.

Andre marched over and wrenched the other pillow from her hand. "The hell it isn't. I like you, Mikayla." He pointed the pillow at her. "I don't say that to many women. And I'm damn sure, not happy about saying it to you considering your connection with my family. I don't lie or play games. I want to get to know you better. Do you want to get to know me, or do you want Ryan and Renee?"

She swiped the pillow out of his hand. "It's not a competition. Renee is my friend. She's only trying to look out for my best interests."

He snatched it back. "She's also Ryan's sister, my cousin that hates me, and a Caldwell, which makes her manipulative as hell. Tell me to go, and I'm not coming back."

She took a step back. "Is that supposed to be a threat?"

"No, it's a simple statement. I will not fight a losing battle for you. " He dropped the pillow on the bed and stepped closer, enclosing her in the warmth of his body. His hand cupped the back of her head. He tilted it up until she meet his eyes. She could barely breathe trapped in his dark gaze. "I'm tired of the games. I'm tired of the pressure to do what's expected. I don't have to do that around you. Every minute in your company is like a five-week vacation. That feeling has everything to do with you and nothing to do with The Caldwell's damn family fight."

He came across as sincere. And a bit uneasy. She doubted Andre made many heartfelt declarations to women.

Her shoulders relaxed. "Please don't hurt me, Andre."

He sucked in a breath and his dark eyes widened. Before she could say more, he eased a strong arm around her waist and drew her against his hard body and covered her lips with his. He tasted like Colgate toothpaste, and the delicious flavor that was him. Her arms wrapped around his neck as she pressed into his firm body.

"Mikayla," Renee's distressed voice cracked through the room.

Mikayla broke from Andre and spun around. Renee glared at Andre. Her face was pulled tight, and slender hands balled into fists.

Mikayla stepped forward. "I know the history. He told me about the fight between him and Ryan in the mountains. I'm going to trust him."

Renee pointed at Andre. "You can't trust that side of my family."

"And he says I can't trust your side."

Renee's beautiful face crumpled. She turned to Mikayla with pain filled eyes. "You're picking him over us. I thought we were friends."

Mikayla shook her head. "We are friends, Renee. I'm not choosing sides in your family feud. I'm choosing what I want, and right now I want to get to know Andre. If you know anything about me, you know I wouldn't say that without thinking things through." Mikayla straightened her shoulders. "Please don't make our friendship a condition of my relationship with him."

Every twitch of Renee's face gave away her suppressing the need to argue. Mikayla never denied Renee's requests before. She usually went along with all of Renee's advice. A part of her feared her friend would reject her. That they still weren't as close as she thought.

Finally, Renee settled cold eyes on Andre. "She's like my sister. If you hurt her, I will jack you up."

Andre stepped up to Mikayla and placed his hand on the small of her back. "The same goes for you and your brother."

Mikayla peered from one to the other. Had she made progress, or just committed to her own eventual heartbreak.

CHAPTER 16

"When are you going to let me know what really happened between you and Ryan?"

Mikayla nearly choked on a buffalo wing. Even though her dad said he'd take her some place fancy, she knew he would be more comfortable at a sports bar. So that's where they were, drinking beers, eating wings and watching basketball highlights on the television screens. She'd even gone so far as to wear her old Clemson sweatshirt and a pair of faded—nondesigner—jeans.

She swigged the beer and focused her eyes on the basketball highlights flashing across the big screen. "What makes you think there's more to the story?"

"I'm not stupid, Mikayla, and I know when you're lying. I also know you don't like when I get in your business, so that's why I left instead of demanding to meet the guy hiding in your bathroom."

Mikayla slid the beer bottle across the table. *Man, I need a cigarette.* Evan raised a brow and leaned his elbows on the table.

"Don't look so surprised. That wasn't Ryan's coat. And you always sleep on the left side of the bed. Both sides were rumpled.

Her cheeks heated. "Do we really have to talk about this?"

"I know you're an adult. And while I may not like the idea that my little girl is having sex, it doesn't mean I can't talk about it with you."

Mikayla ran a hand through her head. "I didn't have sex, Dad," She said, barely checking the annoyance.

"Then what the hell were you doing with a man in your bed?"

Mikayla gripped the edge of the table. "When are you going to let me handle my life on my own? You don't have to know everything that is going on with me."

"Well, excuse the hell out of me," he crossed thick arms across his wide chest. "You're all I've got left in the world. All I ever want, is to see you happy and taken care of. You may view my interest as overstepping boundaries, but I'm making sure the only person I care about isn't getting herself into trouble."

"I'm not getting myself into trouble. I know what I'm doing."

"Then why don't you tell me what you're doing. One day you're going away for the weekend with Ryan. Today, you're in your apartment with a different guy. Please explain. Why shouldn't I find that situation confusing? Why shouldn't I worry about my little girl?

He didn't raise his voice. Evan never did. His firm, no-nonsense tone, always drilled past her arguments straight to her guilty conscious.

Her eyes burned with unshed tears. She didn't know what she was doing. Everything seemed so right when she was with Andre. Thoughts that any relationship with Andre would make her appear desperate resurfaced.

"I'm seeing someone else. It's nothing serious, and we're just friends." She squirmed in her chair.

"A friend that sleeps in the bed with you."

"He came over to repair the disposal. We ate pizza, watched some movies and that was all." Her breathing hitched as the memory of Andre's hands on her breasts.

"Why was he in the bed with you if that was all?"

She cut her eyes at her dad. "I'm drawing the line. We're not discussing what I do in my bedroom."

Evan held up a hand. "Fine, I'll accept that. This guy, were you seeing him before you agreed to date Ryan?"

She tossed a napkin on the plate of wing bones. Might as well get this over and done. "I met him at the wedding. He's Ryan's cousin. They don't get along, but we hit it off. And before you think that I dumped Ryan to hook up with his cousin, you should know that Ryan hooked up with someone else at the wedding as well. I meant it when I said our split was mutual."

Evan's eyebrows clashed over dark eyes. She could tell he didn't believe that part. Damn it! He always knew when she was lying.

"So, you and Ryan split at the wedding and you both hook up with other people."

"Something like that." She plucked the dessert and drink menu from the edge of the table. It sucked that Columbia was a no smoking in restaurants town.

"And this guy is Ryan's cousin. Another Caldwell."

"Yes."

"The two sides of the family don't get along." He scratched his chin. "Are you sure this guy isn't with you just to get back at Ryan?"

She vigorously shook her head. "He's not."

Evan leaned forward, the corner of his mouth twisted. "But how do you know that."

Mikayla slapped the drink menu back on the table. "I just do. Alright?"

Her dad sighed heavily. He leaned back in the chair and took a slow, measured sip of his drink. His eyes assessed her the entire time.

"I taught you how men think for a reason. So that you can understand how special you are, and what you deserve. I'm not going to tell you that you're right or wrong in this situation, but I will say keep your wits about you. Don't get mixed up in the Caldwell family drama. You're not a part of that family."

"I never said I was a part of their family," Mikayla stated in a resigned voice.

"Just remember that. Being friends with your employer is hard enough without thinking you're more important to them than you are."

She balled her hand into a fist on the table. "Why do you do that? Why do you have to talk as if I'm incapable of knowing when someone is taking advantage of me? I'm a smart woman, Dad. Mostly because of you. I finished college, I landed a great job, and I'm successful at what I do. You still think you need to jump in and fight my battles. News flash, I learned to fight in first grade when Stacy McKnight picked on me about the knotty braids on my head."

Evan sighed. His eyes filled with remorse, and she knew she'd hit below the belt. He couldn't help that he didn't know how to relate to a daughter. That's what her mom was supposed to be there for.

"I don't want you to get hurt," he said.

"I'm going to get hurt. Life is full of hurt and pain and bad decisions. But you have to let me make those decisions. I'm fully capable of surviving all three. I'm not your little girl anymore."

Evan sat back in his chair and drummed thick fingers on the table. "Going from one rich man's bed to his cousin's, is that how you show it?"

The easily spoken words sank into her heart like a knife. Evan didn't have to raise his voice to make his point. Just throw out cutting words with an edge of have you lost your mind, and she was twelve again.

Cheers rumbled in the background, a group of guys responding to the game on one of the flat screens. She twisted in the direction of the commotion, unable to face the truth of her dad's words.

She pulled her debit card out of her back pocket and waved the card in the air to catch the waiter's attention. "I'm going to go now," her tone was measured and didn't match the tension pulsating through her body. "I'll call you next week."

The waiter came for the debit card, but Evan pulled out cash and shoved it into the waiter's hand. They stood and walked out. Even with the freezing temperatures outside, several people huddled in groups talking and laughing as they waited for seats inside.

Mikayla quickly patted her dad's shoulder. "Love you." She hurried around him to her car. His grumbled "I love you, too," trailed behind her.

CHAPTER 17

Andre sat across from Curtis and Senator Leventis in the main dining hall of the Capital City Club. Located at the top of the largest building in Columbia, the space provided panoramic views of downtown and beyond. They'd been through the false pleasantries and had just finished eating lunch. Senator Leventis could be a poster child for the corrupt politician but was charming enough to convince his constituents to vote him back in and clever enough to hide his countless dirty dealings.

Curtis Caldwell's shoulders stiffened. Andre readied himself for what lay ahead. The real reason they were here.

Don't hurt me, Andre. Mikayla's words sliced through his brain. His jaw firmed. Senator Leventis was no saint, and this move would help C.E.S., and had nothing to do with his relationship with Mikayla. Mikayla would never discover he helped ruin her project.

"You're going to discourage Dalmtrix from moving into Hartsville County and encourage them to select York County instead." Curtis' sly smile made the Senator's eyes narrow.

Senator Leventis' smile melted from his face. He lounged back in the chair, the rigid set of his shoulders and red color rising beneath caramel skin undermined a relaxed appearance.

"I thought a lot about our conversation last week," Senator Leventis said slowly. "And, despite your...ideas that she'll come forward. I'm willing to bet she won't."

"Women are funny, Senator," Curtis mimicked his opponents position, but his broad shoulders were relaxed. "They'll tell you whatever you want to hear when their bobbing their heads between your legs, then forget the promises when a bigger package comes around."

Senator Leventis's beady eyes narrowed. "She'd never betray me like that."

Curtis chuckled and turned to Andre. "Show the Senator what you got."

Pushing back thoughts of Mikayla, Andre moved his iPad closer to Senator Leventis. With a few swipes of his finger, a video popped up. The

Senator's eyes widened to the size of saucers. Sweat broke out on his brow and the Senator jerked forward in his seat.

"Where did you get that?"

"Sit back," Andre shrugged and cocked his head to the side. "She provided the video."

Andre stopped the video and flipped the cover over the screen. His stomach churned with disgust. She was Laurel O'Neal, a well-known owner of an escort service. Her business had undergone several investigations over the years. Many probes into her connections with wealthy politicians and businessmen and her potential influence on public policy had started over the years. All were promptly shut down. Obviously the woman had connections in high places. Somehow his dad had learned of one of her biggest.

"You're lying," the Senator ground angry words through clenched teeth.

Curtis tented his fingers beneath his chin. "How else would I get the video you two made in her bedroom? Believe me, Senator, I have ways of getting what I want, but stealing videos of people's private moments, isn't one of them." He leaned forward and lowered his voice. "I also know that certain parts of this video were clipped and posted to an amateur porn site. I'm willing to bet the press would love to know that."

"You have no way to prove that."

Curtis laughed. "The birthmark on your belly is all the proof we need. Now, again, you're going to encourage Dalmtrix to move to York County instead of Hartsville."

"But Hartsville is my constituency. They need the jobs. Why do you care where Dalmtrix locates?"

Curtis looked at Andre. Andre sat up and nailed the Senator with a hard stare. "We want Dalmtrix in York County. The reason is none of your business."

"So I'm supposed to forget about three hundred jobs in an area that needs them. Renege on a deal that would benefit the people who voted for me, just because you want Dalmtrix in a county far richer than Hartsville?"

Andre had no argument for that. York County was more prosperous than Hartsville, and there were other businesses who may be interested in using the gas from the landfill. But the potential buy from Dalmtrix was huge. In another year, York County was liable to fail to comply with air quality standards and no industry would locate there. The choices were simple. Either, push Dalmtrix now and get the boost in the expansion of C.E.S., or hope that the current industries in the area would be willing to pay for upgrades required to use the gas from the landfill. Their methods for getting what he wanted were dirty, but Dalmtrix in York instead of Hartsville was the most beneficial for C.E.S.

But Dalmtrix in Hartsville would ruin Mikayla's career. Guilt burned his stomach. Senator Leventis didn't support this project for the good of the people. His support secured votes and provided kickbacks for other projects.

Curtis leaned forward. "Are these the same constituents who dropped their hard earned money into your campaign box two years ago? The same box that you turned around and used to fund an orgy at Laurel's house."

The senator's face mottled a bright red. "That's preposterous!"

"You forget, I was there. I saw your people pull money from that same box and use it to pay Laurel's girls."

Only years of learning not to reveal his emotions kept Andre's jaw from dropping. He thought his dad had paid Laurel for the information. Not that Curtis was also involved with the escort. He wished the truth surprised him.

"And to answer your question," Curtis said. "Yes, we would move three hundred jobs to another part of the state just because we want to. The only question now is will you support the move."

Senator Leventis's gaze flipped down to the iPad on the table. "Do I have a choice?"

Curtis shrugged and turned to Andre. "I think he does."

Andre dug deep and thought about C.E.S. Making this move didn't make him the camera man. Only provided a means to an end. These backdoor maneuvers happened every day in politics. A maneuver which supported the business he worked all his life to grow. Still, his stomach twisted.

Weakness. Something Andre couldn't afford to have in the business world. Something that existed because of the time he'd spent with Mikayla. He couldn't let her make him soft. He'd be her nice guy, but here in C.E.S. business dealings, he had to be ruthless.

Squaring his shoulders, Andre turned to the Senator. "You have until the end of the week to support the protests about the landfill in Hartsville and the concerns that Dalmtrix moving there will make things worse. Otherwise, the video will be released to every major news station in South Carolina."

The senator tugged at the knot of his red and white tie. "What makes you think supporting the protestors will prevent Dalmtrix from coming to Hartsville?"

"Easy," Andre said. "You were the one who convinced the governor to seek Dalmtrix. She'll still support your choice to encourage them to move to another part of the state because it means jobs for South Carolina. You'll still be a champion for looking out for the quality of life of those in your home county. So you see, this benefits everyone."

Except for Mikayla. Andre's jaw tightened.

The Senator's face hardened. "You can sugarcoat this and make it seem like a win, but I know what this is about. I disagree, and that video goes everywhere. I lose my position, my wife and my kids. I go with the move; it looks good on the surface. But I still fail on a campaign promise, to bring jobs to my constituents."

Neither Andre nor his dad responded. After a few seconds of observing the two men, Senator Leventis tossed the napkin from his lap onto the table. "You've got me by the balls. Promise me that if I do this, the video disappears."

"Now why would I give up all my cards?" Curtis asked.

"This is bullshit." The Senator shoved back his chair and stood. "Forgive me if I don't wish you a good day." He spat and marched away.

Andre swirled the water in the crystal goblet on the table. "Though I'm no fan of Senator Leventis, he is right. We could expand our program with a company already in York. There is interest there, especially with the new air standards looming."

Curtis squinted as if Andre had lost his mind. "What the hell is wrong with you? Don't you know this is about more than Dalmtrix and our methane program?"

Andre met his dad's questioning gaze with one of his own. "What else is this about?"

Curtis smirked. "My damn brother purchased land near the Dalmtrix site. He's planning on putting in a development nearby. Moving Dalmtrix kills two birds with one stone."

"You know about that?"

"Looks like you know about it, too. Where did you hear? While you were screwing the hell out of Ryan's ex-girlfriend?"

Andre drew back. "Her name is Mikayla. And for the record, I'm not sleeping with her."

"Then what the hell were you doing arriving in Columbia early? I know it was to spend the weekend with her."

"That's not why I came to Columbia early."

Curtis laughed. "You must think I'm stupid, boy. I could tell by the look on your face last week that you were still thinking about that girl. It was one thing when I thought you slept with her for fun, but you're actually getting feelings for that girl."

"My relationship with Mikayla has nothing to do with this conversation."

"It has everything to do with this conversation." Curtis pointed a finger at him. "You showed that video today without hesitation and laid out what would happen if the Senator disagreed with us without batting an eyelash. You knew what you were doing when you killed this deal. Forget that girl. Ryan isn't going to let you snoop around his ex-girlfriend without getting jealous. He may be enjoying Angelica's delights right now, but he will snatch that girl right back from you out of spite. That's the way my brother and his kids are. Ryan will make sure he stays in this girl's thoughts just to keep you out."

Curtis slid back the chair and rose to his feet. Andre watched him walk away. For Andre, this thing with Dalmtrix only concerned helping C.E.S. Not a way to one up his cousin's family. He'd protected Mikayla after Ryan hurt her, keeping his involvement in the Dalmtrix relocation meant he would also protect her from this side of himself.

But would Ryan abandon Angelica and go back for Mikayla when he learned she was seeing him? Anger and jealousy played around with the guilt in his stomach. Anger he understood. Jealousy baffled him. Jealousy came before love. Love could make him as foolish as his mother. His palms slickened, and his breaths sputtered panicked and short. This thing with Mikayla opened him to feelings he'd hoped never to experience. Feelings that had the potential to do significant damage if they weren't controlled.

CHAPTER 18

Mikayla's Monday morning started with a snide *how are you holding up conversation* with Charity, a passing wardrobe critique from Renee, and proposals for new subdivisions in Georgia and North Carolina from Philip's secretary. When she sank into the chair at her desk, she quickly pulled the nicotine patches from her purse and placed one on her back. Might as well get a handle on the craving before the stress really kicked in.

She stared at the proposals but thought about the Dalmtrix deal. There had to be a way to salvage that land acquisition. She tapped an ink pen on the desk. Maybe they could work something out with the school district. Somewhere she'd heard talk about a new high school, which meant a new subdivision nearby would work. Ryan knew the superintendent. They could approach him. Ideas like this were the type she'd frequently take to him. Now, she'd rather skip hair appointments for two months than work closely with him.

A knock on the door broke through her thoughts. Ryan stood in the doorway wearing a tailored navy suit. Several weeks ago she would have admired him, and while still handsome, she didn't see her friend, only the guy who'd humiliated her.

"Can I help you?" she asked.

He grinned and slowly made his way into the room. "You didn't automatically kick me out of your office. That's progress."

She crossed her arms over her chest. "Don't try me this morning. What do you want?"

Her sharp tone didn't brush the smile from his face. "I've gotten word that the Hartsville school district is considering building another high school."

She nodded. "That's nothing new. It was another reason I pushed the land acquisition."

"Have you thought about how to make the land purchase work out with the new high school so close?"

She dragged in a deep breath and drummed her fingers on the desk. "Actually, I was just thinking about that. Once Dalmtrix announced their intentions, I'd planned to reach out the parks and recreation department to see about incorporating the plans for their new activity center in with our development."

Ryan sat on the edge of the desk. "Good idea. The Hartsville community development department is looking at building an affordable housing community."

Mikayla sat up in her chair. "If we could get in on that deal, incorporate mixed-use housing and commercial near the new high school, we might not net the money we expected but the deal wouldn't be a complete loss. The market for that type of development could work there on a small scale."

Ryan winked. "I knew you'd come to that conclusion. That's why I set up a meeting with the superintendent for late this morning and later this afternoon with their community development director. Are you ready to ride?"

"You want to go to Hartsville today?"

"I don't want to; I'm going to. And since you're the lead on this land acquisition, you're coming to help."

She'd learned to get through the days working with Ryan, but that didn't mean she wanted to spend all day in a car with him. "I've got a busy day ahead. I can't go."

Pain flashed in his dark eyes, and then resignation took over. He straightened and squared his shoulders. "I don't call rank often, but today I am. You're going with me to Hartsville."

She pointed to the stacks of contracts on her desk. "I have work to do."

"And I am part owner of this company. Your work can wait." His firm expression slackened. He leaned on the desk. "I want us to be friends again. I miss talking to you."

Her spine stiffened. "Talk to Angelica."

He stood straight. His eyes hard. "Meet me at my car in five minutes." Ryan spun on his heel and strode out the door.

Mikayla picked up her phone and texted Andre.

Hey, you. Got a long day ahead. I fear I may backslide.

She waited for him to respond. Nothing came. Ryan knocked on her door, asked if she was ready. Mikayla stuck the phone in her purse and followed him out.

*

Mikayla and Ryan returned to the office well past seven that evening. The empty parking lot meant no one had worked late that day. He parked next to her car, turned off the ignition, leaned back in his seat, and blew out a breath. Facing her with a huge grin spread across his face. Mikayla's smile matched his. The day was a success. Though many more details still needed to fall into place, for the most part, they'd secured the agreement from the school district and the community development office. Both entities agreed to begin talks of incorporating their plans with the land Caldwell Development owned.

As much as Mikayla wanted to keep her distance from Ryan during the trip, doing so was impossible. They'd been good friends because they worked well together. Halfway through their first meeting with the superintendent, they'd fallen back into their tag team approach.

"We did it," she said.

"No, you did it. I just sat back and let you do all of the talking."

Mikayla laughed. "Since when do you let anyone do all of the talking. I just brought us back to the topic whenever you began to flounder."

He pressed a hand to his chest, mock disbelief on his face. "I never flounder. Get that right."

"Correction, you tend to go off on tangents and I bring you back on course."

He swiveled in his seat, to face her. "That you do." The smile on his face softened as he watched her. "We work well together."

She broke eye contact. Things were quickly becoming too chummy between them. They may have had a good day at work, but it didn't change the fact that they were no longer friends.

"I'll see you tomorrow." She reached for the door handle, and he placed a firm hand on her arm.

"Mikayla, can we ever get past this?" He asked solemnly.

"Ryan—"

"I know, I shouldn't ask. I shouldn't care, but I do. I care about you Mikayla."

She held up a hand. "You don't care about me. You're mad that I won't fall over myself to forgive you."

"No, I care. I don't want to hurt you."

"Too late, you already did."

He ran a hand over his face then shifted in the seat. When his eyes met hers, wariness reflected in them. "I know I did, but it wasn't just a random incident. You know me, I wouldn't have done that to you if it weren't..." he sighed. "I told you the story, you know, what happened in Paris. Angelica was the one that got away. I was overwhelmed, and I didn't think, just reacted. I love her, Mikayla. You've been in love before. You know how love makes you feel."

His words struck home. She was falling in love right now with Andre. Rational thought went out the window when it came to Andre. All, she wanted, was to talk to him, be close to him, and so she could relate to Ryan's explanation.

Mikayla's phone vibrated. She pulled it from her purse and Andre's name, and number lit up the screen. A giddy grin spread across her face and tingles traveled through her body.

Ryan grabbed her hand. One glance at the screen and his lip curled in a snarl.

"This is who you've been texting all day? He's the one making you smile whenever you check your phone?"

Jerking her hand out of his, she dropped the phone into her purse. "Goodbye, Ryan." Mikayla opened the car door and hopped out.

His door flew open, and he bounded from the car. "Mikayla, I know I was wrong, but you can't do this. He's using you."

"He's not using me." She marched over to the driver's side of her Rav 4.

He hurried around the car and held the door shut. "You don't know how my family works. Andre is only trying to get back at me through you."

"We're just friends."

"No man is friends with a woman unless he's trying to have sex with her."

"Oh really." She placed a hand on her hip. "We were friends without having sex."

He scoffed. "And if you would have given me the time of day I would have slept with you months ago."

She rolled her eyes and shoved his arm from her car. "You're disgusting. Your concern isn't about you being worried about me. You just don't want me sleeping with him when you didn't."

"Mikayla, I know I fucked up, but don't sell yourself short by getting involved with Andre."

His words made her doubts swirl. Her dad thought she'd sold herself to Ryan. Ryan accused her of the same thing with Andre. She took a mental stranglehold on her reservations. She had to trust herself.

"I'm through talking to you, Ryan. Who I see is not your business. Stop worrying about me and concentrate on someone who wants your attention."

She jerked open the car door, jumped in, and sped off.

CHAPTER 19

Andre stepped out of his car and checked his phone to see if Mikayla had called. His disappointment at missing her calls and text messages only increased the guilt after the meeting with Senator Leventis. Guilt, remorse, these were unfamiliar feelings for him.

He'd returned to the office in Greenville after lunch, but he couldn't focus on work. He was curious to know about her day. Mikayla's first text indicated her day had started badly and had upset him. He hated that Mikayla worked with Ryan every day. Ryan posed no threat, but Andre agreed with Curtis. If Ryan discovered he and Mikayla were seeing each other, he might try to work his way back into her life. He doubted Mikayla would fall for any reunion schemes from Ryan. The more he got to know her, the more he trusted that she meant what she'd said about not wanting Ryan back.

Jonathan called right after he exited his vehicle. "What's up?" he asked.

"I'm downtown, near your condo," Jonathan said over the murmur of music and conversation.

"And what do you want me to do about that?" He said just to annoy his friend.

"Just walk your ass over here and meet me for a drink. You probably need it."

More like two, he thought. "What makes you think I need a drink?"

"I know you, you need a drink."

Andre nodded even though Jonathan couldn't see him. He took down the name of the bar and hung up. Putting his bag with his laptop and other work files in the trunk, Andre loosened his tie and walked the short distance to the bar. He would have preferred to drive to the country tonight. As usual, work kept him closer to the office. There were several new contracts he needed to negotiate, not to mention the extra demand since the methane project was moving to the new landfill. Of course thoughts of the new landfill brought thoughts back of the way he was unintentionally hurting Mikayla.

Yeah, he needed a drink.

Within a few minutes, he reached his destination. He walked into the bar and deeply inhaled the smoke filled air. Andre needed a cigarette too. He pictured the way Mikayla's lips curled around the tip of that one cigarette they'd shared. His blood heated, and his crotch throbbed.

The crowd was light and as expected for a Monday. Might as well be the weekend based on the way the top 40 hits blared from the speakers. Jonathan sat at the bar a bottle of beer in hand, watching the television highlights of the weekend's games. While Andre could appreciate a good football or basketball game, Jonathan loved sports.

"What are you doing downtown?" Andre stood beside Jonathan at the bar.

Jonathan shook his head and took a long swig of beer. He was dressed up, compared to his usual attire, in a grey button up shirt and khaki pants. His curls were cut shorter, and he didn't have the hint of a beard he seemed to always carry. Disappointment clouded his friend's eyes.

"You alright?" Andre asked.

Jonathan nodded. "Yeah. I came down to see Karen."

Andre frowned and sat at the bar. The last he'd heard, Jonathan was worried Karen wanted things to progress faster between them. Andre agreed. The woman was always around whenever he called Jonathan. He'd been so wrapped up in his thing with Mikayla, he forgot to ask about her when he visited Jonathan the week before.

The bartender came over. Andre pointed to Jonathan's beer and held up two fingers. The bartender nodded and walked off. "How did it go?"

"Another guy answered the door."

Andre cringed. When the bartender brought the beers, Andre slid one Jonathan's way. Despite the concern of his friend, Andre knew Jonathan cared about Karen. The woman had everything his friend loved. A voluptuous size sixteen figure, she knew her way around the kitchen and looked good without being flossy or high maintenance.

"That's fucked up."

Jonathan scoffed. "Tell me about it."

"That's why we're drinking tonight?"

"Nah. I'll never let a woman get to me like that. I wish her and her new man well." Jonathan drained his beer, then reached for the other one. "Where were you all weekend?"

Andre looked up at the television screen. "You don't want to know."

"That tells me all I need to know. You're still messing around with your cousin's ex-girlfriend. Are you trying to end up like me? Going to your girl's place and having another man answer the door."

"I thought she wasn't your girl. Maybe that's why there was another man up in your spot."

Jonathan scowled. He held up the bottle but pointed a finger at Andre. "We're not talking about me."

"Yeah, well," he brought the bottle back to his lips. "Your problems are the reason we're here, not mine."

Jonathan twisted in his seat and eyed Andre. "Why were you with her? I thought you were through with the family rivalry."

"My family business has nothing to do with her." Andre shrugged. "I like her, alright. What's wrong with that?"

"Nothing would be wrong if she were anybody but your cousin's ex. You've told me how your family works. Do you really want to fall for a woman who has ties to him?"

Andre sipped the beer, remembered the strawberry lager she'd given him over the weekend and smiled. "She's different."

Jonathan snorted. "Famous last words."

"I'm serious, man, she is. Yes, she works for them, but she's planning to leave. She even faced down Renee when she burst into her apartment like a damn eighteenth-century chaperone. I want to see where this goes."

"I get it. You and this woman connected over mutual embarrassment. Maybe you're both even convinced there's something there. But based on what you've told me about your family rivalry, I'd take into consideration that Ryan may try to come between you two out of spite. Keep that in mind."

Before he could respond, his phone rang. Seeing Mikayla's number drove away the day's tension. He turned away from Jonathan and answered the phone. "Hey you."

"Hey you."

He frowned. "How was your day? You sound tired."

"Good actually." She said with a bit of a laugh.

"Really? Your text earlier made me think you were having a bad day."

"It started that way but turned out to be okay. I think I found a way to salvage the purchase in Hartsville." Excitement brushed away the exhaustion from earlier.

He frowned then pressed a finger to his other ear hoping to hear better. After their meeting with the Senator, he doubted anything could salvage Dalmtrix moving to the low country. Unless, for some reason, the Senator doubted his dad would expose what they knew. Foolish of the Senator if that were the case.

"How so?"

"Ryan and I went to Hartsville today. We spoke with the school district superintendent and the community development director. I think we'll have another way to develop the property even if Dalmtrix doesn't locate there."

"Whose idea was it to go to Hartsville?"

"Ryan's, but I was thinking along the same lines. It's not the first time we've been on the same wavelength."

His hands tightened around the cell phone. "So, are you two cool now?"

Mikayla paused. He heard a song playing in the background. She must have been driving. "Not really. We've come to a truce. Since we work together, a professional truce makes sense."

"I thought you were leaving."

"I don't know," she said slowly. "If this new deal works out, it'll be worth staying to see it through to the end. But enough about my day. Where have you been? Before I had to leave town, I'd hoped to see you again. Are you still in Columbia?"

"No, I'm back in Greenville."

"Oh," Disappointment cloaked her voice. "I...thought about you today. Wondered if you were doing wrong."

His heart rate picked up. "Wrong, how?"

"By smoking." She said with a laugh.

Relieved laughter burst from his lips. The guilt over Dalmtrix was out of control. "I haven't had a cigarette. I ate lunch at the Capital City Club then had to get back here."

Another pause. "I see. Do you know when you'll be back in town?"

"Not sure. But when I come back I'll drop by."

"I'd like that." She said quickly.

He smiled at the urgency in her voice. He felt the same thing. Wished he had a reason to be back in Columbia so he could see her again.

"I'd like that too. I'll call you later. Okay?"

"Can't wait."

He heard the smile in her voice. In his mind, he visualized the sexy curve of her lips and the enticing twinkle in those sexy brown eyes. The image brought a smile to his face.

He ended the call and stared at the phone for a few seconds after the screen darkened. He wasn't thrilled with the idea of her spending the day with Ryan, but the tone of her voice said her mind was still on him. Good, because she'd effectively ruined him from thinking of another woman.

"You are really into that woman," Jonathan said, breaking him from his revere.

He took a deep breath, dropped his phone on the bar and sipped from the beer. "I hope this doesn't backfire."

"Let me meet her. I'll tell you in a second if she's no good."

"The same way you figured out Karen was no good."

Jonathan's grey eyes crinkled with his scowl. "Don't start. I knew Angelica was bad news the second I laid eyes on her."

"Worry about your love life, let me worry about mine."

Jonathan shrugged. "Have it your way. But don't get too wrapped up

114

until you know for sure, she's not trying to get back with Ryan. Make sure this woman is worth your time."

"I hear you." Andre focused on the television, and Jonathan did the same. Their heart to heart over. But Andre's concerns this thing he had for Mikayla might backfire, weighed on him and he ordered two more beers to drown out the thought.

CHAPTER 20

"My dad thinks you're taking advantage of me."

Andre's deep laughter came through the phone. Mikayla's skin tightened. The man's laugh could charm a nun out of her panties. Her body buzzed with an electrifying tingle. Lounging on the bed, she rolled over and stared at the ceiling. Even though they'd talked earlier, he'd called again. She wished they were together instead of on the phone.

"My best friend thinks I'm going to come to your apartment and find Ryan already there."

"That will never happen," she said.

"You know that I'm trying not to mislead you," he paused. "Or take advantage of you."

She pulled a pillow close to her chest. "By saying you're trying not to, makes it seem like you eventually will."

"My relationships don't always end perfectly."

Her heart thudded. *We're in a relationship.* "Why?"

He sighed into the phone. She imagined him rubbing a hand across his face. "In the end, no matter how much I don't want it to, the demands of my family pull me back into the bullshit."

She slowly sat up on the bed and clenched the phone. "Are you calling me because you want to talk to me, or because of something else?"

"Because I want too. But my family drama has a way of creeping into every aspect of my life. My dad expects me and my brother to give up everything, do everything, for the betterment of the company. I spend all of my days doing whatever it takes to grow C.E.S. Some of the things I've done aren't pretty." He said in a grim tone.

Mikayla wanted to wrap her arms around him. "Working hard to grow your company isn't a bad thing."

"For most people it isn't. When you're Curtis Caldwell's son, it can be."

"So what are you saying? Are you involved with anything illegal?"

"What I'm saying, is that when you're raised by someone who is incapable of showing decency, indecency can creep into your personal life. It has before. I don't want that to happen with you."

He didn't answer the question. She stopped short of asking again. A small part didn't want to know more. "As long as you're honest with me, that won't happen."

"I'll tell you everything you need to know."

She pulled the phone away and frowned at the screen. "That's cryptic." Mikayla put the phone back to her face. "Are you saying you'll lie to me?"

"No, but you don't need to know everything my family is involved with."

"Why? Because you think I might run and tell Philip and Ryan."

"Because you might run away from me. I don't want you to do that. I want you to come closer to me, not move farther away." His voice lowered to an octave that was like a drug to her system.

Her lips parted with a shaky breath. Slowly her nipples puckered beneath her nightgown.

"I want to see you again. Come to Greenville this weekend," he said.

She glanced at her car keys on her dresser. If only she could go now. Shaking her head, she cleared away the thought. No way would she become a long distance hook up. "How do you feel about me?"

"I told you that when I was there. I want to continue seeing you. Preferably this weekend."

"I can't. I promised my dad I'd visit this Saturday."

"You can come Sunday."

She rolled over onto her stomach. "Or, you can come on Sunday."

"I'd like more than anything to come on Sunday." His words sound a lot naughtier than a simple visit.

She trembled, and wetness blossomed between her legs. "Then come."

"What time?"

CHAPTER 21

Mikayla nearly skipped to the door when Andre knocked late Sunday morning. She pulled in a deep breath, ran sweaty palms down the sides of her jeans and opened the door. Andre's perfectly kissable lips spread into a welcoming grin. His shoulders seemed broader in the brown leather jacket. Beneath it he wore a dark green sweater and tan slacks that despite their casual style still managed to make him look polished. A hot gaze swept over her. She wished she'd chosen something sexy to wear. Instead, she'd chosen a cute, but not sexy lavender V-neck sweater and comfortable flats.

When his eyes met hers, the thoughts of clothing vanished. Desire, hot and potent, darkened his eyes. Her breath caught, and she leaned on the door, to support her suddenly weak legs.

"Hey you." His baritone rolled over her.

"Hey you."

He closed the distance between them, the wonderful scent of Guess Seductive, the cologne he preferred, mixed with the warmth of his large body. She leaned forward lost in the intensity of his gaze. Slowly, he brought his hand up to her hair, gently sank his fingers in the curls then tilted her head back. Mikayla's eyes fluttered closed, and his lips pressed against hers.

The familiar shock that she'd experienced when they kissed swooped through her body. Her arms wrapped tightly around his neck as she pressed closer. Her nipples beaded against his firm chest. She opened her mouth to him, and slowly, initiating a sensual dance, he slid his tongue past her lips.

His warnings and all insecurities faded. This felt right, kissing him felt right.

They finally broke apart, but he didn't release her. It took several seconds after the kiss to get her thoughts back in order.

Lowering her forehead against his chest, Mikayla felt his heart hammering beneath the muscle. "I thought we were just friends."

"I'm feeling a lot more than friendship right now." He pushed back a little until she lifted her head. "It's time to call this what it is. I'm not interested in seeing anyone but you."

"This is really happening."

He nodded. "It is."

She swallowed hard. If everything worked out, this relationship would turn into…what? The love of her life. A possible marriage proposal. Highly unlikely. Right now, she had fiery passion from a guy who liked her. She'd take the fire. She hadn't had fire in a long time.

"I planned a day for us." Mikayla stepped out of his embrace then immediately wanted to crawl back into his arms. "Help me carry some of this stuff into the kitchen."

"I thought we'd spend the day here." The look in his eyes made her breasts ache and heat spread through her belly.

"It's the end of February and a surprisingly warm day. I thought it would be nice to get out. You like hiking, right?"

He raised an eyebrow. "We're hiking?"

"No, but we will walk through Riverfront Park. It's nice, even in winter."

She hurried into the kitchen, and his heavy footsteps followed. She grabbed the small cooler packed with sandwiches, grapes, potato salad and a few slices of pound cake she'd baked at her dad's house the day before.

He took the cooler and peeked inside. "You bought all this?"

"No, I made all that. You've supplied the food for our last few…dates. It's my turn."

"You baked the cake?" Something like admiration flashed in his eyes.

Her cheeks heated, and she smiled. "I can bake and cook when I have to."

He crossed the room and wrapped an arm around her shoulders. "And yet another reason to like you."

"Let's go," she blurted out before she ended up sighing into his chest.

She grabbed a jacket, and they left. It didn't take long to leave her downtown apartment and arrive at Riverfront Park. They entered and walked past the water plant onto the bridge over the canal. The sky was blue, and the temperature offered a spring teaser hovering near sixty. Several runners and a few families were out enjoying the beauty of the river along the park.

"This is my first time here. It's nice." He gazed around, taking in their surroundings much like he'd done in the mountains.

"It is nice. Sometimes I come here to jog." She laughed. "Let me clarify, I came twice when I tried jogging. Other times I came for festivals."

A runner passed on her right side, and Mikayla stepped out of the way. Her hand bumped against Andre's hand. His fingers slowly wrapped around hers as if he were unsure. She tried to imagine him walking hand in hand with Angelica in a park. Couldn't see it. The thought made her smile, and she entwined her fingers with his.

"I was wondering about that. I didn't picture you as the jogging type." He took a leisurely glance down her body. "Good thing. I'd hate to see your curves shrink."

She ran a hand across her hips. "These hips aren't going anywhere. I've tried, and nothing about me will be as thin and attractive as Renee."

He stopped. When she turned to him, there was a frown on his face. "There is nothing wrong with your figure. Renee is too skinny if you ask me. I love your curves."

Pinpricks of heat traveled from her chest, up her neck to her cheeks. "I know I'm not fat. I just…thought guys liked the supermodel type." At least those were always the types of women boys, and now men, chose over her.

"There's a lot to be said for a woman with something to hold on to."

What had to be a silly grin popped up on her face. She turned to keep walking otherwise she'd spend the rest of the morning grinning at him.

"So how was work?"

She glanced over and caught his grimace.

"Work…was work." He said in a dismissive way. "How did it go with your dad yesterday?"

She guessed she didn't need to know about what happened at his job. It irked her a little bit that he didn't want to confide. But they were at the start of their relationship, and she wouldn't push.

"It was fine. He had to help my uncle work on his truck. We spent the day over there. I occupied myself by handing the two of them wrenches until I got bored and went inside and made a cake."

He gently swung their entwined hands between them. "You occupy your time by baking cakes."

"Not really, for some reason we started talking about cakes and that made us hungry. So I volunteered. It was either that or roll up my sleeves and help install a new starter."

He stopped again. "You are full of surprises."

She waited for the frown, or for him to hold up her hand and look for grease under her nails. Something the boy she'd had a crush on in high school had done when she'd worked up the nerve to ask him to prom. To this day, she didn't know what made her so foolish. Probably some teenage movie about the underdog winning the cool kid's love.

Andre grinned at her, but old fears were hard to disappear. She held up her chin. "I'm not the grease monkey I used to be. I don't get under cars anymore, and I'm far enough away that my dad can't drag me out of the house to go hunting at four a.m."

"I don't think I'd mind seeing you in overalls, with grease on your face. You'd probably look sexy."

She grinned and rolled her eyes. "You must be the only guy to think that."

"If I'm the only guy to realize how great you are then I consider that a compliment."

Brenden had liked her, but he'd never seemed delighted to learn about all of the things she could do. Never seemed to view her as a fascinating gift to unwrap. Andre seemed excited about every new thing he learned about her. Would he stop once he realized there wasn't anything fancy to discover?

"Where did you learn to be so charming?"

He grinned and tugged on her arm so they could keep walking. "Definitely not from my father."

They strolled further down the trail and talked about everything and nothing at the same time. One of those fun first date talks that created giddy feelings about the future. A relaxed, easy, two-sided conversation. She'd spent so much of her time with Ryan, and to a certain extent Brenden, listening to them. Learning what was going on in their heads, what bothered them, and their dreams. Andre kept his undivided attention on her. Even when beautiful women jogged by and tried to catch his eye.

They turned and walked back up the Riverwalk, stopping at the brick amphitheater they ate the lunch she'd packed.

"Mikayla," a voice called out from the top of the amphitheater.

She turned and faced a dark skinned woman around the same age as her holding hands with a tall, handsome guy.

Mikayla grinned. "Oh my, God, Caroline!"

The women embraced. When Mikayla pulled back, Caroline gave her the same once over that Renee usually did. Caroline was one of Renee's childhood friends who now lived in New York. She'd come down to visit during the time Renee had orchestrated Mikayla's makeover. Though they were not as close, as her and Renee, Mikayla considered Caroline, a friend.

"I thought that was you," Caroline said.

"It's me. What are you doing here?"

"I'm here for a conference that starts tomorrow. I already called Renee and had planned to give you a call. We're getting together this afternoon at Rowdy's over in The Village of Sandhills. They have karaoke. Come on by. We're meeting at five."

Mikayla glanced at Andre, who sat back and watched the two of them. "I'll see if I can make it."

Caroline turned to Andre. "Mmm, I guess I can see why you might not make it. Hello, handsome." Caroline extended a slender manicured hand.

Andre gripped her hand and gave Caroline one of his charming smiles. "Andre, nice to meet you."

"Oh, the pleasure is all mine."

Mikayla shot a wary glance at Caroline's friend. He shrugged and smiled. "I knew Caroline was a flirt when I met her." He held out a hand. "I'm

Jeremy."

"Now that we've done all the introductions, I insist that you come this afternoon. I must know more about you and this man." Caroline said.

Andre laughed. Mikayla's face burned. "There's nothing to tell, Caroline."

"Then you need to come so that I can tell you what to do with him." Carline crossed her arms and studied Andre.

"She knows what to do with me," Andre said.

"Ahh! That voice!" Caroline turned and grabbed Mikayla's arm. "I bet you do know what to do with him. Girl, the pillow talk must be amazing."

"That's enough, Caroline," Jeremy said with a raised brow. He reached over and pulled her to his side. "I love you, but my limit is reached. Come on, let's leave them to their lunch." He waved at her and Andre. "It was nice meeting you."

Mikayla laughed. "Yeah, you too."

Caroline allowed Jeremy to pull her back up the amphitheater. "Don't forget, five at Rowdy's see you there. If I don't. I know what you're doing!" She sang the last words, her delighted giggle trailing behind.

Mikayla shook her head and sat down beside Andre. Too embarrassed to look at him, she focused on eating her sandwich.

"Are we going?" Andre asked.

"No…of course not. I know you don't want to go."

Andre leaned over and placed a hand on the back of her head. She turned to face him and nearly melted from the heat in his eye. "I think it'll be fun. Besides, your face kind of lit up when she mentioned karaoke."

She grinned. "That obvious, huh? It's one of the things I love."

He leaned over and kissed the side of her mouth. "Then we're definitely going."

And she officially stood one step from tumbling in love with Andre.

*

Rowdy's perfectly described the bar, loud music, not an empty seat at the large wooden tables, and laughter filled voices coming from every corner. Caroline squealed in excitement when Mikayla and Andre came through the door. She had three tables pulled together in the corner next to the stage. She introduced most of those at the table as associates from the conference. A few Mikayla recognized as acquaintances of Renee's.

"Is Renee here?" She yelled to Caroline over the music.

"Not yet, but she said she was coming." Caroline turned and wrapped her arm in Andre's. "You are going to sing next. I've been imagining that voice singing Barry White since I met you."

Before Mikayla could protest, Caroline pulled Andre toward the song selection set up near the stage. Andre shot a helpless look over his shoulder at Mikayla.

Mikayla bit her lip and tried to keep from laughing. *This will be interesting.*

Someone tapped her on the shoulder. She turned and smiled at Renee.

"Hey," Mikayla said after they embraced.

"Okay, don't get mad, but Ryan is here, too." Renee pointed toward the door.

Mikayla frowned and glanced over Renee's shoulder. Ryan stood at the front of the restaurant near the hall leading to the restrooms. He lifted his chin motioning for her to come over.

"Why is he here? What does he want?"

"He's friends with Caroline. When he found out you were coming, he said he needed to talk to you."

"Well, I don't want to talk to him."

"It's about the Dalmtrix deal."

Mikayla sighed, looked over her shoulder to where Andre and Caroline were flipping through the book of songs. She had only a few minutes to get rid of Ryan. With one last blistering glare at Renee, she hurried across the room toward Ryan.

"What do you want?"

"Don't be like that, Mikayla," Ryan said, ushering her down the hall and out of view. "I thought after the trip to Hartsville—"

"That was work. This is not." She shuffled from foot to foot and glanced at the end of the hall. "You should go."

He stood before her, forcing her to look into his face. "Not until I say what I came here to say."

She threw up her hands. "Quit acting as if I owe you something."

"You gave me a knee to the balls," He said as if that meant she really did owe him something.

"Weeks ago, and now you want to bring that up. Why? Because I won't bend over backwards to be your friend."

He opened his mouth, but she held up a hand. "The person caught in a closet having sex with someone else doesn't deserve to be heard."

He pushed her hand out of the way. "You were more embarrassed than hurt. Admit it. We both know we're better as friends than lovers. Shit, Mikayla, you stayed up helping my cousin with her wedding favors instead of coming to bed with me."

Her eyes narrowed. "Is that why you did it?"

"No, I did it because I love Angelica. I'm pointing out the fact that you'd rather spend time torturing yourself than sleeping with me. I knew that going in, but thought because we were friends we could make a good couple. It wasn't meant to be. We both know that." He pointed and took a step forward. "Stop pretending I meant more to you than I did."

A patron came down the hall heading for the bathroom. He eyed both her and Ryan before giving a tight nod and smile. Mikayla lowered her gaze to the floor Ryan was right. She felt more anger than scorned love.

"I am hurt Ryan. I thought we were friends. You know how I feel about being embarrassed or made fun of. I told you about my experiences growing up. You didn't take my feelings into consideration. What you did was a betrayal...I can't easily forgive the betrayal of a friend."

He shoved his hands into the pockets of designer jeans. Though dressed similarly to Andre in jeans and a sweater, he didn't seem relaxed. Ryan always looked as if he were wound up, and waiting, for something to happen.

"I'll take that. And I hope one day you can forgive me."

She closed her eyes, ran a hand across the back of her neck, sucking in a deep breath. When Mikayla opened her eyes and stared at Ryan, a glimpse of the friend, she used to have reflected in his sad dark eyes.

"What did you come here to say?"

His features hardened. "Senator Leventis is being blackmailed. Someone is trying to prevent Dalmtrix from moving to Hartsville."

Her hands clenched into fists, and she took a step closer. "Who?"

"I don't know, yet, but we're going to find out."

CHAPTER 22

"I'm really not a singer," Andre said to Caroline. He'd never sung in front of people in his life. Never planned too. How in the world Caroline convinced him to make his stage debut boggled his mind. The things a man would do to make a woman smile. And the smile on Mikayla's face was worth the ensuing embarrassment. He hoped.

"You don't have to sing really. With that voice, you can just speak the words. And besides," she leaned close and bumped her shoulder against his arm. "You keep your eyes on Mikayla, belt out Barry White, and you can bet you'll end the night happy."

He'd had a similar thought. Though he didn't need Barry. The sexy looks, she'd thrown his way beneath thick curly lashes, were enough to boost his confidence. He stretched his fingers as anticipation tightened his skin.

Caroline searched through the book for a song, and he turned to find Mikayla at the table. Instead, he made eye contact with Renee. Her gaze darted away. He frowned. An uneasy feeling settled in his stomach. He scanned the crowd for Mikayla. She was nowhere to be seen. Andre looked back to Renee, caught her throwing glances in the direction of the bathroom, then back at him.

"Here we go. The perfect song." Caroline said.

Andre nodded but didn't check to see what she chose. "I'm going to the bathroom."

"We've got time. I'll add your name to the list."

He stalked toward the bathrooms. The short distance seemed to grow with each step across the wooden floors. The dread of finding Mikayla and Ryan together weighted his steps.

He froze at the entrance of the hall. Mikayla and Ryan stood close to each other in a corner. Ryan's set jaw and fierce stare, as he gazed at Mikayla, bothered him more than singing before the crowd.

Jealously...and a touch of white hot anger, whipped through him. He rolled his suddenly stiff shoulders, but the angry tension clung like a leech. No way in hell would he let Ryan weasel his way back into Mikayla's life. He didn't give a damn about Ryan snatching Angelica. In the long run losing her improved his life, but he wouldn't lose Mikayla.

He forced the tension from his shoulders and tried to appear relaxed as he walked down the hall. "Am I interrupting something?"

Mikayla spun his way, the remnants of anger in her brown eyes slowly slipped away as she watched him approach. His discomfort ratcheted up a notch. Had Ryan upset her? His cousin backed away from Mikayla, with his fists clenched at his side. Andre secretly hoped Ryan would try something. Ryan deserved to have a few teeth rearranged. Andre expected to be angry when he saw Ryan, but the discomfort of seeing Ryan standing close to Mikayla had him ready to give Ryan a bootleg tooth removal. One that involved Andre's fist and lots of pain.

"Ryan had to tell me something," she said.

Andre slipped his arms around her shoulders. Relief swept through his body when she leaned slightly into his side instead of pulling away.

"Has he said it?"

Her lips twisted, and she frowned. "Yes."

He glared at Ryan. "Now you can go."

"I think I'll go say hello to Caroline," Ryan said easily.

Ryan moved to go around them, but Andre blocked his way. "What are you up to?"

Ryan rocked back on his heels, a smug smile on his face. "Threatened by having me here."

"Keep talking and I'll show you just how threatened I am." Andre's hand balled into a fist. "I'm not playing this game, Ryan. You did me a favor with Angelica. Leave Mikayla and me alone."

"You and Mikayla. As if this isn't just your way of trying to get back at me. I won't let you hurt her."

"The same way you did." Andre said his voice lethal. He took a step toward Ryan.

"I've explained that to Mikayla. We're past that. Did she tell you about the good time we had on our road trip a few days ago."

Mikayla stepped between them. "Okay, that's enough."

Ryan held up his hands. "Oh, I see, you don't want him to know we got along so well. I get it."

"There's nothing to get, Ryan." She propped her hands on her hips. "Andre already knows about our trip and why we went. Save this weak attempt to drive a wedge between me and Andre because it's only going make it harder for you repair the one between us. I heard what you had to say, and now you can leave."

Ryan's words punctured Andre's security. He tried to ignore them. But

126

he wasn't with Mikayla every day. Ryan was.

He pulled Mikayla against him and slid a hand around her waist until it rested on the flatness of her belly. She trembled against him. He hoped with desire.

"You made your choice, Ryan. So has Mikayla. Don't make a fool of yourself."

Ryan grunted then pushed his way around them. Mikayla stepped away. When she turned to face Andre, she briefly met his gaze before glancing away. Dread, ten times worse than the thought of singing in public, settled in his chest. She'd never avoided his gaze before. What the hell had Ryan said?

"What was that about? You didn't have to puff up and try to claim your territory. He already knows I'm seeing you."

Her question grated his nerves. "Knowing and respecting are two different things. Otherwise, he wouldn't have bragged about your trip the other day."

"I told you about that."

"Not about the good time you two had." The music cranked up, and someone started singing a bad rendition of Tony Braxton's, Unbreak My Heart, and Andre had to yell, for Mikayla to hear. A skinny blond came down the hall and glanced nervously at them both.

She grabbed his hand and pulled him away from the bathrooms and out the front door. Fresh air and the setting sun met them.

"We are not going to do this," she said in an even voice. Eyes closed she rubbed her temples. "Ryan and I work together. I can't walk around angry at my boss all day."

Her words made sense, but they didn't calm his unease. Seeing her standing so close to Ryan, knowing his cousin could try and come between them woke up insecurities he'd never felt before. He'd never feared losing a woman. Never cared about losing one, before Mikayla.

"I thought you were quitting your job."

She dropped her hands, and her eyes popped open. "I explained about that."

"Dalmtrix fell through." He pointed to Rowdy's door. "You don't owe either of them anything. You can leave."

She stalked past him to the edge of the walkway. Mikayla spun around and crossed her arms over her chest. "Dalmtrix may not fall through. That's what Ryan came to tell me. Someone's blackmailing Senator Leventis. We're going to find out who."

His tongue went numb while his heart blasted against his ribs. How could Ryan know that? How long before the jackass figured out who, and told Mikayla? "I don't like you working with him." His mind whirled with the idea that Mikayla may discover his involvement in the blackmailing scheme.

She drew back and slightly shook her head. "That's something you'll have to get over. I have to work with him, and, yes, we work well together."

"We?" He slowly stalked toward her. "Since when are you and Ryan a we?"

Her hands massaged her temples again. "I can't believe this." She slapped the back of one hand into the palm of the other. "The acquisitions deal I worked on, might fall through because of blackmail, and you're concerned about me working with Ryan. I thought we were past this."

Andre's stomach and throat simultaneously tightened up. Somewhere in the back of his mind he knew he was acting unreasonable, but he'd never been in this position before. He had no clue how to stop her from looking into the blackmail. If she and Ryan found out, the blackmail would be just the ammunition needed to break up him and Mikayla before they'd really started.

"He's pulling you back in."

She blinked several times, and limp arms dropped to her sides. "Wow. I...can't believe this is coming out of your mouth." She ran a hand through her silky hair and frowned. "This is crazy. I have a chance to fix a problem. Yes, the alternative Ryan and I came up with the other day would work, but it would be even better if we can still get Dalmtrix down there. I'm not going to quit my job, and despite how much of an asshole Ryan can be, I'm not going to stop working with him."

She stepped toward him, her beautiful brown eyes begged him to understand. "I thought we were ready to do this. I thought you trusted me."

He reached out and tucked a few errant strands of hair behind her ear. "I don't trust him."

She pushed his hand away. "So what, you think I'm going to fall out of a closet with him? Damn, Andre, you should know I don't just fall into bed with anyone."

"I don't, your period stopped us."

She flinched and pulled away. *Real smooth, Andre. And stupid as fuck!* He should apologize. The words refused to come. He wasn't upset about that night in her apartment, but he wanted her composure to crack. To see if her emotions were just as jumbled up inside as his.

Mikayla crossed her arms and lifted her chin. "I think you should go."

A good guy would stay. Tell her the truth. Ask her to forgive him. "I think you're right."

She swallowed hard, her eyes glimmered with tears...or anger. He waited for her to give him some hint she didn't want them to end like this.

She stalked around him and back into Rowdy's. His chest tightened. What the hell had just happened? They'd gone from taking the first step toward what's been obvious between them since the mountains, to fighting outside of a bar like college kids. In typical Caldwell fashion, he'd let the jerk come out and ruin everything.

CHAPTER 23

Andre sat at the bar in Buffalo Wild Wings and stared at his cell phone. He picked it up, then put it back down.

He needed fortification.

Picking up the shot glass beside the phone, he downed a stiff gulp of bourbon that burned a fiery trail down his throat. Too bad he couldn't swallow his words that easily. His regret burned worse than the alcohol. Another a new emotion. Something Mikayla had a knack for bringing out of him.

God, that woman made him weak. Forgetting her made the most sense. He rejected the thought immediately. There was no way he could forget her, and frankly he didn't want to. No, he'd been wrong in this situation. He would have to make things right.

He sighed heavily, then picked up his phone to do what he should have done instead of leaving after she walked back into Rowdy's. He called to apologize.

After several rings, the voice mail picked up. He cursed, then texted.

I'm sorry.

If she didn't answer in ten minutes, he was getting into his car and driving to her apartment. He wasn't one to ignore his problems, and he refused to let Mikayla ignore him forever. He signaled the bartender for another drink, and then drummed his fingers on the counter.

He should have been in Greenville. His brother had called earlier asking about a proposal they needed to work on. He couldn't even think about business. Another first, problems with a woman had never distracted him from work.

His phone buzzed on the counter. His heart rate accelerated as he read her response.

You should be. She texted.

Let's talk.

Why?

Because, I messed up.

Several seconds passed. Where are you?

He dialed her number. On the third ring, she answered in a calm voice.

"I'll come to your apartment."

"No, I'll meet you somewhere," she said firmly.

He gave her the name of the restaurant. The bartender asked if he wanted another drink. Andre opted for a glass of soda. No need to further cloud his brain and possibly say something stupid.

He checked his watch and the time on his phone every few minutes. He could fess up and tell her everything about Dalmtrix. Would she understand that this started before he knew of her involvement? Or, would she view the blackmail as him taking the family revenge out on her? Just this morning they'd agreed to forego the just friends label and acknowledge what was between them. If she found out he blackmailed the Senator, their brief relationship would be over.

No, he'd find out who leaked the blackmail scheme before she did and shut them up. He frowned and slid the empty shot glass away. His solution didn't make the regret and alcohol mix any better.

After thirty minutes, Mikayla called to say she was outside. He paid the bartender then went out to meet her.

The night air was cool compared to the heat of the bar, a reminder that winter wasn't truly gone. Mikayla leaned against her car. The yellow lights of the parking lot illuminated her dark hair and softened her brown eyes.

"Before you say anything you need to understand one thing." She straightened from the car and held up a hand when he walked up. "It's bad enough I have to remind my dad I'm a fully functioning adult. I will not," her finger drilled his chest, "do the same thing with you. I like my job, and despite the situation, I'm able to work there without caring about Ryan and Angelica. Part of that is because Ryan and I made better friends than lovers. Something we both," she poked him again, "agreed on this afternoon. The other reason, I can work there and not care is because of you." Another jab. "Because of what we started in the mountains. I'm not going to quit." She took a deep breath and ran a hand over her face. When she met his eyes, determination burned brightly. "You can't think, every time I get along with Ryan, it means I'm running back to him."

His step-sister's demands, Renee's wishes, even her dad's need for control were all things she grinned and bore. But she let loose with him. Her anger and her passion came to the surface with him. Just as she passionately responded when his hands touched her breasts. His dick twitched in his pants as his arousal awakened.

"You're right." He took several steps toward her.

"I'm not flattered by jealousy. If you have a problem, you need just to come out and say it."

He stopped walking. "I wasn't jealous."

Her eyes narrowed. "Then, why demand I stop working with Ryan?"

He opened his mouth. The lie stuck in his throat. Andre coughed, and let out the truth. "Fine. I was jealous."

Her eyes widened, and the corner of her mouth twisted. He closed the distance between them and brushed his hand across her cold cheek.

"Does that make you feel better?" he asked.

Her body trembled against him. "Only slightly."

"Then what would make you feel better."

She took a deep breath, lifted her chin and met his gaze. The flare of passion in her eyes chased away the cold around him.

"You embarrassed me."

He cringed and lowered his head. "I'll never do that again."

"If you do, this is over." She said her voice hard.

Which proved he was right to keep the truth from her.

She stepped closer. Her flowery perfume a crisp beacon in the chilled air. "But you were very close to the truth about why I didn't fall in bed with you last weekend." Her hand lifted to the side of his face. Her small fingers gently brushed his chin. He pictured her slim fingers sliding down across his neck, and chest, and lower to the growing arousal in his pants and his body hummed.

"If it weren't for certain circumstances, I would have slept with you," she said.

He placed a hand on her waist. Nearly closed his eyes and groaned when her breasts touched his chest. "You don't know how bad I want you, Mikayla."

"Then what are we waiting for?"

*

Mikayla's hands trembled. She opened her car door and exited to the parking lot next to the apartment building. Andre stood at her side of the car as soon as she got out. He towered over her in the shadows, dark eyes, tense muscles, and ripe with the promise of ecstasy. A delicious chill skittered through her body.

Andre grasped her hand in his. Heat soared from where they touched and swelled inside Mikayla, the warmth of his body infused hers.

"Are you sure you want to do this?"

His voice, deep and hypnotic, wrapped around her. Quiet, sexy and as so very tempting. He stepped closer until the sensitive tips of her breasts brushed against his chest. Then gently traced his fingers up and down her arm.

Sparks of desire shot straight to her core. "We both want this."

She lifted her chin in a silent invitation. Even in the dark she could see a hunger flare in his eyes. Her mouth opened to suck in a breath, but nothing went to her lungs. Andre's firm lips sealed hers, robbing her of the ability to breathe. His kiss was hard, almost needy as if he were afraid she would pull away.

She wrapped her arm around his neck and pressed her body against his. Her clothing brushed against her skin and itched. Rubbing her chest, legs, thighs against his intensified the itch. Beneath his jacket, she wrapped her arms around his, absorbing his warmth and inhaling the delicious smell of his skin. Andre pulled at the edge of her sweater. Andre's hand, cold from the night air glided up her side and cupped her breast. His cool palm against Mikayla's warm hard nipple made her pulse quicken and sent an answering chill through her that had nothing to do with the cold. Long fingers gently massaged the soft mound. She pressed forward. He lightly rubbed his palm over her stiff nipple. A quick, piercing, pleasure connected straight to the wet spot between her legs.

She pulled her hand from the warmth beneath his jacket and tugged his belt lose. He gasped against her lips when she slipped an anxious hand past his waistband. His body tensed. Eyes popped open. He gave her a look that was both surprised at her boldness and encouraging. The encouraging sent her heart floating, and she pushed her hand through the opening in his boxers.

Her fingers wrapped around his hot shaft. He hissed out a breath. She bit her lower lip and moaned at the decadent feel of soft skin over solid flesh, long and thick. Pulsing with each steady beat of his heart. She pictured his dick sliding within her core, and a charge zipped through her body.

His lips plundered hers again, their tongues sliding together in a decadent glide. Her fingers gripped him, slowly easing up and down in tandem with her fantasy.

Andre slipped the strap of her bra aside and pulled down the cup. His expert hand teased her nipple. Caressed and rubbed the entire mound before finally giving the hard tip the attention it craved. Heat flushed her from inside out. She squirmed against him, moaned for more.

The pad of her thumb brushed the swollen head of his penis. His body jerked. His breath came in ragged puffs after he pulled her hand away and broke off their kiss.

"Upstairs," he said, his baritone hoarse and desire thickened. He gently squeezed her breast. "Unless you want our first time to be on the side of your car."

Right now, she'd take the side of her car. Swallowing hard, she nodded. He pulled his hand from the inside of her shirt. Good, if he kept it there she wouldn't be able to think about making it upstairs to her apartment.

She walked around him and headed for the stairs. He wrapped an arm around her shoulders and pulled her close to his side. Her senses honed in on the heat and tantalizingly masculine smell of his body as they hurried across the parking lot. Her hands shook, and he took the key from her and unlocked the door himself.

They barely crossed the threshold before he spun her around and picked her up. She giggled, and for once didn't care about making the juvenile sound. She trailed kisses across the slight shadow of hair on his strong cheek. Breathed in the seductive aroma of his cologne, tasted the sweetness of the skin along his neck with her tongue and light nips of her teeth.

Andre sprinted down the hall to the living room. Unceremoniously dropped her to her feet before balling the hem of her sweater in his hands and jerking it over her head. Every hitch of his breath, flare of the nostrils, and lick of the lips as he frantically revealed her nakedness made Mikayla thrust out her chest and part her legs for his pleasure. His admiration made her feel sexy, feminine. As if the most important thing in the world to him was making love to her. By the time she stood naked before him, she didn't care about slowly removing his clothes. She just wanted Andre naked.

He helped her pull his shirt over his head and pushed her hand away so he could slide his jeans and underwear down his lean muscular legs. When he stood before her, the lightening rod of his dick standing straight out and center, she grabbed his hand and hauled him to her.

They fell in a tangle of limbs on the couch. Andre's hot naked body covered her front. The chair's slick leather pressed into her back. Grasping her waist, Andre pulled her up until Mikayla's breasts bounced before his face. Thick warm lips closed over her hardened nipple. She gripped his shoulders and arched her back. Never before had foreplay felt this good or made her so aware of the pleasure of skin against skin.

His hips pushed side to side, spreading her legs so that the flat plane of his stomach rubbed against her wet clitoris. Pleasure exploded across her skin. A gasp burst from her lips. He sucked her nipple deeply, switched to the other breast, and moaned. The sound a rumble that resonated deep in her midsection. He reached between them and long fingers parted the swollen folds between her legs.

Mikayla's fingers dug into his arms. "Oh yes!"

He took his time exploring and gliding against every fold of her sex. His thumb traced wide circles around her clitoris. Lithe fingers smoothed both the inside and outside of her lower lips. Teasing her opening, outlining the edge before slowly feeding her heat one long finger at a time.

The carnal massage felt good. Great! Fantastic! But she wanted more. She leaned up and reached for his penis, but her body jerked when he wiggled his fingers inside of her and lightly took her nipple between his teeth.

Her legs quivered. An orgasm looming. *No, not yet.* "Andre, please."

He lifted away and pulled her to the edge of the couch, settling himself on his knees between her legs. He pushed her knees out, exposing her completely. He licked, then bit, his lower lip as he stared down at her exposed sex. She lifted to her elbows, motioned with her head for him to come closer. Slowly, he leaned forward and kissed her. Not with the urgency he had before, but reverently. Cementing their connection.

The full girth and weight of his dick pressed against her slippery center. She shifted her hips, and her clitoris rubbed against his rigid flesh. He groaned, took the back of her head in his hand, and rocked against her. The smooth pleasure of his sex as it glided across the wet nub of her clit radiated to every cell in her body. Needy fingers sank onto his muscular arms, and she ground her slick heat against him.

Back and forth, back and forth, he rubbed. Trembles racked their bodies. Her toes curled into the carpet. Andre's hips shifted further back, and the wide tip of his penis tumbled down to her dewy opening.

Mikayla's head fell back. "Oh my, God!"

Andre froze. "Damn, you make me want to..."

All it would take was a shift of her hip, and he'd slide in. Their gazes collided. He wanted to. Tension tightened every hard muscle pressed against her. Mikayla bit her tongue to keep from telling him to do it.

He pushed away and reached for his pants and pulled a condom out. Once he covered himself, he turned back and spread her legs open. Slowly, and to the hilt, his long thick erection filled her. Sweat beaded along his face, a grimace that was both pleasure and pain marring his handsome features.

"Touch yourself," he said in a voice deeper and infinitely sexier in the throes of lovemaking. "Spread your lips, let me see while I'm inside you."

She hesitated, but the smoldering look in his eye pushed her to let go. She trailed her hand down her body to where they were joined. He pushed her knees further apart and licked luscious lips and stared down.

"Use both hands." He gritted out.

Ignited by his desire, her other hand joined the first to open herself up to his view.

"Yes, just like that. Damn, Mikayla, you look so good."

He let out a long sigh, bit his bottom lip, and started long slow strokes.

One of his hands left her knee to gently grasp her breast. He alternated between kneading her fleshy mound and pinching her nipple. His head dropped back then fell forward again. Her body tightened, her toes once again curled into the carpet. Her heart rapped against her ribcage like a deranged woodpecker.

She closed her eyes. Blocked out everything but the fullness of him inside her, the smell of his desire surrounding her, the sensual feel of her body pressed into the leather couch, and the awed way he moaned her name.

Then he pulled out. Her eyes flew open. "Nooo, what are you doing?"

"I've got to taste you." His mouth closed over her center.

She slapped the couch and cried out. Breathing, thinking, became difficult as his expert tongue lavishly attended to every inch of her trembling core. It was the most decadent experience ever. The way he grabbed her hips and lifted her. The carnal sounds of pleasure he made that rumbled through her body. The pinch of his fingers as they dug into her body, pushed her to the edge.

A violent tremble shook her legs. Andre lifted his head, resumed his position, and slid his wonderful length back inside.

The nerves in her body, already hypersensitive, vibrated with each deep, steady, push. "Andre! Yes!" she cried.

The pace of his thrusts increased. He leaned forward until his body rubbed her clitoris with every push. That was all it took.

An orgasm seized her muscles. Her eyes popped open. "Andre!" Wave after tremendous wave of pure ecstasy fell over her like spilled grains of sand.

The rhythm slowed but didn't stop. Prolonging her release. More and more trembles racked her body. Then, with a few solid thrusts, he shouted his release. Deep inside her his body jerked, sending more sprinkles of pleasure across her skin.

He collapsed on top of her. Their sweat combined as he laid his head upon her breasts. She felt the pounding of her heartbeat throughout her body. Or was that his?

Wrapping her arms around him her hand traced across the back of his head. Incoherent thoughts swirled in her brain as she tried to regain composure.

"I think...we both...deserve a cigarette," she said between breaths.

Andre's laughter was a deep rumble against her body. He lifted his head a devilish smile on his face. "We may smoke several before the night is over."

CHAPTER 24

"This week has been particularly terrible. What are we doing this weekend to recover?" Renee pinned her friend with a questioning glare.

Mikayla inwardly cringed. She dropped a red-lined contract on Renee's desk for further review. Outside of their bi-weekly Saturday morning hair appointment, the two barely had time to see each other away from work. Over the past six weeks, they'd been swamped with several new projects breaking ground in South Carolina and Georgia.

She sat in the chair across from Renee's desk, stretched her feet and kicked off her shoes. Usually, she wasn't so informal, but her feet were tired from running around putting out fires all day.

"Sorry, Renee, but I'm busy this weekend."

Renee rolled her eyes heavenward. She leaned back in her chair and flipped the bang from her face. "This thing isn't over yet?" She whined like a vegan at a bar-b-que buffet.

"Nope," Mikayla shook her head. "Not yet, so you might as well get used to it."

"I don't know what you see in him." Renee draped a well-toned arm on the hand rest of her leather executive chair and toyed with her diamond drop earrings that sparkled brightly against her yellow Michael Kors blazer.

"It's been six weeks and in that time he's been caring, generous, and an all-around good guy. If you got to know him—"

"I don't want to know him," Renee's tone was razor sharp.

"He's your cousin and we're seeing each other. I don't like having my only female friend roll her eyes and suck her teeth every time I say I'm going to be with my man." Mikayla leaned forward and rested her hands on the edge of Renee's desk. "Forget this stupid rivalry. It's your dad's fight anyway. Be happy for me."

Mikayla watched Renee with baited breath. The past few weeks with Andre were great despite the distance between them. He'd visited every weekend and even spent the past weekend with Mikayla, visiting her dad.

Evan begrudgingly gave Andre his nod of approval after Andre identified what was wrong with the catalytic converter on her cousin Tyrone's car. An accurate diagnosis that surprised both Mikayla and her dad.

She was filled with all of the thrills that came at the start of a relationship. The one downside was Renee's disapproval. Renee's daily dire warning that everything would soon come to a devastating end were taking a toll on her patience. She no longer feared her friendship with Renee wouldn't survive, but still she wanted Renee's approval. What could she say? Old habits die hard.

"I want to be happy for you, Mikayla. You deserve to be happy. I just can't see that happening with Andre."

"Why not?" She leaned back. "Because he and Ryan used to cheat with each other's girlfriends? That was years ago. They've both moved on."

Renee flipped her bang again. "I don't like Angelica."

"Well, don't pin your hopes on a reconciliation between me and Ryan. We've come to a work truce, no less, no more. Whatever attraction there was is completely gone."

Renee's eyes lit up. "So you admit there was an attraction. Ryan is convinced you were never attracted to him."

She rolled her eyes and stood. "You're hopeless, Renee. I'm with Andre, and I really like him. I feel like I did with Brendan…but more. I want to see where this goes."

The fight left her friend's eyes. A heavy sigh sagged her shoulders, Renee stood and walked around her desk. "If he hurts you—"

"I know," she said before Renee could finish.

They hugged, and Mikayla felt a small weight lift from her chest. This wasn't a stamp of approval, but at least they were inching toward the right direction. When she left Renee's office, Ryan and his dad walked out of Philip's office. Ryan waved her over.

"Are you free Monday morning?" Ryan asked.

She pulled her phone from her pocket to check the calendar and nodded. "I am, why?"

Philip gave her a reassuring smile. "Because, we'd like to discuss the specifics of your new position before announcing the news in the staff meeting."

"New position?"

Ryan smiled. "Congrats, Mikayla, we've agreed you're the best person to run the acquisitions department."

She gaped at them, and then a smile fought its way across her lips. "Seriously? What about Dalmtrix?"

Philip waved a hand. "The way you worked with Ryan, to turn the project around, proves you deserve the job. Congratulations, I couldn't have picked anyone better." He gave her a pat on the shoulder. "Now if you'll excuse me, I'm running late for a meeting."

Mikayla turned to Ryan. "Did you do this?"

"No," Ryan said. "Dad came to me this afternoon. He always wanted you to have the position."

An excited laugh tumbled from her. "This is fantastic."

"I know, and once we find the blackmailer and get Dalmtrix back, everyone will know why you're our new manager."

Her smile withered away. "How are we going to do that? Everyone, we asked, said they knew nothing. Including the Senator himself." Mikayla had hounded his secretary enough to get five minutes with him. His shifty eyes and sweaty palms told her he had lied. Whatever info the blackmailer had on the Senator must be good.

Ryan wrapped his arm around her shoulder. "We'll worry about that after Monday. Tonight we need to celebrate."

She laughed and was about to pull away when Angelica came down the hall escorted by Charity. Both of their eyes narrowed in on her wrapped in Ryan's embrace. Mikayla hastily pulled away, but the damage was done. Once they announced her promotion on Monday, Charity would re-start rumors that she was considered because of her relationship with Ryan.

"So what are we celebrating?" Charity stuck the tip of her tongue out the side of her mouth as if she could taste the awkwardness in the air.

"You'll find out soon enough," Mikayla said. She turned a tight smile toward Angelica, who hurried to Ryan's side and linked her arm through his. "You all have a great weekend."

Ryan opened his mouth as if he was going to say something, but Angelica jerked on his arm, and he closed his mouth. Mikayla smirked and turned away. She brushed past Charity and hurried down the hall to her office. It was past time to get out of the office and call Andre to firm up their weekend plans.

Wrapping up the work week, she shut down her computer and organized a few files before grabbing her purse and rushing to the door. Angelica blocked her path just as she was about to walk out. Mikayla's grip on her purse tightened.

"It's funny how the Caldwell men tend to want what they can't have. Isn't it?" Angelica's Parisian accent flowed past her lips like silk. She eyed Mikayla from head to toe. "But if we're honest with ourselves, it's how most men operate."

"What do you want, Angelica?"

Angelica laughed and pushed past Mikayla into her office. The cloying smell of her thick perfume invaded Mikayla's lungs. Angelica's black and beige halter dress clung to her slim figure as she glided across the office with an effortless seductive walk. So effortless, Mikayla wondered if she'd earned a master's degree in hip swinging.

"I want what you have." Angelica turned slowly and cocked her head to the side. "I didn't think much when Andre and you hooked up. I mean you're cute, but not really competition. For whatever reason, he's stayed with you."

Frowning, Mikayla crossed her arms over her chest. "What about Ryan?"

"Ryan is a very sweet boy, but we both know Andre is a man." She strutted across the room. "I just thought it fair to warn you, before you get too wrapped up in this game. I will get him back."

"You haven't contacted him since the mountains."

She raised her hands. "Oui, I thought he would contact me. I underestimated his attraction to you. But I won't anymore."

Mikayla's muscles trembled, with the need to smack the smug smile off of Angelica's face. One one-thousand, two one-thousand…She tried counting, telling herself things would be okay that this woman's threat meant nothing. But beneath the anger, a very real discomfort settled like a lump of old oatmeal in her stomach. She tried to push her emotions aside, tried to be the bigger woman.

She failed.

Mikayla dropped her purse and took a step in Angelica's direction. "Andre doesn't give a damn about you, never did."

Angelica laughed. "I saw the receipt for the ring."

"Then why sleep with Ryan."

"Unfortunately, I found it after the closet debacle with Ryan. Oh, don't look so upset. You must have realized this little dalliance wouldn't last long." She arched an eyebrow.

A knock on the door prevented Mikayla from responding. She turned to find Ryan standing at the door watching them curiously.

His wary glance bounced between the two women. "Is everything okay?"

Angelica hurried around Mikayla and pressed against Ryan, "Oui, mon cher. Just girl talk." She kissed his cheek. "Shall we leave?"

Ryan glanced at Mikayla, then turned back to Angelica. When Angelica smiled up at him, his eyes softened, and he nodded.

"See you later, Mikayla." Ryan pulled Angelica out of the office.

The lump of oatmeal began to swell.

She shouldn't feel bad for Ryan being used by that vulture, but she did. They'd been friends. Even though he'd done her terribly wrong, shouldn't she do something?

The harder question was, should Mikayla say anything to Andre. A cold sweat broke out over her skin. He'd said he only considered marrying Angelica because she made the perfect hostess. But who really considered marrying someone without feeling some affection for them?

Her phone vibrated. Absently, she pulled it out of her pocket and answered.

"Hey you," Andre's baritone greeted her.

She cleared her throat. Slowly she picked her purse off the floor and once again headed out of the office. "Hey you."

"I'm stuck at the office, and really I should be available in Greenville this weekend."

A lump of disappointment settled in beside the oatmeal. "Can't make it this weekend?"

"No, but I think it's really a shame you've never seen my home. Come to Greenville."

She bounced on her feet. "Yes!"

His deep laughter filtered through the phone. "Great. I'll text you the address to my condo. We'll spend the night there, and then tomorrow I'll take you to my house in the country. Sound good?"

"Sounds perfect. I'll pack a bag and be on my way."

"Can't wait. See you soon, baby."

His sweet words warmed her heart. To hell with Angelica and her childish games.

CHAPTER 25

Mikayla straightened her shoulder and gave herself a mental pep talk outside Andre's condo door. No way would she let Angelica's weak threat ruin her weekend. If she planned to trust what was between them, she'd have to trust him. She knocked on the door.

Andre swept the door open, cell phone plastered to his ear. He grinned broadly, and the sexy gesture sent a frisson of delight across her skin. The man was delicious in a crisp white shirt unbuttoned at the base of his throat and tucked into the waistband of charcoal grey slacks.

He grabbed her hand and squeezed ushering her inside. Mikayla dropped an overnight bag beside the door and let him lead. He lived in a beautiful condo with an excellent view of downtown Greenville, and the Reedy River was visible through the large windows. The combination of beige walls, dark wood floors and cream tones complemented the tan modern furniture. A large television screen and an array of electronic devices adorned one wall. No pictures anywhere. Typical bachelor's space.

"I don't have time for this," he snapped into the phone. Andre leaned over and kissed Mikayla's cheek, pointed toward the couch, then stood gazing out the wall of glass windows leading to a balcony. His shoulders stiffened, and he ran a hand across his face.

She crossed the room and wrapped her arms around his waist. Resting her head against the rigid muscles of his back, she closed her eyes and relished the enticing smell of his cologne. She'd missed him. The way he smelled, the way he towered over her but touched her as if she would break, the deep rich sound of his voice. Missed him so much that all she wanted now was to forget about her conversation with Angelica and concentrate on relieving his tension. She hated seeing the people she loved upset.

Her eyes popped open. She loved him!

He turned around and wrapped his arm around her shoulders and cradled her against his side. "I don't give a damn what you have to say. Don't bother me with this anymore." He ended the call then tossed his phone on the couch. "Hey you," he lowered his head and pressed a kiss against her temple.

She giggled…a trait she started around him. "Bad phone call."

"I don't want to talk about that phone call." His seductive lips slid from her temple, down her cheek, then to her jaw. His voice was smooth and rich as honey. "I want to reacquaint myself with your body."

Her breathing hitched and pulse increased in tempo. "You got to know it pretty well last weekend."

His deep chuckle penetrated her body with the intensity of a hypodermic needle. Shooting her up with a desire that hardened her nipples and sent a river of warmth between her legs. "I can never know enough. Every moan you make drives me crazy."

She opened her mouth, but Andre's tongue flicked across the pulse of her throat. "I…bet you say that to all the ladies," she said her voice breathless.

Andre lifted his head, and all humor left his eyes. "I've only said that to you."

Her smile fell away as her lips parted with a heavy breath. "Then make me moan."

That was all the encouragement he needed. All her uncertainties faded away when his lips touched hers. They'd spent the past month and a half becoming familiar with each other's body. She'd never been a selfish lover, but giving Andre pleasure turned her on more than she ever would have expected. The thought of the sweet taste of his skin on her tongue and the feel of his body under her fingertips had her wet, and aching for him.

She made quick work of releasing the buttons of his shirt and ran her hands over the strong muscles of his chest. A curly mass of chest hair tickled her fingers, and she gently scratched her nails against his hot skin. He broke their kiss and nibbled along her jaw and down the side of her neck. Quickly unbuttoning her pants, he pushed them past her waist. When his nimble fingers touched the wetness between her legs, a satisfied sigh seeped through his lips. Andre leisurely drove one long finger into the depths of her center driving her to elicit a long sensual moan.

"That's it, baby, let me know you like it." He pressed her back against the cool glass balcony window. He slowly lowered to his knees. "I want more than moans. I want to make you scream."

Lifting her right leg his hand ran up and down her sensitive skin, and he rested her trembling leg over his shoulder. Her head fell back against the glass then he parted the swollen lips of her core.

"You've got the prettiest pussy on the planet," he murmured before his tongue did a long stroke across her erect clit.

Mikayla's knees buckled, and she pressed against the glass for support. Pleasure bounced inside of her from head to toe. One hand grabbed his head, the other splayed against the window. No words came, only loud cries while his firm tongue explored the wetness between her thighs. The extreme pleasure more than she could bear, her fingers clenched against his scalp, and her leg trembled as the start of an orgasm pulsed a frantic beat.

"You've got to stop," she gasped.

"Not yet." Thick lips surrounded her swollen nub followed by the steady pressure of him sucking.

Her orgasm exploded. "Andrrreeeee," she screamed his name. Slapping the glass and bucking against his mouth. Before the waves could pass, he pulled her away from the window onto the floor. She lay panting on the hardwood floor while he pulled a condom from his pants, lowered them and covered his erection. Quickly, he covered her body with his then buried his face in her neck and his thick erection into her trembling flesh. His thrusts were fast, urgent and slid against her walls perfectly. Her hips lifted to meet his, long nails dug into his back. Primal grunts and moans the language of her heart.

He rode the wave of her orgasm until another rose. Strong hands gripped her hips, and he pushed steadily in and out. Her toes curled, her mouth went dry, and when he turned his head to kiss her neck, she shattered again. His body tensed and then his dick jerked deep within her with his release. She gasped, "I love you."

*

Forty-five minutes later, Mikayla forced herself to leave the shower and look for Andre in the living room. After her whispered confession, he'd avoided eye contact, she figured they both needed a few minutes alone. *How the hell am I supposed to fix saying I love you way too soon?*

Mikayla found the living room empty. Reflected in the glass door, Andre stood illuminated by the glowing end of a cigarette on the balcony. She made a quick detour back into the bedroom to grab a sweater out of her overnight bag before joining him. The days were warming up, but the nights were still cool. A steady breeze greeted her when she walked outside, and she pulled her sweater tight. Andre glanced over, the corner of his mouth lifted, but it wasn't exactly a smile.

"I like your orange head wrap," he said.

She patted the makeshift turban. "I couldn't let my hair get wet in the shower." Her toned peaked defensively.

He motioned with his hand for her to come closer. "I wasn't trying to be sarcastic, I meant it. You're comfortable enough with me to wear it." He shook his head then brought the cigarette to his lips. "You shouldn't be comfortable with me."

She leaned against the balcony ledge beside him. Moonlight glistened on the surface of the river in the distance, and the faint sounds of life in the city drifted their way. She thought of Angelica and her earlier confidence wavered.

"Why not?" She held out her hand, and he passed over the cigarette.

Pulling in a deep breath, he stood straight his shoulders rigid and faced her. "I need to tell you something."

The cigarette shook when she raised it to her lips with a trembling hand. The nicotine did little to calm her racing heart.

"Let me guess, it's been fun but now it's time to move on," she said.

"No. Where did that come from?"

She wasn't relieved. "I saw Angelica today. She wants you back." She watched closely for any sign that the news made him happy.

He frowned. "How do you know that?"

She pretended it wasn't excruciating to tell the man she'd fallen in love with that his beautiful ex-fiancé wanted him back, with a flippant shrug. "She told me."

"Typical." The single word reply was followed by a humorless chuckle. "Angelica likes to play games. She's upset I don't give a damn about what she did in the mountains. Telling you was her way to get me to reach out and ask her to come back." He took her arm and pulled Mikayla against the warmth of his side. "Don't worry."

"You say that, but do you mean it? You did plan on asking that woman to marry you." She handed the cigarette back to him.

He took a draw and handed it back. When she shook her head, he crushed the butt in the ashtray beside him. "She was good looking, fit in with my family, and willing to accept that I couldn't give her more than the security that comes with my wealth."

She lifted her head and looked into his eyes. His handsome features were clear in the silver light of the moon. It struck her again how much she'd grown to care for him.

"You'd still planned to spend your life with her. Are you sure you didn't love her just a little?"

Andre peered into Mikayla's eyes. "I don't know how to love." His tone implied more than what he said. Those dark eyes screamed a demand she wished she could misunderstand.

Pain erupted in her heart. Tears stung her eyes, and she turned away. They'd made no promises to each other. She'd made the choice to be with him and let her feelings slip in over the past weeks.

"It's a good thing I don't love you then, huh," Her voice rippled like the moonlight on the river.

He slipped behind her and wrapped strong arms around her waist. She wanted to resist, but the heat from his body pulled her in. She rested her head on his shoulder, and he lowered his lips, pressing them against her temple.

"Maybe you could show me how to love," he whispered.

Hope exploded inside her. "You have to want to learn."

"That's the difficult part. I've never wanted to be in love before."

She squirmed in his arms in an attempt to turn, but his grasp tightened and prevented her from moving.

His voice took on a wistful tone. "Mom puts on a brave front, but she still loves my dad after all of these years, and he knows it. Whenever she comes to visit, he asks her to spend the night with him. Not because he cares or misses her, but because she lets him. It proves he still has power over her. My stepmom used to get angry, now she accepts his infidelity. Love makes you do stupid things."

This time when Mikayla turned, Andre didn't stop her. She wrapped her arms around his neck and trembled when his hands ran up and down the curve of her back.

"Some people can't distinguish between a person loving them and a person taking advantage of them." Her fingers brushed the hairs on the back of his neck. "It doesn't mean everyone who falls in love, is willing to be treated badly."

"I'm my father's son. I've cheated, broken hearts, and taken advantage. I don't want to do that, not to someone I could love."

Warmth spread beneath her skin, she barely contained her smile. "Admitting that means you won't. You already know the value of having someone love you."

He slowly kissed her. When he lifted his head there was a tight smile on his face, but no joy. "I'm glad you think that."

Before she could reply he kissed her. Harder. Aggressive this time. He slid his large hand past the waistband of her pajama bottoms and firmly cupped her behind. A stirring against her stomach meant his arousal was increasing, and her body heated in response.

"Have you ever made love on a balcony?" His deep voice rumbled seductively against her lips.

She moved her head from side to side. He grinned. "Let me introduce you to the delight."

CHAPTER 26

Mikayla squealed happily when Andre's country house came into view at the end of the long driveway. Her joy brought a satisfied smile to Andre's lips. He rarely took women to his sanctuary from work, family, and life in the city. The one time he'd brought Angelica she'd complained of boredom.

"The house is beautiful," Mikayla stepped out of the car.

"It's alright." He tried to play it off as no big deal, but couldn't hide the pleasure in his voice.

Early morning sunlight filtered through the tall oak trees surrounding the two bedroom cottage. He didn't need a lot of space while out here, and the woods blocked the view from both the road and Jonathan's house that was a few acres over. Andre considered the place functional and structurally sound, but not beautiful.

"Did you plant the roses?" She walked over to the green stems that would produce yellow flowers in a few months.

He cocked his head to the side. "Me, plant roses?" He chuckled. "No, mom did right after I bought the place. She insisted on adding color."

Mikayla fingered one of the stems and looked around the yard. "She did a good job. Even though winter is ending, there's color and beauty."

"I'll be sure to let her know you like it. The inside isn't as nice. I didn't let her decorate."

She left the roses and came back to his side. "If she did this good with the yard, why not?"

"My mom loves butterflies. All of her decorations have them. I refused to let her defile my man space."

Her laugh echoed in the solitude of the early morning. "I like butterflies. Maybe I'll put a few on the walls."

He grinned, reached out, took her elbow and pulled Mikayla against him. He enjoyed the feel of her soft breasts against his chest and couldn't resist palming the lusciousness of her behind. She ran her hands up his arms and squeezed his biceps. He liked the way she got excited when she touched him.

"You keep rubbing me like that and I'll let you put up pink butterflies."

She giggled, the lovable sound luring his head down to her lips. The curves of her body pressed against him, and her eager tongue darted out to meet his.

He liked her, a lot. Wanted to spend too much of his free time with her. The fact that she loved him was scary as hell. The Dalmtrix deal was effectively killed, and that didn't hurt her. She'd found a way to persevere, but things could still go bad if she discovered his involvement.

Her hand wormed its way to the front of his pants. Getting her inside as soon as possible was all that mattered right now. The roar of a motorcycle engine interrupted them.

Mikayla raised a brow and glanced his way.

The black and chrome Harley stopped beside his car. He pushed back his frustration but didn't smile at Jonathan's impromptu visit.

Jonathan removed his helmet and strolled over. "I thought that was your car." He gazed at Mikayla with an appreciative gleam in his eye. "And you brought an angel with you."

Andre wasn't prone to eye rolling, but Jonathan's Prince Charming routine could be nauseating. "Mikayla, this jackass is Jonathan Wright."

Her eyes widened, and she grinned. "The petri dish defender?"

Jonathan laughed. "You told her about that."

Mikayla pointed her thumb in Andre's direction. "I only got his side of the story."

Jonathan winked. "I'll be sure to tell you the truth one day."

Andre raised his brow. "I told her the truth. I always tell the truth." The lie nearly stuck in his throat.

"Then she knows I kicked your butt?" Jonathan asked with a look of surprise.

Andre pushed Jonathan's shoulder. "She's about to see me kick your butt. What are you doing here anyway?"

"You didn't mention coming up this weekend, and when I saw your car I figured I'd stop by and see what's up." Jonathan smiled at Mikayla. It was the same smile Andre had seen turn women into stuttering fools.

"Just showing Mikayla my place. You can leave now." He swept an open hand toward Jonathan's bike.

Mikayla playfully swatted at his arm. "Don't be rude. It's nice to meet you, Jonathan."

Jonathan's teasing look meant he wasn't planning on going anywhere anytime soon. "That's right, Andre, don't be rude. Have you been inside yet?"

"You know we just arrived," Andre said.

"Then she doesn't know your fridge is probably empty. You know you should come to my house for breakfast."

"I had groceries delivered yesterday," he cut in before Jonathan could head to the door.

"Even better, I'll cook." He took Mikayla's hand and placed it on his arm. "Andre's a terrible cook. When we were roommates in college he damn near gave me food poisoning every time he stepped in the kitchen. I still don't know why I bless him with my friendship."

Mikayla laughed and peeked over her shoulder when Jonathan led her to the door. Andre sighed but smiled and followed. Jonathan had bugged the hell out of him to meet Mikayla. As annoying as Jonathan's arrival had been, Andre appreciated his friend looking out for him.

Andre's cell phone rang as soon as they entered the house. His brother's number flashed on the screen.

"I've got to take this," he said to Mikayla and Jonathan.

Jonathan grinned. "Go ahead, I'll entertain Mikayla."

"That's what I'm worried about."

Jonathan winked before escorting Mikayla to the kitchen. He leaned down and whispered in her ear. The sound of her laughter trailed behind them. Andre would have to remind Jonathan to turn down some of that charm.

Andre frowned as another bout of laughter came from his kitchen and he answered the phone. "Yeah?"

"I just got word that Dalmtrix is still considering moving to Hartsville."

Andre spun away from the kitchen. His fingers tightened around the phone. "Where did you hear that?"

"I spoke with someone at the Chamber of Commerce. Apparently Caldwell Development is working out a new project with the school district and Community Development Department. Early buzz about this project is making the area more enticing for their relocation."

"What about the worries of increased contamination if they move?"

"They've sent representatives down to talk with the county council and promised to go the extra mile to prove their commitment to the environment. Even if Senator Leventis disagrees with the deal, it's going to go through."

Andre scowled over his shoulder toward the kitchen. Mikayla and Jonathan were engrossed in an animated conversation. He couldn't make out their words, but knowing Jonathan, the joke was at his expense.

"It's not worth fighting anymore," Andre said. "Let Dalmtrix go where they want and we can pilot the landfill gas program somewhere else."

"I'm almost willing to agree," Isaac said. "But Dad is taking this as a personal attack from Uncle Philip."

Andre spun away from the kitchen and gripped the phone. "That's preposterous."

"Convince him of that. He's got dirt on the governor and wants to use it to force a tax deal to get Dalmtrix to move to the Upstate."

Andre's pulse hammered in his ears. "What?"

"And there's more. He's got information on mishandled funds in the Hartsville school district that could threaten the new development."

Andre's hand balled into a fist. He reared back to hit the wall but held back. "We can't do that."

"It's already being done. We've got a meeting with the superintendent on Monday morning."

"I'm not going."

"You know how this goes. Either you're with Dad or against him." Isaac said in a tone weighted down from years of hearing that statement.

The constant threat from their father grated Andre's nerves. "My loyalty to this family shouldn't be questioned."

"I'm not the one you need to convince."

Andre ended the call without another word. Frustration and anger crashed like waves inside him. This bullshit was going to blow up in his face. Going with his family on this would surely mean losing Mikayla. There was no way his dad would kill this deal without letting Philip know he was behind it. If he fought his dad, he knew what would happen. Curtis wouldn't hesitate to snatch away Andre's rights to the company. He'd lose everything.

Andre stared at the phone then the kitchen. He'd worked so hard to help build the company. If he kept Mikayla, he'd risk losing everything. If he gave her up, he'd definitely lose the only woman who made him even think about love.

But love is a fleeting emotion.

Mikayla popped her head around the corner. A beautiful smile brightened her face and shot an arrow of happiness through his chest.

"Good you're off the phone. I think Jonathan is about to ask me to marry him."

"Get it right," Jonathan's voice came from the kitchen. "I already asked."

"Jonathan wants me to break his arms." Andre walked toward Mikayla. He tried to sound lighthearted, but his words came out gravelly and gruff.

Mikayla frowned and reached up to place her hand on his cheek, concern reflecting in her brown gaze. "Are you okay?"

"Yeah," he leaned down and gave her a fleeting kiss. He walked around her and approached Jonathan. "I hear you're making moves on my lady?"

Jonathan laughed. "Just pointing out that she could do better."

They continued the good-natured taunts, but Mikayla's worried glances darting his way didn't help the unease clenching his gut.

*

"I like her," Jonathan said when he and Andre walked outside to his motorcycle.

"Maybe a little too much."

Jonathan took his helmet off the bike and propped it between his arm and side. "Worried she'll realize the grass is greener?"

"Not hardly. But it wouldn't hurt to tone it down."

A serious look replaced the smile on Jonathan's face. "You like her, too. A lot."

He did but was it enough to fight over with his dad? Enough to stir up Curtis's fears that his sons would turn against him the same way Phillip had?

"I'm thinking about ending things." The words put a sour taste in his mouth.

"The look on your face says you're not really considering that."

Andre ran a hand across his face. "I don't like it, but it's for the best."

"What crazy ass notion put that into your head? You don't bring women up here. Angelica came because she begged, and I saw the relief on your face when you said she hated it. Mikayla didn't hesitate to help in your kitchen, and she seems comfortable curled up on your couch right now, I don't think she's going to complain. I didn't believe it, but now that I've met her, I see the connection. Why in the hell would you end it?"

Jump right to the point, why don't you? Without a second thought, Andre relayed the conversation he'd had with his brother. The entire time he told the story he could hear how unreasonable it sounded to ruin a relationship with Mikayla over his dad's need for retaliation. Even though Jonathan didn't agree with him going along with the Caldwell anything goes business model, he knew Andre's family well enough to understand how difficult it would be to go against Curtis.

When Andre finished, Jonathan put his hand to his chin. "So expose a few scandals, prevent the move of a major manufacturer and push them to go somewhere that profits C.E.S., loose Mikayla, but keep your dysfunctional family intact."

Andre rubbed the back of his neck. "That sums it up."

"Do you realize how asinine that sounds?"

He held his head back and groaned. "Yes. It's asinine. It's unethical, and it'll ruin my relationship with Mikayla. I turned against my dad once, and not only was it a disaster, but it proved in the end, I was just as bad as him."

"You're a grown man now."

He pushed aside past regrets. "I put everything I had into making C.E.S. successful. Am I supposed to walk away from the company for a woman? Then do what?"

Jonathan smirked and tapped him with the helmet. "You are the C.O.O. of a major corporation. It shouldn't be hard to find another job. Or, use that damn M.B.A. you have and start another one. Take a few people from your dad's company and launch your own waste recovery and recycling business. You've said yourself small business need better solutions."

"It's not that easy."

"Yeah, it is." Jonathan slipped onto the back of his bike and fired up the engine. "Give her up and become what you swear you're not. Your dad."

Andre stood in the driveway until the sound of Jonathan's motorcycle faded. He turned back to the house, thought of Mikayla lying on the couch wrapped up in a quilt watching television. She didn't have many options. He didn't have cable or satellite. Just a converter box, but she hadn't complained. Just smiled that adorable smile of hers and kissed him before he walked Jonathan out.

Back inside, Andre found Mikayla dozing on the couch. He smiled and strolled over and kneeled in front of her. She always fell asleep in seconds. He understood her exhaustion. She often worked late and spent her days traveling across the state. But whenever he called she stopped to talk to him. Whenever he visited, she gave him her undivided attention. Amazing and selfless, and he was about to give all of that up?

He brushed the hair away from her face. She stirred, her eyes opened slowly and blinked several times before focusing on him.

Mikayla smiled. "Sorry."

He shook his head. "You work too hard."

"Don't we all." She looked around his sparsely furnished living area. "Maybe that's why I like your place out here. Just the basics, and enough peace and quiet to get your brain refreshed for another work day."

"I don't get very much quiet with Jonathan around."

She laughed and sat up. "He's nice."

"And he likes you."

"Hmmm, there may be hope for us. Renee has agreed to stand down on bashing you, and your friend has taken a liking to me." She leaned forward and kissed his cheek.

He sat beside her on the couch. "I'm thinking of leaving my job."

"That phone call. Was it about work?"

"For the most part." He leaned back on the couch and brushed his fingers through her hair. "My brother called to tell me about one of my dad's ideas. Something I don't agree with."

"If you left, what would you do?"

He shrugged and toyed with a few threads escaping the back of the couch. "Find another job or start a business. I'm not worried about that as much as how my dad will handle my leaving. He strikes out at those he perceives disloyal. He'd consider my leaving C.E.S. a betrayal."

"How so?"

"When my dad cheated on my mom, he kicked her out and completely cut her off. No house, no money, no anything. She tried to fight, but he had enough money to hire lawyers that had her held up in court so long she finally gave up."

He frowned and balled his hands into fists on the back of the couch. "I was angry and hated him for what he did. So I left to live with her. After six months of struggling and not knowing where our next meal would come from…I became resentful."

"Of your dad?"

"No, of my mom." He turned away from her and rubbed his face with his hands. "I would lash out and could barely hide my anger. I wondered what had she done to make him hate her…us…so much. I guess he knew my limit because a few months later he reached out to me. Invited me to visit." He scoffed. "I jumped at the chance. I realized everything I'd given up. He asked me to stay for good and I did. Mom wasn't angry. In fact, she wished me well and said she couldn't stand to see me suffer with her. Dad's only requirement–my loyalty. He didn't want to lose his son the same way he'd lost his brother."

He turned back to Mikayla. She stared at the floor.

"I've gone along with everything he's asked of me. A part of me even enjoys the money, the power. I reveled in bending the rules, making people give me what I want. I let myself believe dad's tactics of abusing power and privilege were okay because we were building an empire. An empire I'd inherit one day."

"What is he asking you to do now that's finally pushed the button?"

The truth burned his throat, but telling her would require revealing what he'd done already. Instead, he opted for part of the truth. "It would require me to give you up."

Her head snapped up, and questions swirled in the chocolate centers of her eyes. "He asked you to do that?" Confusion was evident in her voice.

"No, but doing what he expects means the end of our relationship. I'm not ready to let you go."

She studied him, her brows drawn together while she bit her lower lip. Sadly, a small part of him hoped she'd say his family was worth more. But then she leaned over and kissed him, all doubts were pushed aside.

She pressed against his chest until his back leaned against the couch. Her soft lips made a sensual trail from his mouth to his ear and down his neck. Need jumped through him, his muscles became rigid, blood rushing to his crotch. Andre's breaths staggered when her gentle hands unbuttoned his pants. Her palm, soft and warm, enclosed around him. He pressed his head into the back of the couch and her confident hands massaged him into a frenzy.

The sound of Mikayla's erratic breaths made his dick swell. He loved that she loved touching him. He wanted to return the favor and worship every inch of her body. He moved to get up, but her hand tightened. Slowly, she lowered her body until she came face to face with his need. Wet lips enclosed his swollen lower head, followed by a slow sweep of her tongue along his length. She took him in so deep he touched the back of her throat. A low groan rumbled from his chest. To hell with his family, he chose her, Mikayla Sanders was worth more.

CHAPTER 27

After spending the day with Mikayla, and regrettably watching her leave close to seven that evening, Andre went straight to his dad's mansion. It was better to get this over with in private instead of in front of the entire staff Monday morning at the office. He'd spent so much of his life trying to make C.E.S. successful, he couldn't imagine not working there. Not only because of his loyalty to the family. Over the years, he developed a deep sense of pride in C.E.S.'s success. Together they'd turned C.E.S. into a powerhouse.

If he walked away, for what? Love? The same emotion turned his mother from a self-assured woman to her ex-husband's mistress. He couldn't be that weak. If he left the security of C.E.S. and he and Mikayla didn't work out, he had no idea who he'd be. Or if fighting his dad was really worth this new love, this new sense of morality.

A vision of Mikayla's soft eyes and a beautiful smile flashed through his mind. A sense of peace settled over him, just like he felt whenever she was around. Something he didn't get much of from his job or his family. He had to trust that choosing her was the right decision.

Classical piano music greeted Andre when the butler opened the door. He didn't recognize the man. His dad must have fired the previous one, likely for some minor slight. His determined footsteps echoed on the white marble floors. Andre made his way down the hall lined with portraits of his father and stepmother to the source of the music, Curtis's study.

He didn't knock, but entered and shut the door quietly behind him. Curtis Caldwell sat at his desk, his feet propped up, a Rogaska crystal highball in his hand. Brown liquid nearly filled to the brim. Probably Marnier Cognac, the senior Caldwell's favorite. His eyes were closed, and his lips pressed tightly together and his feet swayed with the surges and regressions of the music.

"What do you want?" His dad asked without opening his eyes. Grabbing the remote he cranked down the music.

Anxiety settled over Andre. This visit wasn't going to go well. Fights with Curtis never did. He crossed the room, the luxurious carpet muffling the sound of his footsteps, but he didn't doubt his dad knew every move he made.

"Isaac called. Your efforts to keep Dalmtrix out of Hartsville have expanded."

"Why shouldn't they?" Curtis took a sip from his glass. "No need to let all our hard work go down the drain, not over some low-income project."

"That project will serve the area well." Andre tried to keep his voice even. "We've already pushed Dalmtrix away—"

"They're still considering locating there. I thought you were working on getting the tree huggers riled up."

Andre gritted his teeth then forced his jaw to relax. "The story was spilled. There wasn't anything else to do." He sat down opposite his dad.

"Oh, there's a hell of a lot more that we can do." Curtis dropped his feet and nailed Andre with a hard stare. "You're just too whipped to do it."

"We can start our gas project without Dalmtrix. You know that. You're just sticking to this plan because you're trying to derail Uncle Philip's project. This infighting has to stop. People other than your brother are affected."

"Like who," Curtis sneered. "That secretary of his you're screwing every weekend."

Andre leaned back in his seat. He held his dad's stare, but his heartbeat increased. "Her name is Mikayla, and yes, I'm referring to her."

"I know good and damn well she's the one pushing this project. Her and your playboy cousin. I'm surprised she hasn't fallen back in bed with him. I guess you're keeping her busy." Curtis indulged in another long sip.

Andre clenched his hands to keep from responding to the insults. "If you know it's her project, then why keep trying to kill it."

"You need me to kill it. What the hell are you thinking sleeping around with her?" Curtis slammed his glass on the table. "Running to Columbia every weekend like a pussy whipped schoolboy." He scowled at Andre.

Andre's anger bubbled inside like lava. "I care about Mikayla. Something I don't expect you to understand, but I hoped you would have enough respect for me to leave her out of this."

His dad scoffed and surged up from his chair. "Enough respect for you. You always were soft. Just like your damn momma."

"If you don't leave this alone I'll quit."

Curtis laughed, then gulped downed the rest of his drink. "No, you won't."

Andre stood. Fist planted firmly on the Brazilian lacquered wood and glared at Curtis. "Yes. I. Will." Each word loaded with the power of his rage.

All humor left his dad's face. Wrath replaced the smug expression, but there was a glimmer of worry in his eyes. "You'd turn your back on family for this girl. You'd actually join my brother's side and work against me."

"I don't want to, but don't push me. I'm invested in C.E.S. just as much as you. I've joined you in the blackmail, the bribes, the outright threats." He pounded the desk with each statement. "All in the name of securing new contracts. I've been with you since I was sixteen and you know I've been loyal. But I'm tired of the way we do business."

"What are you saying? You want to become one of those broke we are the world love everyone business men?" Curtis fluttered his fingers and twisted his lips. "Are you going to build a life with that girl who comes from nothing in your shoddy shack in the country? You'll give up all the comforts and benefits that come with being a Caldwell so that you don't hurt this girl's feelings."

Andre's back stiffened, and he stood straight. "I'll do all of that because I care about her. I've made my own money, and I've got enough saved to get by. I know enough about running a large corporation to get another job. It won't be like last time, I won't come running back just because you jingle the keys to a Porsche in my face."

The doubt in his dad's eyes turned to full blown fear. Like any fearful animal forced into a corner Andre knew Curtis would strike soon. *Time to get the hell out of here.* Andre pivoted on the balls of his feet and walked toward the door.

"You forget, son," Curtis said easily. "I've got just as much dirt on you as you have on me."

Andre whipped around. "I don't plan to use what I know against you."

"Soft! Just as I thought." Curtis stalked around his desk. "I will use everything I know to ruin you. I'll make sure no corporation will take a chance on you. I'll spread rumors of mismanagement and complaints about the way you treated co-workers."

"If you start a mud-slinging war I'll throw so much dirt you and C.E.S. will never recover. You destroying my reputation will equal the end of yours, Isaac's, and the company we worked so hard to build. I learned from the best, so don't test me."

Andre stormed to the door, composed himself and turned back to Curtis. "Dad, find another way to lash out at your brother. Leave Mikayla's project alone. Hurt her, and I swear you'll pay." He slammed the door shut. Adrenaline rushed through his body as if he'd just gone ten rounds with a heavyweight champion. Unease settled heavily in his chest. He knew where his dad would hit next. He only hoped he could block whatever blow Curtis threw towards Mikayla.

CHAPTER 28

"A toast to Caldwell Development's new head of acquisitions." Renee lifted her martini and grinned.

Mikayla pushed aside the empty tapas plates before raising a glass of red wine. "Thank you, even though the rest of the office may not join us in celebrating."

"To hell with Charity York. She's the only one who's jealous of you getting the position. Finally, we're having a girls' night. We have all this good food, good wine, and we're going to have a damn good time." Renee's hand wavered, spilling a splash of the martini while she leaned sideways onto one of the beaded blue silk pillows spread throughout the booth of the wine and tapas bar. "Everyone in the office knows you're great at what you do. I couldn't be happier."

"Not just because I'm your best friend."

"Heck yeah, because you're my best friend," Renee laughed. "But also because you deserve it. Now toast."

Mikayla shook her head and clinked glasses. "You're one in a million, Renee."

"I know that already." A devilish gleam in her eyes, she leaned in close to Mikayla. "What I don't know is how things are going with you and my cousin."

"You don't really want to know."

"Normally I would agree, but considering I haven't had sex in months, and these martinis have severely impaired my judgment I'm going to ask. Are you spending all your time with him because the sex is that good?"

Mikayla giggled, and Renee's eyebrows rose to her hairline.

"Oh my goodness, you're giggling. I don't think I've ever heard you giggle." Renee giggled too.

"I don't...unless it comes to Andre." She sighed and leaned back onto a red pillow. Slowly she swayed to the rhythmic music playing softly through the speakers and thoughts of Andre took hold. "I'm comfortable around him. I would never have expected it, but from the moment he took my hand in the mountains I felt it. We clicked. We talk, we don't talk, we go out, we stay in, my dad likes him, and the sex is amazing."

"You're falling in love," Renee whispered.

"I'm in love," Mikayla said eyes glued to the smooth ceiling. "And I let it slip out."

"What did he say?"

"Something about not knowing how to love, but that maybe I could show him."

Renee sat up. She curled her martini glass against her chest and gave Mikayla a sappy smile. "For him to say that means a lot. That side of my family isn't known for romantic gestures."

"Then you won't believe this." She explained Andre's willingness to step away from the family business.

"Did he say what my uncle has planned?"

"No, but I was so moved that I," her face burned, and she lowered her eyes. Just thinking about her show of thanks made her core constrict, but she wouldn't go into detail about that. "Let's just say I was overcome with emotion and desire." She met Renee's eyes. "Do you think he loves me?"

Renee brows drew together. "Umm let's see, I think he has to be close if he doesn't already. The reason my dad and uncle don't get along stems from some weird sense of broken loyalty. My uncle always demanded that Andre and Isaac stay loyal to him. For Andre to consider stepping away from the family, means he's certifiably crazy about you."

Happiness rose inside her chest like bubbles in champagne. There was hope for the relationship. Hope that he actually loved her and was too afraid to admit his feelings. His actions proved more than words. Still, to hear him say I love you, would mean everything.

"I also met his friend, Jonathan. Very handsome, very flirty, you should meet him."

Renee shook her head and waved a finger. "No, ma'am. I don't have time for matchmaking. Especially with a friend of my cousin."

"He's a nice guy. You shouldn't judge him before you meet him. Besides, you said yourself it's been awhile."

Renee lifted her chin. "That's because I have discerning tastes, not because I can't find a man on my own." Renee slowly lowered her glass to the table, and the smile on her face morphed into a flat line. "I had an ulterior motive for asking about Andre."

"Okay, what?"

"I wanted to be sure that you were completely over Ryan." She held up a hand before Mikayla could interrupt. "I get it. You were never in love with Ryan. My dad and I wanted that more than you, but you must admit it would have been great if you became my sister one day."

Mikayla reached over and squeezed Renee's hand. "I don't need to marry Ryan for me to be your sister."

"Yeah, yeah, still. I don't want the news to hurt you."

"What news?"

Renee pulled her hand back. "Ryan asked Angelica to marry him," she said in a rush. "Dad is going to go ballistic and mom can't stand the woman. He hasn't said anything to them yet because I think they're going to run off to Vegas."

Mikayla shot up in her seat. "No! He can't marry her."

Renee's eyebrows peaked in a steep V. "Why do you care?"

"I shouldn't after what he did, and I don't care, for the reason you think. Angelica confronted me last Friday to say she wanted Andre back. Her marrying Ryan is a way to try and make Andre jealous."

Renee nodded slowly, a thoughtful look on her face. "That could work."

Mikayla picked the olive out of an empty martini glasses and tossed it at her friend. "Didn't you just say he loved me?"

"Sorry, forget that. What are we going to do about Ryan?"

"I'm not going to do anything. It's his problem, and he needs to fix it." Renee's face screwed into a frown, and Mikayla held up a hand. "And don't look at me like that. If I tell him, he's going to think it's because I still care."

"You do still care."

The truth landed in her gut with a heavy thud. She didn't have romantic feelings for Ryan. But knowing how much he cared about Angelica, and how hard it was for him to get over her when she'd broken his heart, nagged the one sympathetic bone she had left for Ryan.

"I don't want to see anyone hurt, but I'm not getting in this. I told you. You're his sister, you say something." She waved, for the server to bring the check.

Renee presented her case like a top notch defense attorney as they left the restaurant and on the cab ride home, but Mikayla held her ground. She refused to get in the middle of Ryan and Angelica's phony relationship.

Andre's Mercedes sat parked in front of her apartment building when she arrived home. Thoughts of Ryan and Angelica drifted from her mind. Mikayla had given him a key the prior week. Mikayla's cheeks ached from her wide grin, she shoved the cash at the driver and jumped out. Andre hadn't said he was coming this weekend, and he knew she was going out with Renee, but it didn't diminish her delight that he'd surprised her.

She struggled to get the key in the lock, and several curse words worked their way out of her mouth. The door flew open.

She sagged with relief when she saw him, and tilted her head. "Hey you."

Andre's broad smile sent warmth dancing under her skin. "Hey you."

They quickly fell into each other's arms. Vaguely, she noticed the door closing, and Andre moved her further into the apartment as they kissed. Breathing in the wonderful mixture of his cologne, her hands, ran across the buttons of his dress shirt. He must have just arrived. Otherwise, he would have taken off the work clothes. Though she had no problem removing them herself.

"You taste like wine," he said against her lips.

"I drank a lot of wine."

He lifted his head and frowned. "Then drove home?"

"I'm not stupid. Renee and I called a cab." She wrapped her arms around his neck and grinned, swaying her body against his.

His erection slowly rose against her stomach. A sexy grin brightened his handsome face. "Good. I'd hate to punish you."

"Ooh, please punish me." She leaned up and sucked on his lower lip.

Andre grabbed her thighs and easily lifted her while Mikayla shrieked and giggled like an adolescent birthday girl wrapping her legs tightly around his waist.

"Just remember, you asked for it."

*

Three hours later Andre sat on the edge of the bed and handed Mikayla a cigarette. She could barely catch her breath, but she didn't turn down the smoke Andre offered.

"I'm glad you came," she said.

"So am I." He leaned down and slowly kissed her. Even after loving his body for several hours the soft glide of his tongue stirred her arousal.

Fire simmered in his dark eyes when he lifted his head. Her body would hate her in the morning, but she looked forward to the promise of more punishment.

"What made you come down?"

He reached for the cigarette. Once he settled himself against her headboard, she flipped over so that her chest rested on his thighs. His large hands gently rubbed her exposed backside, and she had to fight the urge to arch and purr like a kitten.

"I planned to come but didn't say anything after you mentioned going out with Renee. I know you guys haven't spent a lot of time together."

"That's sweet, but I wouldn't have dumped her if I knew you were coming."

He took a draw of the cigarette then grinned. "I know that. I wanted to surprise you."

"I like the surprise." She swung her feet back and forth.

He handed the cigarette to her, then patted her behind with his free hand. "So what did you two talk about? I'm assuming she grilled you about me."

"She did, but not in a bad way." Mikayla's brows knitted together, and she stared at the smoldering tip of the cigarette.

Andre's hand stopped its gentle petting to shake her softly out of her reverie. "What's wrong?"

"Nothing...just," she turned, on her side to face him. "I'm worried about Ryan."

His body tensed beneath her. "You shouldn't be thinking about Ryan."

Andre's icy tone caught her off guard. "I work with him and am best friends with his sister. I can't exactly keep him from ever popping into my mind."

"That convenient excuse again," he nudged her to the side and stood up.

"Are you still upset about that? I'm not quitting my job over some stupid jealousy."

Anger radiated intense waves from his naked body as he towered over the bed. "It's not stupid when my woman says she's worried about another man right after we have sex."

Mikayla rose to her knees. Her movements were jerky when she wrapped the sheet around her body. This would not turn into another argument. With a deep breath, she started over.

"I didn't mean to offend you. I was only trying to explain what happened with Renee. Ryan is going to marry Angelica."

He laughed. Hard. Bent over with his hands on his knees hard.

She expected him to frown, say that was a messed up situation, or at least apologize for jumping to the wrong conclusion.

"Serves both of them right," he said after his mirth dissipated. "Where are they registered, I'll send them a gift."

Mikayla placed the cigarette in the ashtray on the nightstand. "You can't be serious."

"I'm dead serious."

She stepped off the bed and searched for words. "But...she doesn't love him. Doesn't care about him. She admitted she wanted you back."

He threw up a hand as if what she said meant nothing. "She called me with that same bull and I told her never to call back. I don't give a damn what Angelica wants, and if Ryan is dumb enough to marry her then more power to him."

Those words were very familiar. "That was her on the phone last week. Why didn't you tell me?"

"You didn't need to know."

A jolt of pain twisted in her heart like a rusted saw blade. "I didn't need to know. If anyone needed to know, it would be me. Especially after I told you what she said to me."

"Don't be dramatic, Mikayla, it's not your style. Angelica approaching me has nothing to do with you. If something doesn't concern you, I don't mention it."

Her anger soared. "Is this how you view our relationship? That if you decide something doesn't concern me just keep it to yourself. How am I supposed to trust you if you won't share with me."

"I don't need to share with you. I've been more open with you than any other woman." He grabbed the cigarette and pointed at her. "And I drew a line with my dad that I never wanted to draw."

"Yes, over something else you won't tell me about."

Andre's hand stopped halfway to his mouth, and he regarded her through the haze of the smoke. "Because it doesn't matter. All, that matters, is my actions toward you. Don't come to me asking for more because that's not going to happen." He looked away then took a drag. "Be happy with what you get."

That wasn't good enough. "Tell me you love me."

He grimaced then paced angrily to the nightstand and stubbed out the cigarette. "Don't start that."

Her throat constricted, but she had to know. "Actions may speak louder than words, but I need to hear it."

"If you're waiting to hear it then I'm never going to satisfy you."

Tears stung her eyes. She turned away. "I want more than that."

His footsteps came up behind her, and then warm hands clasped her shoulders. "Please," he blew a weighty breath, "give me time."

Her heart weakened, but the part of her that wouldn't settle for second best rose. She shrugged out of his embrace. "Give you time now. And then, what? Put up with it later when you say you can't change."

He rubbed his eyes then groaned. "Mikayla, I told you I'm not good at this." His hand dropped. "I won't be forced into saying something."

"Andre, relationships are about compromise, trust, and mutual respect. If I don't feel confident in this relationship, then it's best to move on."

The cold anger and disappointment that settled over his features sent a chill skittering across her skin.

"Oh, so you don't feel confident in this relationship anymore," Andre bit out.

Not completely. Not when he kept things from her

She crossed her arms over her chest. "I don't know."

His face hardened as he took two steps back. He turned and slid into his underwear. The silence hurt worse than if he'd yelled. Mikayla's heart rammed against her rib cage the sound of her own harsh breaths echoed in her brain. She watched him dress. Not once did he look at her. *Just that quickly and we're through.*

Andre walked out of the bedroom. The front door opened then closed with a resounding thud. She flinched then swiped at the steady flow of tears.

CHAPTER 29

Hair corralled into a ponytail and dressed in an old pair of overalls, Mikayla skipped her hair appointment and went to visit her dad. Doing yard work, he'd staunchly refused her offer to help. But when she showed up and grabbed the weed eater, thankfully he didn't comment. The mindless chore was just what she needed to keep her mind off Andre and the way he walked out.

The burn of her arm muscles and sweat pouring into her eyes seemed to be the perfect distraction.

The weed eater hit the back fence and jerked her arm. She tapped the damn thing on the ground to get more line, but nothing came out. Increasing her efforts, Mikayla hit the trimmer harder and harder her frustration growing.

"You planning to buy me a new one, baby girl," her dad's voice came from behind.

She froze. The urge to throw the stupid machine on the ground and kick it for good measure pummeled with her beating heart. She inhaled a deep breath. *People break up every day and survive. I will too.*

Pasting what she hoped was a smile on her face, her stiff facial muscles protested the attempt at the illusion of happiness.

"Sorry, I was trying to get more string."

Her dad took the weed eater and flipped the contraption examining its head. "Beating it won't make more come. The roll is out." He grinned and turned it back to face her.

Great, she was a failure at relationships and weed eating too. Her lips trembled and then the tears spilled. The panicked expression on her dad's face made her turn and wipe them away with the back of the rough work gloves she wore. *Get yourself together.*

"I'll grab the rake and start gathering up these clippings." She tried to walk around her dad, but he placed a gentle hand on her elbow.

The concern in his eyes nearly made the tears return. "What's wrong,

Mikayla."

"Nothing I can't survive."

"Trouble with you and Andre?"

She looked towards the sky, pulled off a glove and used her thumb to wipe the remaining tears. "Andre and I are over."

"Since when?"

The frantic look on his face was almost comical. Her dad's usual response after she broke up with someone: *"Oh, well, better for you anyway."*

"Since last night." She grabbed the weed eater back from him and headed for the shed.

Her dad followed. "What happened?"

"We're on different levels. We want different things. So I did what you taught me, move on instead of staying with a guy who's not right for me."

She put the weed eater on the shelf and took down the rake. When she turned, her dad was leaning against his truck and staring at her as if she'd just said unicorns played on his Pop Warner team.

"He's perfect for you."

Mikayla had to fight to keep her jaw from dropping. "Just because he knows about cars and can fix stuff with you over a few beers doesn't mean he's perfect for me."

"I know that."

"Then what makes him perfect for me, dad? The man likes to keep things from me. He has no compassion when it comes to other people. And has told me to forget him ever saying he loves me. That sounds like the perfect guy."

Her dad sat on a stool blocking Mikayla's escape route by pushing the matching stool her way. "Time to talk." His tone said Coach Daddy was on the job.

Sitting she held the rake between her legs and pushed the handle from one hand to the other, instead of meeting her dad's stare.

"Tell me what happened."

"I thought we agreed to keep conversations about what happens in my bedroom out of our relationship."

He grabbed the rake with one hand. When she met his glare, Mikayla groaned, not ready to deal with that no-nonsense live-under-my-roof-you'll-do-as-I-say look from her teen years.

"What happened?"

She pulled on the rake, and he let go but crossed thick arms over his chest. Quickly she went over the highlights of what happened the night before. Putting extra emphasis on the fact of how easily Andre walked out. Her dad listened silently and rubbed his chin a thoughtful expression on his face.

"I know I raised you to know how men think, but I guess I didn't do a good job of explaining the complexities of a man."

She frowned. "What are you talking about?"

Her dad grunted and leaned backward until he was resting against the side of the truck. "Yes, for the most part, men are simple. We know what we want and go after it. We say what we feel and leave out all the fluff. But that's on the outside, inside there's a lot more complicated stuff going on."

"I don't understand."

"From what I've learned about Andre I can tell he's old school and pretty straightforward. Not prone to big romantic gestures, but he'll show you how he feels. I'll start with the situation with his family. Regardless of what it is, he obviously felt strongly enough about not wanting it to hurt you to go against them. There are a lot of things a man will do for a woman he cares about, but picking a fight with his family isn't one he'll go into lightly."

She hit the floor with the rake. "Then why won't he tell me what they're planning?"

"No man wants to see his woman hurt. Just telling you would more than likely upset you."

"How do you know that?"

"I've been there." A nostalgic smile creased his face. "Your uncle Tommy never liked your mom's cooking. I made excuses for him, but eventually she asked. Like a fool, I told her. She tried to play it off, but her feelings were hurt. She never said anything to my brother, but I noticed that her actions around him were different. To this day, I wish I'd just left well enough alone. The same thing goes with you and Andre. You'll look at his family differently. Maybe even look at him differently. He wants you to know he's willing to fight them for you but wants to protect you from the hurt that'll come from knowing what they're capable of."

Mikayla studied the dirty floor. That made sense, she got it, but she wasn't some weak person who couldn't handle the truth. He never said his family did anything illegal, but he never said they didn't. The one thing, he did say, was that his dad demanded loyalty. Going against his father must have cost Andre a lot.

Evan leaned forward and rested his elbows on his knees. "Now on to Ryan and that Angelica woman. Yes, he should have let you know she was calling."

Mikayla's head snapped up, but her dad held up his hands to prevent her from interrupting. "But it's the same thing. Does knowing she wants him back make you feel any better? Especially knowing she's calling." She shook her head, and he continued. "Never let another person get in the middle of your relationship. If you want to be a friend to Ryan and let him know what Angelica is doing, fine. But you've got to consider the drama that comes when you put yourself in someone else's situation."

She twirled the rake's handle. "It seems wrong to say nothing."

"You did the right thing telling his sister. You may be close to the Caldwell's and they like pretending as if you're part of their clan, but remember that you aren't. Leave it to Renee to warn him."

"Okay, but that doesn't change the fact that Andre doesn't love me."

"Obviously the man cares a lot about you. He's not going to say the words because you forced him. I got that the first day I met him. I want you to find love like your mom, and I had. I told her I loved her three times. The day I realized it, the day we got married and the day you were born. I wish I'd said it more, but she knew how I felt."

"How can you be sure?"

"I showed her every day." A smile came across her dad's rugged face. "She'd say she loved me, I'd squeeze her shoulder and she'd grin and say 'yeah, I know.' Do you know that I love you?"

"Of course."

Evan raised both brows. "When was the last time I said it?"

"At the sports bar," she said with a raised brow.

Her dad narrowed his eyes. "Not after an argument."

The day she graduated from college. After the commencement, when she was celebrating with Brenden. He'd walked over and pulled her into his arms then whispered the words right before telling her to go out and have a good time.

"Point taken," she said.

"I'm not saying to take him back. If you're not happy then you're better off without him. I never want you to settle for a guy who treats you bad, or makes you feel less than what you're worth."

"Just think about what I said." He stood and placed a hand on her shoulder. "And, Mikayla, I love you." His pat was awkward, but it warmed her heart.

He took the rake and left the shed. Uncertainty weighed heavily on her heart. *Should I call him or not?* Admit she was wrong, and accept the relationship he could offer or move on and wait for someone else. Another guy who made her feel as comfortable in her skin, and didn't mind that she had a bit of a tomboy inside. One that set her body on fire whenever she heard his voice and didn't expect her to be someone she wasn't.

She hurried out of the shed. Inside the house, Mikayla pulled her cell phone out of her purse. Before she could think about her actions, she sent Andre a text. Calling and having him hang up was far too scary.

*

Andre stared at Mikayla's text. I'm sorry.

Immediately he wanted to text back with the same. This simple fact made him angry at himself.

He stared out the balcony window. The cool glass brought memories of her first night in the condo. Then came the desire to have her there again.

"Shit!" He swung around and grabbed the highball glass on the coffee table and raised the midday cocktail to his lips. Ice and the vestiges of rum and coke hit his lips. He headed to the kitchen, to make another. He poured the rum then slammed the bottle on the counter.

Why does she still care about Ryan? Didn't she know how much Andre risked going against his family and still Mikayla's concern was for Ryan. Not a thought of Andre going against his family for her. All she cared about was her punk of an ex-boyfriend possibly getting hurt.

Adding the cola, he took a sip. Time to move on. Time to forget her. His chest tightened along with his grip on the glass.

His phone chimed like a bell. It was the tone he'd set for her text messages. Light, happy, just like Mikayla. He wanted to ignore the sound, but the damn emotions she'd ignited in him, drug his feet across the floor to the phone.

I love you.

The tightness in his chest loosened. Her words excited and scared the hell out of him. They sat in the back of his throat like a dry piece of bread. Too tough to swallow to uncomfortable to cough up.

He called her back. She answered on the second ring.

"Hey you." Her voice trembled.

Hearing Mikayla eliminated the tension in his chest. "What are you doing?"

"Cutting grass at my dad's house." She exhaled heavily. "He asked about you."

"What did you say?"

"That we were through."

He knew that when he walked out on her, but the words still hurt. He wasn't through with her. Didn't honestly know if he'd ever be through with her.

Andre brought the glass to his lips for another fortifying sip. "Are we?"

"I don't want us to be."

He sank onto his couch. "Neither do I. But I can't do this with someone else in our relationship."

"He's not. But I know what you're saying. I'm staying out of Ryan's relationship. Renee knows, and it's up to her to tell him. But if you want Ryan out of our relationship then the same goes for Angelica. What if she was the one to let me know she called instead of you? She's already laid her cards on the table. If you don't do the same, then it's easier for her to come between us."

The truth of her words settled heavily in his chest. He pinched the bridge of his nose. "She can't come between us."

"If we aren't on the same page then she can."

"What about the other reason you kicked me out?"

"Excuse me? I didn't kick you out. You left without saying a word."

"There wasn't more to say."

"Yes, there was...is." She whispered.

Time to cough up the words. Say what he felt and move forward. The words remained lodged in his throat.

He pictured her after a day of cutting grass, dirty and sweaty. Probably annoyed that her hair was getting messed up, but helping anyway because she loved her dad. Mikayla was willing to make that small sacrifice for her father. Andre sacrificed all his life for the loyalty of his family. Deserted his mom when she needed him. Supported his dad's decisions even when they made him feel sleazy. All people he loved, but only knew how to show it in equally fucked up ways. Why couldn't he sacrifice for someone who'd only made him feel good?

His heart raced, and he rubbed a sweaty palm over jeans. "I love you, too." He blurted, pushing aside the feeling of sinking into a hole, he couldn't escape.

"Where are you?" The smile in her voice brought a cheesy grin to his face.

"Back home. I have some work I need to do."

"Oh." Her voice shrank to nearly nothing.

Longing burrowed deep in his bones. "Take Friday off. Let's go out of town."

"Where did that come from?"

"I've seen you wrapped up on a mountain, dressed for work, dressed casually, and in all your naked glory, but I haven't seen you in a bikini."

"It's March, that's too cold for a bikini, even in South Carolina."

He stood and paced back and forth across his living room. "Then we'll spend the weekend in Miami, at my family's beach house."

"That's too much."

"It's not. Tell your bosses that I said you can't work on Friday. We'll fly out Thursday night spend all weekend there. How does that sound?"

"Sounds perfect...and like I won't see you until Thursday."

"Believe me, it'll be worth it."

CHAPTER 30

Mikayla knocked and waited for the okay before entering Philip's office on Monday morning. She entered the office and paused at the sight of Philip, Renee, and Ryan sitting around the small conference table in the corner. Philip wore a fierce frown. Renee appeared thankful for the interruption, and Ryan's features twisted with frustration.

"I can come back later," she reached for the door knob.

Philip pushed away from the chair and stalked to the fully stocked bar. "No, come on in. Maybe you can talk some sense into Ryan." He jerked the decanter of brandy off the top shelf and poured the brown liquor into a highball glass.

She glanced at Renee, who nodded. Great. Right after promising to stay out of the mess, she walked smack dab into the middle of the storm.

"I think I should come back later."

She turned, but Philip's voice stopped her. "No, you ought to hear this."

Mikayla shot Renee a please save me look. "Really, I shouldn't."

Renee shrugged her shoulders, and Philip kept talking. "Ryan's gotten it in his head that he should marry Angelica. That isn't the worst of it, for some reason he's figured he doesn't need a prenuptial agreement."

Her eyes flew to Ryan. "You can't be serious."

Ryan sprang up from the chair. "I trust Angelica."

Renee spun her chair around and watched Ryan pace back and forth across the room. "Why, because she screwed you in a closet."

"Why is it so hard to believe we're in love?" Ryan asked.

Philip slammed the highball glass on the bar, sloshing liquor over the polished surface. "I don't give a damn if you love her. You are not giving that gold digger the legal right to spend all your money, divorce you, then suck in alimony payments for years."

"We're not going to get a divorce. This is our second chance."

Mikayla lowered her eyes to the floor. The sincerity and hope in Ryan's voice shot daggers of guilt through her. She tried calling on her anger from the mountains in an effort to prove she didn't owe Ryan anything. But the outrage didn't surface.

"Ryan, you need a prenup. Angelica isn't what she seems," Renee said.

"And how do you know that? You won't spend any time with her. Mom won't give her a chance. I know our reuniting came at a bad time, but you can't hold the closet fiasco against her forever. We're getting married."

"She doesn't want you," Renee shot back.

"I can't be your man forever, Renee. Get off your high horse and find a man, and then maybe you won't be so jealous of me."

Mikayla sucked in a breath. She, Ryan and Renee privately joked Renee's love life was so dismal Ryan would forever be her date. Though the three of them all laughed about Renee's picky taste in men, they both knew, behind Renee's beautiful exterior, there was a real fear she'd end up alone.

"Don't talk to your sister like that," Philip said.

"It's true. She's lonely, and that's why she's against me marrying Angelica. She doesn't want to lose her twin."

Renee slowly stood. She raised her chin and glared at Ryan. "I've already lost him. You have my blessing to marry her. I hope you get everything you deserve." Renee stalked to the door. Mikayla placed her hand on Renee's arm, but Renee just patted Mikayla's hand before stomping out.

She spun to face Ryan. "That was unfair."

"No, it's the truth and it's time we stopped coddling her." Ryan crossed his arms. "Let me guess, you're going to tell me why I shouldn't marry Angelica as well."

"That's none of my business." She looked at Philip. "I'm sorry for interrupting. I can come back later."

"Is something wrong?" Philip asked.

"No, I'd like to take Friday off. If that's not a problem."

Ryan stepped into her line of vision. "Why do you need Friday off?"

"That's none of your business," Mikayla shot Ryan an angry glare.

Ryan crossed his arms and frowned. "You're still with him aren't you?" He sounded more concerned than angry. "Do you know he's only using you?"

Her fists clenched, but she reined in her anger. She would not get into this with Ryan. Andre was right, they didn't belong in the middle of the Ryan and Angelica drama. "I could say the same for Angelica."

Philip walked over. "Wait, you're still seeing Andre. Have you both lost your minds?"

Mikayla turned to Philip and fired off a frigid stare. "With all due respect, Mr. Caldwell, you have no right to comment on my personal life." His hurt expression diminished her anger. "I am truly appreciative of everything you've done for me, but I have to draw the line somewhere."

"Take Friday off," he said in a disgusted voice. Then turned hard eyes to

Ryan. "But you are not marrying that woman."

Ryan's chest puffed out, his eyes narrowed to slits.

Time to go. Mikayla hurried out the door. On the other side of the door, Mikayla bumped head-on into Charity.

Mikayla raised a brow. "Eavesdropping?"

Charity's lips twisted, and she stared down her nose. "You're really making your way around the family. Aren't you? Didn't work out with Ryan, so you moved on to his cousin."

Mikayla moved left to step aside, but Charity blocked her path.

"I don't have time for this." Mikayla pushed Charity out of the way. Remorse swelled in her chest. Now *I'm behaving like a juvenile.* Toxic. The only way to describe this office. She needed a new job otherwise the atmosphere would poison her further.

*

Andre and Isaac were discussing the new proposal in Kansas City when the door to Andre's office opened. Andre turned to remind whoever was interrupting them he wasn't to be disturbed, but froze when his dad strolled through the door. Today was the first time Curtis had come into his office since Andre confronted him at his house. Since then, they'd operated under business as usual, but Andre's tension only increased with each passing day. Nobody threatened Curtis Caldwell and walked away unscathed.

"Discussing the Kansas proposal?" Curtis asked. He walked casually over to the table and pushed the papers around on the surface.

"Yes, I think we have a good chance of winning the bid," Isaac replied.

Andre guessed his brother knew about the fight he'd had with their dad, but he doubted Curtis went so far as to reveal how bad.

"Great, that'll be more money in the coffers. C.E.S. will continue to grow and prosper, making all of us rich men."

"We're already rich men," Isaac said.

Curtis dropped the paper in his hand and stared at Andre. "That we are son. But you can't get complacent. Some people get comfortable and think their wealth will always be there. There are no guarantees in life. The only guarantee is if you work hard you'll be successful."

Andre turned in his chair and leaned back. "And throw in a little blackmail."

Curtis's dark eyes hardened. "I do what's necessary to ensure success. It's not always pretty, but the strong survive, and the weak wither."

"I've always supported you and this family. I want C.E.S. to survive as much, if not more than you do."

"No, you don't. You're willing to toss everything I worked for aside because of the sweetness you've found between a woman's thighs."

Isaac spun to Andre. "What's he talking about?"

Curtis's thin lips rose with a dirty grin, and he turned to Andre. "You haven't told your brother you're willing to bring down the entire family business because you're sleeping with Ryan's leftovers?"

"It's not like that."

Isaac sat forward in his chair. "Then what's it like? Because it sounds like I'm being left out of some important discussions."

Curtis pointed at Andre. "Your brother here wants us to forget the fact that Dalmtrix may move to the low country after all."

"I know, and I agree," Isaac said. "We've found an alternate landfill in Virginia that's a perfect fit for C.E.S.'s expansion into landfill gas."

"But you know it's more than that," Curtis said with a vengeance. "It's about putting my brother in his place. They think they're better than us. Ruining their new development deal proves we have the upper hand."

"Do you hear yourself?" Andre bolted from his chair. "This rivalry is stupid, it's old, and it's time for the nonsense to end. You want to prove you're better than Philip. Then live your life and make C.E.S. successful. Hell, you've already proven you're more than a garbage man. Forget this competition and move on."

"He's right dad," Isaac said quietly.

Andre wanted to collapse with relief, and surprise, when Isaac agreed with him. Andre guessed Isaac was as tired of the rivalry as he. Although Andre also knew anything that distracted their dad from the true purpose of growing C.E.S., would annoy Isaac.

Curtis pointed a finger at his oldest son. "So are you ready to walk away from me, too?"

Andre slapped the back of one hand into the palm of the other. "It's not about walking away. It's about focusing on what's important, and C.E.S. is important. Not fighting with our cousins."

Curtis's eyes narrowed to razor sharp slits. "Your brother threatened to report all of our not so savory dealings to the authorities."

Isaac stood. "Tell me that's a lie, Andre."

"I said I'd leave the company if he kept pursuing this. My threat came after he threatened to blackball me."

"Regardless," Isaac said. "You're willing to compromise everyone. For what?"

"That's what I said. He's lost his mind." Curtis cut in.

Ignoring his dad, Andre turned to his brother. "Would you stand back and let him smear my name?"

"See," Curtis yelled. "That woman's already tearing this family apart. Is this woman worth it?"

Andre frowned at his dad then his brother. Wondered how he ended up in this position. When he'd issued his threat, he'd barely considered the effect on Isaac. Or the hundreds of people employed by C.E.S.

"I won't tear down the company or betray my family," Andre said.

"Your secrets are safe with me."

Isaac's shoulders relaxed. A calculating gleam lit Curtis's eyes.

"But my promise hasn't changed," Curtis said. "You chose this woman over the family and I will make sure you never work again."

Isaac shook his head. "Dad—"

"No!" Curtis pointed at Andre. "You're either with us or against us. You decide."

Curtis strolled out of Andre's office as if he hadn't threatened his son.

Frustration itched along Andre's body and grew until he thought he would tear off his skin. With one angry sweep, he knocked all of the papers off the table.

"Whoa, calm down!" Isaac raised his hands.

"I'm sick of playing his games."

"You and me both, but he's our dad. He built this company for us. It's shocking to know you'd suddenly give that up for some woman."

"It's more than that…"

"I don't care what it is. It's not worth it," Isaac said. "Family is more important. The business is important. This woman isn't."

Isaac's face, full of confusion and disappointment brought home the degree to which his father and brother refused to comprehend what Andre felt for Mikayla. Which meant eventually, he would have to make the choice between love and loyalty.

CHAPTER 31

By Thursday afternoon, Mikayla wished the plane to Miami was waiting for her right outside of the office. Bags packed and in the backseat of her car, she hurried out of the office without saying goodbye. She planned to meet Andre at the Columbia Owens Airport where his private jet waited.

The tension in the office during the week was thicker than congealed bacon fat. Renee was angry at Ryan. Ryan was angry at everyone. And Philip's frustration with his family came through in every conversation. The dynamite on the bomb came when Mikayla learned Charity had filed a complaint claiming she'd been attacked by Mikayla.

All the tension from the week evaporated when she spotted Andre leaning lazily against his car. He wore a denim shirt that clung to his broad shoulders and khaki cargo shorts. His enticing lips spread with an effortless sexy smile that sent her heart into overdrive. She barely shifted the car into park before jumping out.

He strolled over and wrapped her into a warm hug before sliding his delicious lips over hers for a deep soul-stirring kiss. Everything that happened over the week no longer mattered. All that mattered was the upcoming weekend with the man who loved her.

"Hey you," Even after breaking off the kiss his sensual baritone turned her insides to mush and skin to prickly gooseflesh.

Her face ached from the big goofy grin she wore. "Hey you."

"Ready for the weekend?"

"More than you know."

He frowned, "Bad week?" Andre motioned two attendants over that she hadn't noticed before.

Mikayla handed her keys to Andre, and he popped open the trunk. The attendants approached and retrieved the bags.

"I don't want to talk about it." She rolled her eyes and pushed her bangs out of her face. "How was yours?"

A shadow crossed his face. She reached up and ran a hand across his

175

cheek. "Forget it. This weekend isn't about work."

He smiled. "Then let's get to it."

*

Mikayla gasped at the spectacular view of the ocean from the spacious open-air living room of Andre's home in Miami. She hurried across the brightly tiled living room floor to the large patio and pool. A lush wall of palm trees encased the outdoor space.

"The view is beautiful."

He wrapped her hand in his and kissed the back. "I'm glad you approve."

"Approve." She turned back to face him with a smile. "I love it."

"Enjoy the ocean now because I'm not sure if you'll see a lot of it."

"Why is that?"

He slowly pulled her back into the living room. Desire brightened his dark eyes and sent heat skimming across her skin.

"Because I may want to keep you in the bedroom all day."

She wrapped her arms around his trim waist. A gentle breeze mingled his cologne with the scent of the ocean.

"I may let you."

He swept her up into his arms. She shrieked then giggled. When his warm lips kissed along the column of her throat, her laughter turned into a low moan. The awesome view forgotten, he carried her up the stairs to the bedroom.

*

Finally, on Saturday afternoon Mikayla convinced Andre to leave the bedroom. They'd agreed to try and break their habit of smoking after sex and, as a result, had sweated off numerous nicotine patches. Spending hours in bed with him was wonderful, but she didn't want to miss the opportunity to swim in the pool.

"You know you'll have plenty of time to come back and swim." Andre grumbled as they walked down the stairs.

"I don't know. You may not invite me here again."

"Hmm, and I was thinking of bringing you here every weekend."

She grinned at him over her shoulder and caught his eyes assessing her backside in the new dark green bikini. The bikini that delayed the pool trip by forty minutes. The bikini that he'd stripped from her body in less than a minute.

"Let me guess, so you can see me in a bikini more often."

They walked through the living area onto the sunny lanai. One of the housekeepers smiled at them and placed a tray with chilled champagne and strawberries on a table between the lounge chairs near the pool.

"That would be another perk." He picked up a glass and handed one to her. "But that's not the reason. Since we'll be together for a while, it would

176

be nice to get away more often."

"A while...How long is a while?" She took a sip of the champagne. The bubbles tickled the inside of her mouth.

His face became serious. "A while. Indefinitely. Far into the foreseeable future."

Time stood still before erupting in a sputtering of her heart and a rush of happiness. "That sounds a lot like forever."

He tilted his head and gave her a teasing, puzzled look. "It does. Doesn't it?"

"Don't tease me like this, because right now I want forever with you." Her breath stuck in her throat after she blurted her feelings out. The guy just admitted, with great difficulty that he loved her and now she hinted at a lifetime together.

He didn't smile, there was no teasing glint in his eye, and instead his eyes locked into an intense almost determined stare. "I'm sacrificing to make this work, so we can't be for a fleeting moment. We have to be for the long haul."

Screw the pool. Mikayla wrapped her arms around him so quickly he stumbled. He easily steadied himself then returned her kiss with full fervor. Her hand snuck past the waistband of his swim trunks to grasp the stiffness of his erection. Once again, he lifted her and headed back inside toward the stairs.

*

Andre watched Mikayla swim across the pool. Tomorrow they would go home and this fantastic weekend would be a memory swallowed up by the crap that came with being a Caldwell. He and his brother were leaving for Kansas City then Dallas on Monday. A last minute trip that would take him away from Mikayla and put his focus back on C.E.S., something he'd neglected in the past two months.

That's why he'd needed her to understand where his feelings were. That he wanted to make the relationship last.

Her head, covered by the ugliest green swim cap he'd ever seen, popped out of the water. She blinked several times before opening her eyes and grinning. Who was he kidding? She could wear a hat made out of old banana peels and still look beautiful.

"Aren't you going to get in?"

He spread his legs and rested his elbows on his knees. The tops of her breasts floated on the surface, their soft swaying stirring desire through his groin. "If I get in, it won't be to swim."

"You'd have to catch me first."

In a flash, he sprang up from the chair and dove into the pool. The water muffled her delighted shriek and she scrambled to swim away. He caught her quickly and pulled her above the surface.

"You could have warned me you're faster than a submarine." She said breathlessly.

"Then you wouldn't have dared me to catch you." They were in the five-foot section, and he wrapped an arm around her waist and walked her to the side of the pool. The drops of water on her skin sparkled like diamonds in the afternoon sun. He lowered his head and kissed them away from her chocolate shoulders.

"This weekend was perfect. I don't want to go home."

He lifted his head. There was something more than just regret about returning to work. "What's going on?"

"I don't want to talk about it."

His need to protect, find out who or what threatened the smile on his woman's face reared up. "Is there anything I can do?"

Water slapped against his chest, and she readjusted her arms around his shoulders. "No. It's normal work stuff. That's all."

The look in her eyes said there was more. He pushed aside his annoyance she wouldn't confide in him. He'd laid down the ground rule that if it didn't concern her he wouldn't bring it up. There was no doubt she'd call him on his own rule if he insisted she spill her guts.

He pulled her back to the middle of the pool. Kissed her and let his hands ease away the strings holding together the back of her bikini. She grinned and responded by pulling on the waistband of his trunks. All the encouragement he needed to make love to her in the pool. But beneath his desire he couldn't shake the feeling he'd missed something by not being able to hear everything going on in her head.

*

"Ready to go?"

"Not really," Mikayla said with a sad smile. "But, I might as well be."

Andre gave her a knowing look before handing her bag to the waiting limo driver. He turned back to her. "I'm going to do one last check of the room before we go."

"I never knew you were this OCD."

He laughed. "You've got a long time to learn everything about me." He turned and took the stairs two at a time.

Mikayla watched him go with what had to be the widest *I'm in love* grin on her face. She'd never been this happy. With Brenden, the love had come easily. They'd both been excited about their relationship, ending college and taking the next step. But the deep, overwhelming, hot burning feelings that were invoked when she thought of Andre made her relationship with Brenden seem like a high school crush.

Her cell phone rang. She pulled it out of her purse and Renee's number flashed across the screen.

"He did it." Came her friend's frantic greeting. "That fool ran off to

Vegas with that tramp."

Mikayla turned to check for Andre. There was no sign of him. Still she walked out the front door.

"That's his mistake to make. Plus you gave him your blessing."

"That was given in a fit of anger. He had no right to go there with me."

Mikayla could imagine Renee pacing across the room. When riled up, she couldn't keep still to save her life.

"I agree, but you said it yourself. Your brother can be an ass."

"He's still my brother, and I do care about him. Mikayla, I can't let him marry her. She's going to break his heart, again. You remember, Ryan was broken when he returned from Paris. How's he going to handle it when she's back with Andre?"

"Hey! She's not going back to Andre."

"Well, if not him then someone else. What are we going to do?" Renee's apologetic tone didn't alleviate Mikayla's annoyance.

"I'm not doing a damn thing," Mikayla said. She tried to push back the anger. Tried not to let her friend's flippant dismissal of her relationship with Andre bother her. But it hurt with the pain of a mutant bee sting.

"You should have told him instead of hinting around. It's not my place. I'm out of this."

"Mikayla, I'm sorry. I shouldn't have said that. You love Andre, and I made a promise to be nice. And after everything you've said, he has to care about you. Old habits die hard. But, please, you've got to understand this is driving me crazy. Ryan is making a terrible mistake."

"I can't help you, Renee. The moment Ryan stepped in that closet, he relieved me of all responsibility toward him." Andre opened the front door and stepped out. He saw her on the phone and frowned. "Look, Renee, I've got to go. I'll be home soon. We'll talk later."

She ended the call and slipped it back in her purse. He glanced at her purse then met her eyes.

"Everything okay?"

She nodded and gave him a tight smile. "Mmmhmm. Ready?"

His lips pressed together while he slowly tapped his phone against his hand. Questioning eyes bore into her, and she knew he waited for her to elaborate. Unable to take the scrutiny, she turned and strolled down the stairs to the limo. Mikayla wasn't about to ruin a perfect weekend by mentioning why Renee had called.

Several seconds later, she heard his sigh before he came down the steps. The driver opened the door for them, and they slipped into the back of the limo.

CHAPTER 32

"Mikayla, come to my office." Philip Caldwell gave the order and turned away taking long strides down the hall to his office.

Instead of dropping her purse to the floor and letting out a frustrated sigh, she gritted her teeth and followed. Easing into the week with a cup of coffee and the memories of her weekend in Miami with Andre was out of the question.

Philip sat behind his desk and motioned for her to sit across from him. She set her purse on the back of the chair and sat on the edge.

"Before you get started," she said. "Renee called yesterday and told me about Ryan. My position hasn't changed. I won't get involved."

Philip held up a hand. "Though I think you and Renee could have talked him out of being so foolish. That's not the reason I called you in here. It's about Charity."

"What about her?"

"She's threatened to sue the company if we don't take disciplinary action against you."

Mikayla slid back in the seat. She blinked several times as her mind tried to comprehend what she'd just heard. "You can't be serious. She was blocking my way out of the office. She refused to let me pass."

"That's not the story she's telling. I believe you, but she's spoken to a lawyer." Philip pinched the bridge of his wide nose. When he met her eyes, his were full of remorse. "She's documented instances of our family showing favoritism to you. And gone so far as to say we encouraged you to prostitute yourself to Ryan in order to secure your promotion."

Don't sell yourself to Ryan Caldwell to get what you want. Her dad's voice rang through her head.

"I didn't."

"I know that, but she's serious about filing suit. She must have been planning this for a while. She's gathered evidence and even taken statements from other employees."

Which explained Charity's frequent break room gossip session with coworkers.

"What are you going to do?"

"If we don't fire you, she's going to the media with this story."

Years of trying to hide her discomfort crumbled. Her hands shook, and her jaw dropped. *My apartment. My car payment. My bills.* She had some savings, but not nearly enough to cover expenses for more than a few months.

"Are you firing me?"

"No. I would never go against you. You're Renee's best friend and after what Ryan did to you," Philip shook his head. "I pushed you two together. You were the first woman who held his attention after Paris. I shouldn't have been so obvious in my approval of his attraction."

"You couldn't talk me into doing something I didn't want to." She'd been so focused on living the perfect life, she'd thought her and Ryan together was a good idea.

"We can trade blame all day. Despite Charity's accusations, you received the promotion because of your work."

"I almost cost us millions in Hartsville."

"But you worked out a solution. Did you ever find the blackmailer?"

Mikayla shook her head. "Apparently no one knows anything. After things had begun to work out, I let it go."

Philip nodded. "I've got to do something to pacify Charity. As much as I hate dealing with people like her, if she goes to the press with her lies the bad publicity could ruin other deals we have under negotiation."

"Then what are you going to do?"

Philip glanced away, the first time she'd ever seen him appear hesitant. "I'm making Charity deputy director of acquisitions and increasing her pay."

Mikayla's spine stiffened. She sat up. "By how much?"

"I'd rather not disclose her salary."

Meaning, she'd make the same as Mikayla if not more. Then hold this threat over the family's head every time she disagreed with Mikayla on anything. Work would become a living hell instead of the joy it once was.

Mikayla clenched the arms of the chair. She wanted to lash out, demand Philip fight back. Or go find Charity and show her a real shove. But Mikayla understood what had to happen. Philip and his family were pillars of the community. This scandal would tarnish that reputation and leave a dark cloud over the company name.

Slowly she pried her fingers from their death grip on the chair. Her heart went from a fast, angry pace, to a slow, reluctant thud. "You'll have my resignation by the end of the day."

Philip's jaw dropped. The shock in his eyes provided comfort in knowing he hadn't expected her to resign.

"You can't quit."

"You and I both know it's easier to pay Charity off than fire her. I also can't work with Charity after this. I care about Caldwell Development and its reputation. I won't let my lack of judgment jeopardize the company."

"That's not necessary."

Mikayla stood. "Yes, it is." She picked up her purse and calmly placed the strap on her shoulder. She tried to appear rational when inside her emotions threatened to explode. She didn't know what she would do. There were no other job prospects. Her resume hadn't been updated in years. Tears burned her eyes, and her throat tightened.

No. She would not break down. She would get through this.

"If you think about it," she said, defeat wrapped around her words. "You'll realize I'm right."

She turned and hurried out of the office. There was nothing left to say.

Renee stood just outside of her office door. One look at Mikayla and Renee's smile mangled into a frown. "Are you okay?"

"I quit."

"What are you talking about? Is it because of Ryan?"

Mikayla shook her head. "For once, this has absolutely nothing to do with your brother or your cousin." The tears she fought ratcheted up the burn factor. "I'll call you later, okay." She rushed around Renee and down the hall. *I have to get out before I make a fool of myself.*

On the way to the car, Mikayla pulled out her phone to call Andre but ended the connection before the second ring. He would be on his way to Kansas City right now. No need to burden him with her problems while he tried to get a new contract. Plus, there wasn't much he could do to help. Though right now, having his shoulder to literally lean on wouldn't be so bad.

She stopped for a six-pack of strawberry ale, a large bag of cheddar and sour cream potato chips, and a pack of gummy bears. Being forced to resign from your job was a good enough reason to eat horribly. Her eyes strayed to the cigarettes behind the counter, and she purchased a pack of those too.

Mikayla changed into yoga pants, and a tank top then parked her behind on the couch. She stared at the ceiling with one hand in the chip bag and the other holding a cigarette. The situation required a plan of action. Finding a new job was at the forefront, but her body was numb from shock, discouragement, and anger. Everything she had worked for gone.

This was her fault. One irrational moment and Charity took the opportunity to go after what she'd wanted. Things never turned out the way they should when she spontaneously reacted.

Andre was the only anomaly. She popped another chip in her mouth and hoped their relationship didn't end in disaster as well.

She would look for, and find, another job.

Tomorrow.

Her cell phone rang as she reached for the bag of gummy bears.

"Hi, Renee."

"Hi, Renee. That's how you're answering the phone after my dad just made the biggest mistake of his life letting you walk out the door."

Despite the seriousness in Renee's voice, Mikayla laughed. "It's not the biggest mistake in his life. If you calm down and look at things rationally, you'll realize my leaving is for the best."

"What are you going to do, Mikayla?"

Mikayla took a long drag on the cigarette. Like one of Pavlov's dogs, the sensation stimulated her a craving for Andre.

"I'll figure it out. People lose jobs every day and survive. I will too."

"I don't understand how you can remain so calm when things go crazy. I'd be screaming about the unfairness of it all."

Mikayla glanced at the half eaten bag of chips and the smoldering cigarette in her hand. She grabbed another gummy bear and popped it in her mouth. If Renee could see her, she wouldn't think she was handling the situation very well.

"Then I'd have a sore throat and no job."

Renee sighed. "Between you not being here anymore, and Ryan running off with that woman, things couldn't be worse. Do you want me to come over?"

Mikayla's phone beeped. Andre was calling her back. "No, I'm just going to decompress then start the job search. Look I'll call you later, okay."

"Do that, or I'll come by after work. We'll figure this out."

Renee's concern brought a smile to her face. "Thanks. Talk to you soon." She switched the call over. "Hey you."

"Hey you. Sorry, I missed your call earlier. The plane was landing. Isaac and I are getting ready to get in the car." There were muffled voices in the background.

"No, biggie. I just wanted to hear your voice."

"Is everything okay?" Concern filled his voice.

"Yes. I quit my job today, but it's no big deal. I can find another job." Her attempt at breezy just sounded nervous.

"You quit!" He snapped. "What happened? Did Ryan do something to you?"

"No, nothing like that." She took another drag off the cigarette then stubbed it out and stood. Pacing back and forth, she relayed the events of the previous week and how the situation had blown up that morning.

"Why didn't you tell me about that?"

"It didn't concern you."

"I hate I ever said that." His voice rattled as if he were walking fast. "Look, Mikayla, I don't know a lot about love and positive relationships. But I'm learning. I don't like seeing you upset and not knowing what's wrong. Forget that rule, no more secrets. If something is bothering you, let me know."

She paused in her pacing and sat on the end of the couch. "Does that mean you'll do the same?"

"If you ask, I'll let you know what's going on."

She rolled her eyes but accepted his word. "Same here."

A heavy breath came through the phone. "Fine, Mikayla, I'll let you know what's going on with me."

"And what your family is planning that may hurt me?"

"Don't push it. Our car is here, and my brother is on his way over. I don't like the idea of you being alone."

His concern was the only bright spot in a terrible day. "I'll be okay."

"Go to my cottage."

Reaching for the bag, the last of the gummy bears went into her mouth. "I don't remember how to get there." She mumbled around the candy. "You live in the country."

He laughed. "Fine, go to my condo in the city. I can't be with you, but it'll make me feel better to have you lying in my bed."

"I can take care of myself." She washed down the sugar rush with a swig of ale.

"I know, but it's all I can do for you right now. Jonathan has a key, I'll call and ask him to leave it beneath the mat before you arrive. I've got an extra credit card in the safe. Call me when you're there, and I'll give you the code. Order whatever you want, make yourself at home, and I'll be there at the end of the week."

Her fear began to ease. Going to Andre's house wasn't a plan for the future, but it was a plan for now. "You know this isn't necessary." She popped up off the couch and headed to the bedroom.

"No, but it makes me feel better."

She pulled her overnight bag out of the closet. "I'm the one who lost my job."

"And I'm the one who's going to take care of you. Now pack your stuff and leave."

CHAPTER 33

Isaac entered the back of the car, and the driver shut the door behind him. He faced Andre and scowled. "Is something wrong?"

Andre glanced at his brother but didn't answer. Flipping through the contacts on his phone, he searched for the name of the family's private investigator Ted Levant. A former Army Ranger, Ted now offered his services to those who needed information and didn't care how they got it.

"Mr. Caldwell," Ted's cool voice answered.

"I need you to find everything you can about a woman named Charity York. She works for my Uncle Philip, at Caldwell Development."

"Anything else?"

"We got the information about the key players in Kansas and Dallas last night. Good job."

"As always," Ted said with confidence. "When do you need the information on this woman?"

"End of the week."

"You got it."

The line went dead. Andre clenched his cell phone and tapped the device against his chin. Mikayla was always good under pressure, but the sound of her voice wasn't the same. There was a definite lack of assertiveness. She didn't say it, but today had thrown her off course.

He'd threatened her job once, the least he could do was get it back.

"Who's Charity York?" Isaac asked as the car moved forward.

Andre tossed the cell phone in the cup holder. After unbuttoning the jacket of his sports coat, he reached for the brandy decanter in the car's mini bar.

"She's blackmailing Uncle Philip."

Isaac frowned. "And we should care because…"

"The threat cost Mikayla her job." He took a sip of the warm liquid. The burn settled his jumbled nerves. He couldn't believe he was actually helping his uncle.

Isaac turned in his seat and studied him. A mixture of concern and disbelief clouded his brother's face. Not surprising, if Isaac had suddenly come to the defense of the other side of their family for the love of a woman, Andre would think his brother had lost his mind.

"What is it about Ryan's ex that's got you so twisted?"

"Will you stop referring to her as Ryan's ex? Her name is Mikayla."

"She was in Ryan's bed."

"No, she wasn't. And since when do you care what bed a woman once slept in? The rotating door of women you go through can't be described as innocent."

Isaac took the decanter from Andre and filled a glass. "A woman's past is just that, her past, except when it includes conspiring with our trifling cousins."

Andre held up his glass and stared at the fractured light reflected in the amber liquid. "Is it really that side that's trifling? My conflict with Ryan started when Dad pushed me to steal his girlfriend. The rift in the family came when dad refused to acknowledge Uncle Philip after he started his development company. Dad pushes us to strike. It's his sick way of making us prove loyalty to him when the man doesn't deserve it."

Isaac sank back into the seat. He took a sip then pressed the glass against his forehead. "We both know dad is the root of the dysfunction, but why fight now? We've put in too much blood, sweat, and tears to grow Caldwell Environmental Solutions. Push Dad and we're both out, and assholes like Scott Morrison or our step sister take over and reap the benefits."

"Or we walk away and start something else."

Isaac shot up and slapped his hand against the door. "I'm not giving up my legacy because you're crazy about some woman. You've always pushed against him, always tried to pretend you're better somehow, but you're not. What are you going to do with the information you dig up on this Charity woman?"

Andre looked away, and Isaac laughed. "Exactly. You're going to use that same killer instinct we inherited from dad, to threaten her. The dirt Ted pulled, on the people we're meeting with today, are you're going to use that, too."

"We don't need Ted's information to get the contracts." Andre put his glass down and ran a restless hand over his head. "Our work speaks for itself. We didn't get where we are just from back door dealing and unsavory compromises."

"But the scheming didn't hurt."

"I didn't care about who got hurt before. Going along with what Dad wanted, nearly cost us our mother, has made us compete with our cousins at every turn and honestly compromised our business." Andre lifted a finger with each point. "Just like this woman is using what she knows to threaten Uncle Philip, someone can do the same with us. It's only a matter of time."

"C.E.S. is all I have," Isaac said in a determined voice. "I'm not walking away from this company. Our company."

"And if I do, am I going to lose my brother?"

Isaac's face hardened as he stared at Andre. "You know the answer to that. I won't turn my back on you."

Andre kept his cool, but relief rushed through him. He didn't want this decision to take away the only ally he'd ever had, outside of his mother and Jonathan.

"I wasn't sure that would be your answer."

"Just because I don't understand your decision doesn't mean I won't respect you for making it. I won't let Dad blackball you if you do walk away."

"No need for you to go against him, too."

Isaac leaned back against the seat and tapped his finger on his glass. "We've always stuck together when it came to him. He won't run the risk of having us both walk away. If he threatens you, I'll step in."

Andre nodded. It was good to know Isaac had his back. The pack they made when they were young never to become like their dad and uncle was still intact.

"But I need to know why. What is it about this woman," Isaac held up his hand when Andre glared at him. "Mikayla that has you questioning everything? One minute you're normal, and after a weekend with her you're changed."

"I'm not changed. She just helped me realize I want more out of life. It's not all about loyalty, hustling, and work when I'm with her. I can just relax and be still." He shrugged. "I guess we can fall in love."

What appeared to be envy flashed in Isaac's eyes. He turned away so quickly and finished his drink Andre couldn't be sure.

"You must have gotten that from Mom," Isaac said. "Everything dad has against commitment is inside of me."

"Maybe you haven't met the right one."

"I wouldn't do right if I did find her." Isaac frowned.

Andre considered his brother. "So what are we going to do with the information Ted sent last night?"

Ted had not disappointed. He'd not only found out who would be on the review panel selecting the new waste contractor. He'd provided proof of adultery, misplaced money, addictions, everything down to how many times a day they went to the bathroom. The information would go a long way toward ensuring everything went in favor of C.E.S. But lives would be destroyed if they used the information.

Isaac cocked a brow. "What do you suggest?"

"Let's try securing the contracts the old fashioned way. Going in and introducing ourselves. Learning their needs and expectations." Andre leaned over and pulled up his work bag. Unzipping the front pocket he pulled out a file folder. "I've researched the history of their previous contracts. They've had a problem with reliability and complaints about the lack of professionalism of the drivers. We can win this on that alone."

Isaac took the file and flipped through the papers. After a few tense seconds, he finally nodded.

"I guess you're not giving up on C.E.S. We'll do it your way."

Andre tipped his head to his brother, then pulled out his cell phone to call Jonathan.

*

Once they checked into the hotel suite, Andre left to walk around downtown. He stopped in a coffee shop and ordered a plain black coffee, then went back outside to drink it at one of the sidewalk tables. Pulling a carton of cigarettes from his jacket pocket, the smell of tobacco made him long for Mikayla. If the information Ted came back with helped her keep her job, he'd have to leave C.E.S. Fighting that side of the family would only hurt her, and the thought of hurting her repulsed him.

"Do you mind if I bum one of those off you?" A male voice asked.

Andre turned toward the tall light skinned man sitting at the table next to him. The man's face was vaguely familiar, but Andre couldn't place where he knew him from. He tossed over the pack and watched as the man pulled out a cigarette.

"Thanks. I'm trying to quit, but not doing too well."

"I quit years ago," Andre replied.

"Not doing to good then, huh?"

Andre tossed over his lighter. "Not quite."

The man lit his cigarette, closed his eyes and grinned. "Just like going home."

Andre nodded and took a drag of his own. He missed Mikayla. She should be at his condo by now, and hopefully the bouquet of flowers and the chocolates he'd ordered had arrived. He'd call her later and let her know he'd hired a masseuse to come over in the morning.

"You're Andre Caldwell."

He glanced back at the man. Took another good look at him. The guy had features a woman would consider handsome, his grey button up shirt and black pants were simple, but had the cut and fit of tailoring. But Andre still didn't know why he looked familiar.

"Why do you want to know?"

The man sat forward and rested his arms on the wire table. He motioned to Andre with the hand holding the cigarette. "Because, you're the man I want to run my company."

Andre shifted in his seat until he faced the guy. "I'm not looking for a job."

"You don't have to be looking to find the right opportunity." The guy rested the cigarette on the table and reached out his hand. "I'm Steve Harden, owner of Harden Composting."

The light bulb of recognition flashed. Steve Harden submitted a proposal for C.E.S. to fund the startup of an indoor composting facility. Andre was interested in learning more about how to make money in that little explored market in the Southeast. He'd checked the former biology professor's research on potential streams for organics and understood how funding Steve could benefit C.E.S. and him.

Of course, Curtis had been staunchly against the idea. Regardless of how much money they could have potentially made, Curtis disagreed with any idea he didn't come up with.

"You started the indoor composting."

Steve took a drag off his cigarette, then sat back in his chair. "After C.E.S. turned me down, I sought seed money to start on my own. No need to be a subset of a larger conglomeration when I could branch out. I secured a federal research grant, and some money from a few foundations to start my first facility in North Carolina. Now I'm ready to branch out to other locations."

"Why do you need me?"

"I'm not a businessman. The success of my first facility is great, but I'm not afraid to admit trying to run two is above my head. I'd rather be running the facility itself, making sure things are working the way they should. I need someone like you to help my business grow."

Andre slowly leaned forward. "Tell me what you've got going."

Several hours later, Andre shook Steve's hand and walked back to the hotel a bounce in his step. Though he'd made no promises, from what he learned, taking over as the C.E.O. for Harden Composting was just the challenge he needed. Taking the position would mean a significant pay cut short term, but the opportunity had the potential to pay off in the long run. There were plenty of opportunities to expand the marketing and sales for the material. His dad would try to buy them out if he left, but he could handle that when the time came. As soon as Isaac finished with his investigation into Charity, he'd have him investigate Steve. If it all panned out, Andre would make the move.

When he made it back to the hotel suite, he knocked on Isaac's bedroom door and got no answer except for the murmur of voices. No telling what, or who, his brother had gotten into. Pushing aside thoughts of his brother, Andre pulled out his phone to call Mikayla. There were two missed calls from her and one from Angelica. Ignoring the voice messages from Angelica, he called Mikayla. He couldn't wait to share the good news, and hear the sound of her voice.

CHAPTER 34

After lounging for nearly an hour in the luxury of Andre's large tub, Mikayla finally pulled herself out of the lavish bubble bath. She'd nearly burst with delight when she'd entered the condo to find four dozen roses and a huge basket filled with scented bath accessories. A much needed bright spot in a disappointing day.

Humming softly, she wrapped up in his navy bathrobe and pulled the lapels up to her nose to breathe in his scent. Warm desire spread through her as the soft material brushed against her naked body. The end of the week couldn't come soon enough.

The bedroom door was closed, but the sound of the front door opening and closing made her stiffen. She glanced around for something to defend herself with, and then laughed at herself for being foolish. It was probably Jonathan checking on her.

Still, she picked up the solid glass ashtray next to the bed and her cell phone from the dresser before walking out.

"Hello?" she called. Her heart thumped heavily in her chest as she walked down the hall to the living area. After entering the room, she stopped. Andre's father stood without the slightest hint of surprise.

He slowly pulled off a navy suit jacket and glared. "I can see the appeal, but you're no match for Angelica's beauty."

Her fist clenched around the lapels of the robe. She hadn't expected her next meeting with Andre's dad to go well but also didn't expect insults. "How did you know I was here?"

"There isn't a step my son takes that I don't know about."

"What do you want?"

The sick chuckle he let out spread unease across her skin. Dark eyes that were similar to Andre's raked over her body from head to toe. "Got a little fire, too. Do you let that out when you're screwing my son? Is that why he's willing to walk away from the family for you?" He stalked toward her. "I won't let him."

Clammy sweat covered every inch of Mikayla's body after his thorough inspection. But she didn't back away. "Andre's a grown man. I don't make him do anything."

"No need to be coy with me, girl. Angelica wasn't afraid to brag on her bedroom powers of persuasion."

He stopped in front of her, wrinkling his nose as if she were trash. Her throat threatened to close up. She didn't know much about Curtis except that he was a ruthless businessman and could hold a grudge for years. Though she'd never heard of him being violent, she was thankful Andre and Jonathan knew she was here just in case something happened.

"I asked why you're here," she said in a tight voice.

"Simple. Leave my son alone."

She raised her chin. "That's up to him."

"Do you think this thing between you two is will last?" He laughed the same full on laugh Andre gave when she mentioned Ryan marrying Angelica. The similarity sent a chill down her spine. "He did a good job convincing you he's in love. You're not the first woman not worth the socks on my feet who's tried to weasel her way in. Andre always chooses his family."

"Andre is ten times better than you."

"Really?" Curtis asked with a sly grin on his face. "He wasn't better than me when we worked together to blackmail Senator Leventis."

Mikayla gasped, her hand lost its grip, and the ashtray hit the floor with a thud. "What?"

Curtis raised an eyebrow. Full lips curled into an evil smile on what would be a handsome face. "I'm taking it you didn't know about that."

"He said he was trying to stop you from hurting me."

"Oh...you must mean his small stance against destroying your contract with the school district and community development office down there." He gave her a patronizing look, even patted her shoulder as if he cared. "Andre put on a good show, but in the end, he chose what's best for the company."

She jerked away from Curtis. "How is this possibly good for your company?" Her hands trembled, and she clenched the ends of the robe.

"We have plans to expand our landfill gas program and need Dalmtix to locate where we can provide it to them. The landfill in Hartsville wasn't the ideal place. That was the reason for the senator's blackmail. Going after the district and community development office was simply to ruin my brother's plans. Cost him a few million dollars."

"At my expense."

He shrugged. "You don't matter."

She sucked in a breath. "I do matter."

"Maybe to your dad and for some reason to my brother...but he did tend to take in strays." Curtis walked away picking up his jacket and draping it over his arm. "But to me and my son, you don't. In fact, Angelica is on her way to Kansas City right now to be with him."

"Angelica is in Vegas with Ryan."

"The marriage ploy was our effort to get Andre back in line. She called and gave him one last chance to get her back before marrying Ryan. Her last text to me said everything was a success. I booked her a flight to Kansas City before coming over here. To take out the trash."

Mikayla trembled. Curtis' words singed her body and blow torched her heart. Andre had betrayed her. Every time she mentioned Dalmtrix, he would say things would work out. When he was working behind her back to make sure, they didn't.

Her phone rang. She eyed Curtis, and he chuckled. "Answer it. Might as well hear it from him."

"He invited me here." All of her pain spilled out in those words. She didn't want to believe Curtis's nasty, hateful lies.

"That was before knowing he could get her back." His eyes turned cold. "Answer the phone."

Pulling the phone from the robe pocket her arm felt like lead. Andre smiled up at her, a picture of him beside the pool in Miami filled the screen. Her stomach heaved. His lies. His betrayal. His love. All poison.

"Hello," she couldn't force their usual greeting from her lips.

"I've got something to tell you." He said in a rush.

Tears welled in her eyes. She squeezed them shut. She would not cry. "Let me guess, Angelica called."

There was a pause that hurt her more than his dad's words ever could. "How did you know?"

"Your dad is here. He's told me a lot of things. Things you insisted I didn't need to know. Like blackmailing Senator Leventis and trying to ruin my chance to salvage the deal by getting back at your uncle and Ryan."

"Mikayla, listen—"

"First tell me if it's true. Is it all true?"

"It is, but you've got to understand—"

"I understand perfectly. I can't trust you…and you don't love me. Goodbye, Andre." She ended the call. Tears streamed down her face. With her eyes closed, she couldn't see him, but she felt Curtis standing in front of her.

The humiliation of this betrayal was larger than any she'd ever known. At least Ryan's betrayal had been spontaneously stupid. This betrayal was deliberate and meant to hurt her.

She opened her eyes to Curtis's satisfied smirk. "Are you happy now?"

He slipped on his coat. "Actually, I'm ecstatic. This isn't a hotel. Get out before noon tomorrow."

He walked away and slammed the door behind him. She flinched. A sob clawed its way up her throat. This pain warranted tears. This pain left her hollow and broken.

*

Rage surged through Andre's body. He dialed Mikayla's number right after she hung up. The call went straight to voicemail. He dialed his dad's number, and no surprise Curtis's phone went straight to voicemail too. He should never have invited Mikayla to the condo when he wasn't there. He knew Curtis would strike eventually, but never expected him to approach Mikayla directly.

He dialed both numbers again. Same response.

"Shit." His tone was lethal, and he lunged off the bed. He'd leave a note for Isaac and take the jet back home.

He wrenched open the bedroom door. Across the shared living space, a woman marched out of Isaac's room.

"You sorry bastard! Don't ever call me again!"

Isaac rushed to the door of his room and yelled back. "I damn sure won't. I need a woman who knows what she's doing."

"To hell with you." She spun on her heels and stormed out.

Andre frowned. Women yelling at his brother was nothing new. Isaac yelling back was another story. Andre rushed over.

Isaac turned to him. He swayed on his feet and blinked several times. The smell of alcohol filled the space. Panic increased Andre's heartbeat. His brother never drank to excess, and he damn sure never raised his voice.

"What the hell was that?" Andre asked.

"What? That?" Isaac pointed in the direction the woman had taken. "That was a mistake."

"Is it the type of mistake that's going to involve the police?"

Isaac blew air between his lips. Andre cringed at the foul smell. "Nah...Allison's just mad because I didn't want her."

Isaac swayed again, and Andre caught him before he fell over. He helped his brother into the bedroom. Mini liquor bottles were spread out over the floor. That explained the alcohol, but not the why. He dragged Isaac into the bed.

"Sounds like more than that," Andre said, dropping his brother on the bed.

Isaac groaned and draped his arm over his eyes. "I couldn't...I tried, but ever since..." A humorless laugh escaped his brother. "It's all her fault."

Andre stiffened. "Who?"

Isaac leaned up on his arms, gave Andre a look that said he'd spoken too much. "I'm good now. Just going to fall asleep." He fell back on the pillows.

Andre wanted to know what the hell was going on but didn't have time for his brother's drama. He'd figure it out after he fixed things with Mikayla.

"I've got to get back to South Carolina. Dad's done something to Mikayla, and I need to go put him in his place. Can you handle things tomorrow?"

"Yeah…sure…" Isaac jumped up and rushed to the bathroom. The sound of his brother's retching soon followed.

Damn! He could still leave. If Isaac's drunken stunt ruined the deal in Kansas City tomorrow, then it wasn't his problem.

He pulled out his phone and called Mikayla.

Voicemail.

Shit!

His brother threw up again. Andre rubbed his nose as a headache roared to life. He couldn't leave Isaac like this. He didn't give a damn about his dad, but he did care about Isaac. For Isaac to get this drunk, something was up. His conscious would never recover if he left and something happened. Something bad.

He pulled out his cell phone, he'd call Jonathan. Maybe his friend could go over and catch Mikayla before she left.

Voicemail.

Fuck! What is the point of cell phones if people don't answer them?

Isaac retched, then groaned. Andre shook his head and went to check on his brother. How could things get so bad, so quickly?

CHAPTER 35

Andre didn't leave Kansas City until late the next day. He'd alternated between worry over his brother getting so drunk and annoyance at the delay it caused. Isaac wouldn't say exactly, what had made him get so drunk. He'd get to the bottom of that later.

He'd tried calling Mikayla repeatedly, but she never answered. He hoped she'd listened to his voice messages as he attempted to explain. By the time he reached Jonathan and asked him to try and catch her, she was gone. Instead of asking him to go after her, Andre decided it would be better to talk to her in person. He didn't try calling his dad again. He'd handle Curtis in person.

During the flight home, Ted forwarded him the first bit of information he had pulled on Charity York. More than enough dirt for his uncle to stop her threats. He debated going to Mikayla first but chose to handle Curtis.

Andre landed in Greenville and went straight to his dad's home. He burst through the door, and the butler crossing the entryway jumped at the sudden intrusion.

"Where is he?" Andre bit out.

"On the upstairs balcony," the man said in a shaky voice.

Andre took the stairs two at a time. He marched across the hall and pushed open the glass doors leading to the balcony that spanned the entire second floor of the house.

His dad glanced up from the magazine he was reading. Slowly, Curtis set the magazine on the table next to his chair. "I'd expected you sooner."

Anger and frustration pulsed inside of Andre so strong he thought his skin would burst. He wanted to yell, scream, and even fight his dad for what he'd done. That was exactly, what Curtis would want.

Andre took a deep breath, and then squared his shoulders. "Isaac got sick, so I stood in to make a good impression with the stakeholders in Kansas City. C.E.S. stands ready to expand. He's gone to Dallas to do the same there."

Curtis stood and walked over with a confident smile on his face. "I knew you would come around."

Andre stepped back before his dad could pat him on the shoulder. "I let him go to Dallas, on his own. I came to resign in person."

The smile on Curtis's face quickly turned to a dark scowl. "You can't resign."

"I can, and I am. I've given up too much of myself to watch your dream succeed."

"This isn't just my dream. It's for you and your brother. I built this company for my sons to carry on."

"No, you built this company as a slap in the face to your brother. You've raised me and Isaac to follow you completely or not at all. You claim, all you want is loyalty, but you're not loyal. What you did to Mikayla was the last straw."

Curtis scoffed. He turned away from Andre with a look of disgust and paced to the edge of the balcony. "You don't need that woman. She's not worth being on your arm."

"The money you made, doesn't erase the fact that our family started with nothing except the land grandpa won from cheating in a card game."

Curtis spun toward him. "Where you come from doesn't matter. It's where you're going. And we can go far. You can have any woman, and you're settling for your cousin's leftovers."

"You see everything as a rivalry between our families. You can never understand what I feel about Mikayla."

"We'll see if she's worth it when you find her back in Ryan's arms. I'll give you your job back only because you're my son, but you'll hear from me every day how you almost lost it because of some foolish emotion."

Andre clenched his fists. At that moment, he knew he would never work for his dad again. "I will pack up my office next week. Goodbye, Dad."

Panic swept across Curtis's face. "Where the hell do you think you're going? What are you going to do? I meant what I said. I'll ruin your name."

Andre glared at him. "Ruining my name ruins yours, too. It'll be proof that you're so incompetent at running your business you let your son mismanage funds and lead the company astray."

Curtis' eyes narrowed into slits. "I'll ruin you."

"And lose both sons in the process. Isaac already has my side in this. Let it go. Leave me alone."

He turned away from the surprise on his dad's face.

"This isn't over," Curtis yelled.

Andre didn't bother to look back. "It is for me."

He walked out. Fought the urge to slam the door behind him. He trusted Isaac would keep his word and try to prevent Curtis from blackballing him. Still, he'd fill Steve in on the situation that might arise due to his departure from C.E.S.

Nervous energy jetted along his skin. The future was uncertain. It would be a lie to say he wasn't afraid of leaving the comfort of C.E.S. Fear always accompanied new ventures. But as he walked away from his dad's house, free of the ties to him and the company, a sense of liberty settled over him. It quickly turned that fear into determination.

*

It was nearly five when Andre walked through the doors of Caldwell Development. A receptionist greeted him and called his uncle's secretary to announce his arrival. He glanced around the lobby. He'd never been there before. Except for the receptionist desk and a large fountain of water along one wall, the interior looked like a tastefully decorated living area of a model home instead of the headquarters of a major corporation.

A few minutes later he was lead down a hall lined with offices that opened into another large reception area with three doors, his uncles, Ryan's and Renee's names on the doors. He wondered where Mikayla's office had been.

The receptionist opened the door to the middle office and motioned for him to go inside. His uncle stood behind the desk. His hard face a mask of distrust.

"I would never have expected you to come here," Phillip said.

Andre crossed the room and stared, at the man he'd been taught to hate most of his life. He felt neither hate nor love. Just the freedom of knowing he wasn't bound to him by a rivalry he didn't want.

"I have something for you." He dropped the envelope with the preliminary information Ted had found on Charity on the desk.

Philip nudged the envelope with a finger. "What's that?"

"Proof that Charity is working with someone in your accounting department to embezzle funds. There's more coming, but that should be enough to fire her and give Mikayla her job back."

His Uncle frowned and grabbed the envelope. Tearing it open, he quickly scanned the papers. "Where did you get this?"

"We have our sources."

Philip stopped examining the papers a knowing look in his eye. "I've heard about my brother's sources. What I don't know is why you're giving this to me."

"I told you, so you can give Mikayla her job back."

"From what Renee says, you don't want her working for us. I thought you'd be happy to learn she resigned."

Andre crossed his arms, wrestled back the guilt that he'd had that exact reaction initially. "It's not easy knowing the woman, you love, is working with the man she used to date. I know you want them together."

Philip dropped the paperwork and walked over to his bar. "But…"

"But, I trust Mikayla. And she loves this job." He followed Philip to the bar and met his Uncle's gaze with a direct stare. "She doesn't love Ryan."

Philip nodded and poured dark liquor from a crystal decanter into two glasses. "I know that. But you've got to realize that our family loves her. She's Renee's best friend, and for some reason, she helped Ryan get out of that mood he was in the first time he lost Angelica. I admire her work ethic and her determination."

"Then why didn't you fight this Charity woman?"

"Because, our company is one of the largest development firms in the Southeast. Our name is everything, and fighting a public battle with Charity would hinder, not help, our brand." Philip handed a glass to Andre. "I didn't want to fire Mikayla or demand her resignation. I couldn't turn it down either."

Andre swirled the contents of the glass. He didn't like Philip's reasoning, but he understood where he was coming from. His dad was the king of handling things behind closed doors instead of fighting the battle in public.

"Now you can make Charity quietly go away." Andre took a sip of the alcohol. His lip twisted with a sad smile. Phillip drank the same bourbon as Curtis.

Andre placed the glass on the bar. "I'll leave now."

"Wait a second," Philip said. "You're helping me because you love Mikayla. I know my brother. He's not going to like it."

Andre's shoulders stiffened. "I no longer care what my dad wants or thinks. I resigned this morning. I'm done with this rivalry and living up to his expectations of loyalty."

Sadness filled Philip's eyes. "I wish I could say the same."

"You can if you want too."

"Curtis will not stop until I concede I was wrong for starting this company or admit his empire is greater than mine. It's something I can't do. Our dad may have gotten our land through shifty means, but I turned that cheating hand at cards into something I could be proud of. If it means fighting my brother for the rest of my life to prove it, then so be it."

Andre shook his head at the stubbornness of old men. "Goodbye, Uncle Philip."

Philip raised his glass. "If you're going to be in Mikayla's life, then I'll say see you around, Andre."

With a nod, and a sense this move had somehow pulled him further into the fight than away, Andre turned to leave.

He ran into Renee coming in. Her eyes narrowed. "What do you want?"

"Hold up, Renee," Philip said. "He's come in peace. Gave us what we need to fire Charity and get Mikayla back."

She crossed slim arms over her chest and glared at Andre. "I thought you were back with Angelica."

Andre flinched. "I don't want Angelica. I'm on my way to tell Mikayla that now."

"What's this about?" Philip asked.

Renee held up a hand. "Wait a second, Daddy. I'll fill you in, soon." She turned back to Andre. "I had a feeling Curtis was lying. Do you really love her? Is this really not about the stupid rivalry anymore?"

"It was never about the rivalry. But, if it'll make you feel better, I quit working for C.E.S. today. What does that tell you?"

Renee's shoulders relaxed. "She's not at home. She went to her dad's house, but she's supposed to meet me at Rowdy's tonight at seven."

"I thought you didn't like us together."

She shrugged. "Don't get too excited. I'm only telling you because I want to be there when she rips your balls off."

The corner of her mouth lifted. Andre smiled back. Hell must be freezing over. He might actually grow to like Renee.

CHAPTER 36

Mikayla stared at her reflection in the bathroom mirror at Rowdy's. Renee would just have to be upset because Makayla didn't try for cute today. Her hair pulled up in a ponytail she'd opted for an old Buffalo Bills t-shirt and jeans, and the closest she came to makeup: cherry ChapStick. She had no plans to return to the days when she didn't know what to do with a curling iron. But she was no longer going to spend endless amounts of time prepping herself to go out in public. The new Mikayla didn't want that life anymore. It came with too much stuff she didn't need. Growing up, she'd thought people with more had perfect lives. Now she knew perfection came at a cost. Mikayla wanted simple again.

The loud music from the karaoke stage increased in volume then decreased as women came in and out. The place was packed for a Monday. If she had known tonight was the night for the monthly cash prize to the best singer, she would have suggested they go somewhere else. But the crowd and the noise was good, she guessed. More of a distraction.

She patted around her eyes. Maybe she could have at least put on mascara or dabbed some concealer around her eyes. Lack of sleep and crying all night made her look exhausted. She deleted all of his voice messages, unable to stand hearing his voice or any hollow excuses that were easier for him to say into a phone than to her face.

What was there to explain other than he'd tried to ruin her development idea in Hartsville not once, but twice? His dad made it perfectly clear he expected his son to continue to work for and support the family. To continue to participate in the rivalry, he'd fostered for years.

But the love in her heart wouldn't go away. And her love wanted an explanation even more than she wanted to forget. Why did he do it? Had he ever planned to walk away from the fight? Had anything they'd felt for each other been real?

Renee texted to say she'd arrived and had a table. Mikayla had only arrived a few minutes ago and headed straight to the bathroom instead of sitting and watching everyone else be happy and carefree. Why the hell did she pick this place?

Mikayla slipped the phone in her pocket and left the bathroom to go meet Renee. She ran into Ryan on the way to the main area. He looked almost as bad as she did. Except, the dusting of a beard on his chin that increased his good looks and his designer clothes were only slightly ruffled.

"I didn't know you were back in town. I heard about Angelica."

Bloodshot eyes met hers. "Renee told you?"

"No, Angelica called Andre."

He leaned against the wall. "She wanted him all along. It was all a ploy to get him back." Regret and sadness filled Ryan's eyes. "I hurt you for her. I'm sorry."

It was the first time she'd actually believed his apology. Despite herself, she empathized with what Ryan was going through.

"Are you going to be okay?"

He nodded, but he didn't look very convincing. "I keep waiting to find the woman who looks past my name, and what happens? I end up getting shafted. Twice. By the same woman."

Mikayla winced. She could have prevented this.

"I should have said something about Angelica. She let me know she wanted Andre." She turned to face Ryan. A confused frown marred his features.

"Why didn't you say anything?"

"It wasn't my place to get in your relationship. I let Renee know figuring she would tell you."

"As my friend you should have told me."

Mikayla placed a hand on her hip. "Yeah, and as my friend you should have said something before sleeping with Angelica in a closet."

His defensive stance withered. Ryan groaned and leaned his head against the wall. "I guess we both need a refresher course on friendship."

She clasped her hands behind her back. "We made a worse couple."

Ryan laughed. "We did. Our kisses were okay. I think we would have been decent in the bedroom." He lifted his head to grin at her.

She shook her head. "I don't want decent. I want amazing."

"I agree with that. I had amazing. And more than that. Or at least I thought I did." He took a deep breath. "So it's true, she's back with him?"

"I hoped you could tell me."

"When I left she was angry Andre hadn't returned her calls. She'd thrown her plans in my face before talking to him. My only consolation was that I'd come home and find out you and Andre were still together."

The smallest spark of hope, which she tried to tamp down, flared in Mikayla's chest. Even if he weren't back with Angelica, he'd done other things that were unforgivable. "I haven't talked to him." She quickly relayed what happened with Curtis.

"I wouldn't put too much into what my uncle says," Ryan said. "The man lies as easily as I breathe. It's his way of controlling everyone around him. I can't say I'm thrilled you're with Andre, but I will say putting your trust in my Uncle is like trusting a rattle snake not to bite you when you have it cornered."

Hope flared up again. "I don't know."

Ryan reached over and took her hand in his. "From the way you've fought us to prove what you have is real, I think it's worth finding out the truth. I do love you, Mikayla, and I want you to be happy."

She turned her hand to entwine their fingers. Mikayla searched for the animosity she'd felt just a few short months ago after he'd embarrassed her in the mountains. None was there. They'd both been wrong to enter into that relationship. But she did love him, and Renee, as if they were her brother and sister.

"Same here." She grinned. "Sorry for the knee to the nuts."

He laughed. "I deserved it."

"Yes, you did." She squeezed his hand.

The microphone on the stage squealed. She and Ryan both jumped and covered their ears.

"Sorry, everyone, it's my first time on stage."

Mikayla's jaw dropped. The blood rushed from her head. Was that...Andre's voice?

"I came here tonight, not to win the cash prize," Andre cleared his throat. "But to win something far more important. Mikayla, stop talking to Ryan and come out here."

Her body turned hot, cold, tingly, and numb all at once. She turned from Ryan and slowly walked down the hall. Across the room, Andre stood on the stage with a microphone in his hand, shifting from foot to foot and looking uncomfortable as hell.

"There's my prize." His deep voice, helped by the microphone, reverberated throughout the room and bounced intently against her heart.

People at tables turned to follow his gaze. Everyone's eyes were on her. Her hand went straight to her hair. Renee shot her an I told you so look. She could almost hear her friend's thoughts. *Always be cute.*

"You look beautiful," Andre said. "I'm not good at...grand romantic gestures. But today I'll try. My family is full of shit. For too long I played into that. We've hurt you, embarrassed you, and taken your friendship for granted. The least, I can do, is stand up here and embarrass myself in front of all these people and let you know that I love you."

Her eyes watered. Mikayla's heart couldn't pump blood fast enough to deliver oxygen to her brain. She thought she'd either faint or burst.

Then the music started, Lenny Williams, Cause I Love You, blared through the room.

Women swooned and one man yelled out "Yeah, man, that's how you do it."

She watched in both disbelief and bliss as he sang the words. When he got into the song and actually swung his hips, a shocked laugh escaped her.

Oh my, God, he's really doing this. He was really up there, singing in front of everyone, so she'd take him back.

When he went into the full "Oh, oh, oh, ooooh!" and stamped his foot, Mikayla knew her answer. She was his forever.

Instead of recounting the speaking part in the song, Andre stared at her.

"Mikayla, I'm sorry. My dad lied. I did not take Angelica back. But I lied to you before that." His dark gaze pierced hers from across the room. "I have no excuse for what I did. It was all that I knew, but you showed me another way. You make me want to be better, for you." His gaze swept the room and the people watching them. "I walked away. I quit my job today." He zeroed in on Mikayla. "I'm starting over in North Carolina, and I want you to come with me. To hell with this family drama. Let's start over, away from both sides. Forgive me." He took a deep breath. "Marry me."

The crowd erupted in cheers. Tears streamed down Mikayla's face. People chanted "Say yes. Say yes. Say yes."

She turned and ran out the door.

Outside she pulled in deep breaths of air. Did she forgive him? Marry him? Move to North Carolina or wherever? Trust him never to betray her again? Oh, man, she wanted too. But was going with him right?

The door to Rowdy's opened and closed. She knew it was him without turning around.

"I warned you my family doesn't fight fair."

She kept her back to him. "So you did."

She listened as his footsteps neared until he was right behind her. "The blackmail of Senator Leventis began before I knew you were involved with the deal."

"But you still went through with it."

"I did."

She brought a hand to her temple. "Why?"

"You and I weren't official. I wasn't in love with you at the time. I convinced myself ruining the deal made sense. No different than how I operated before I met you and that if you never found out we could be friends, and it wouldn't mean a thing. Then when you figured out a way to salvage the land purchase, I thought things had worked out."

She spun to face him. Her defenses almost melted at the pleading in his dark eyes. "You tried to ruin the deal again."

"No, my dad tried." He took her arm in his. She didn't pull away, and he drew her close. "That's what I couldn't tell you. I knew you'd be hurt if I told you, and I'd have to confess everything for you to understand. By then

I realized I cared and couldn't do that to you again. I told my father, and he threatened to ruin my name if I walked away."

"You didn't walk away. Your trip to Kansas City proves that."

"I did today. Him lying to you was the last straw. I'm taking a job in North Carolina."

"Angelica?"

He wiped away a tear that slipped from the corner of her eye. "I didn't answer her calls or listen to her voice mail. I haven't talked to her since that day she called me weeks ago. I'm so sorry my dad did that to you. I want to start over. I want the two of us to be together. Away from my family and the craziness they pull into our lives. I want to become that good guy you thought I was."

"What if I don't want to live in North Carolina?"

He winced, and the pain in his eyes pulled at her heart. He nodded and seemed to force himself to accept it. "I found out Charity is stealing from your Uncle. If you don't want me, you can have your job back."

"You got my job back, even though you hated me working for them."

"I only want you to be happy. If you can't move past this, at least I know I tried all I could to get you back."

"Will that satisfy you?"

The hand on her arm tightened its hold. "No, but I'd learn to live with it."

The war over what to do was over. He had her the moment she heard his voice in Rowdy's. Still, she took a second to search deep in her heart. To make sure that she was ready to try and trust him again. She stepped closer to him and grabbed the front of his shirt. "Don't lie to me ever again. Because I love you, Andre." His body sagged with relief. "I forgave you the second you stepped on that stage. I missed you from the moment I hung up the phone. I only want you."

The corner of his mouth twitched. Then his eyes stirred with something else. Heat and love filled her. She'd missed him.

"I'll never lie to you again. I love you too much to risk losing you."

She stared at him. "This wasn't supposed to last."

"No, they said it wouldn't last. But we both knew from the start that no matter how unlikely it should be, there is something real between us. I need you, Mikayla. You showed me how to love. I want to spend the rest of my life loving you."

"Yes."

"What?"

"Yes, I'll marry you."

He lowered his head and kissed her. A crowd of Rowdy's patrons spilled out the bar, watched and cheered. Mikayla barely heard the cheers. She pulled Andre closer.

ABOUT THE AUTHOR

Synithia Williams has loved romance novels since reading her first one at the age of 13. It was only natural that she would begin penning her own romances soon after. It wasn't until 2010 that she began to actively pursue her publishing dreams. When she isn't writing, Synithia is working hard on water quality issues in the Midlands of South Carolina and taking care of her supportive husband and two sons. You can learn more about Synithia by visiting her website, www.synithiawilliams.com, where she blogs about writing, life and relationships.

Facebook: http://www.facebook.com/synithiarwilliams
Twitter: http://www.twitter.com/@SynithiaW

Books by Synithia Williams

<u>Crimson Romance</u>
You Can't Plan Love
Worth the Wait
A Heart to Heal
Just My Type
Love's Replay
Making it Real
From One Night to Forever

<u>Harlequin Kimani</u>
A New York Kind of Love

www.ingramcontent.com/pod-product-compliance
Lightning Source LLC
Chambersburg PA
CBHW032128170626
46808CB00006B/2141